SOLDIER OF THE QUEEN

SOLDIER OF THE QUEEN

Philip McCutchan

Chivers Press • Thorndike Press
Bath, England   Thorndike, Maine USA

This Large Print edition is published by Chivers Press, England, and by Thorndike Press, USA.

Published in 1999 in the U.K. by arrangement with Severn House Publishers Ltd.

Published in 1999 in the U.S. by arrangement with Chivers Press, Ltd.

U.K. Hardcover ISBN 0–7540–3593–X (Chivers Large Print)
U.K. Softcover ISBN 0–7540–3594–8 (Camden Large Print)
U.S. Softcover ISBN 0–7862–1667–0 (General Series Edition)

The text of this Large Print edition is unabridged.
Other aspects of the book may vary from the original edition.

Set in 16 pt. New Times Roman.

Printed in Great Britain on acid-free paper.

British Library Cataloguing in Publication Data available

Library of Congress Cataloging-in-Publication Data

McCutchan, Philip, 1920–
    Soldier of the queen / Philip McCutchan.
        p.   cm.
    ISBN 0–7862–1667–0 (lg. print : sc : alk. paper)
    1. India—History—British occupation, 1765–1947—Fiction.
    2. Large type books. I. Title.
    PR6063.A167 S65   1999
    823'.914—ddc21   98–44364

THE CHAIN OF COMMAND

Lieutenant-General Sir Iain Ogilvie (James Ogilvie's father) General Officer Commanding the Northern Army at Murree.

Major-General Francis Fettleworth, Divisional Commander, commanding the main column of advance from Peshawar, including the Royal Strathspeys.

Brigadier-General Forrestier, Chief of Staff to Fettleworth.

Lieutenant-Colonel Lord Dornoch, commanding the Royal Strathspeys.

Tom Archdale, Staff Major

Major John Hay, 2 i/c Royal Strathspeys

Captain Andrew Black, Adjutant

Captain Rob MacKinlay, B Company Commander

Lieutenant James Ogilvie

'Bosom' Cunningham Regimental Sergeant-Major

Hamish Barr, Colour-Sergeant

Brigadier-General Preston has the independent command of the column marching from Gilghit.

CHAPTER ONE

On the parade men from B Company had been busy all morning erecting the gallows. Now the pipes and drums of the battalion were rehearsing, beating out a slow march ahead of two exercising companies, a mournful highland dirge that drifted towards the distant foothills of Himalaya and which would be a fitting tribute to the terrible solemnity of the next day's ceremonial. Looking out of a window of the Officers' Mess ante-room across the parade and the cantonments, watching the Highlanders move through the clouds of dust that hung in the air beneath a high, hot sun, James Ogilvie thought with dread of that next day. It was a side of army life that frankly sickened him. He knew by now that he would never be entirely happy away from the barrack sights and sounds—the sounds of the military music, the bugles that signposted every one of his days, the hoofbeats of horses, the jingle of harness, the metallic banging from the farrier-sergeant and his men, the loud voices of the drill-sergeants . . . and also the glitter of British uniforms that held the Raj in fee and kept the Empire set astride the gorgeous East, finest jewel in the crown of the Queen Empress. Ogilvie had by now been long enough on Indian service to see quite clearly that initially

1

he had had a romanticized view of the British Army and of the North-West Frontier wars in particular, a view that was not always borne out by the facts; he had no complaints that his eyes had been opened to reality. But everything inside him revolted against next day's ceremony. Already there had been talk of more unrest along the Frontier, of warriors coming in from Afghanistan to lead the men of the hills against the Queen's soldiers. There would be enough of death to come, without adding to the toll in hidebound ceremonial.

Ogilvie turned away from the window, caught a glimpse, through the door into the Mess, of the white jackets of the servants preparing for luncheon, of the magnificent regimental silver on the long table. He paused, momentarily. There was history on that table; silver that had been with the regiment since the days when his father, and before him his grandfather, had commanded. Before that, even. It was something to think about. History and tradition had not been built up the easy way.

Leaving the ante-room, he was hailed by one of his brother subalterns. 'Time for a drink, old man?'

Ogilvie shook his head. 'I'm due out there.' He gave a jerk of his head towards the parade and its wreathing dust, its rising, choking heat.

'Don't like it, do you, James?' The speaker grinned, rested his kilted rump on the arm of a vast leather chair. 'Can't be too damned squeamish, you know. India's no damn kindergarten, old man.'

Ogilvie flushed, seemed about to say something in reply, but thought better of it and swung away angrily. As he left the ante-room and marched down the passage buckling on his Sam Browne belt, the subaltern smirked and said to no one in particular, 'Touchy so-and-so at times, what? Takes himself too damn seriously, if you ask me.'

* * *

Next morning James Ogilvie's servant stood back, looking critically at his handiwork. His officer's scarlet tunic was beautifully brushed and pressed, the set of the kilt was just right; the belt buckles, the hilt of the broadsword, the two stars on either shoulder—all shone as befitted a lieutenant of the 114th Highlanders, the Queen's Own Royal Strathspeys. The *skean dhu* was pushed to precisely the right depth into the stocking and the white spats gleamed.

'You'll do, sir,' the man said.

Ogilvie nodded. His face was white and set and he was unable to keep the shake from his fingers. As a solitary bugle sounded from the parade ground he took a deep breath and reached for his white pipeclayed helmet. The foreign-service full-dress headgear was as immaculate as the rest of his accoutrements, with the bright, blue-green flash of the Royal Strathspey set into the dip of the *puggaree* above the regimental badge. Ogilvie turned to his servant, who was also, that morning, dressed in what amounted to review order—though, by God, Ogilvie thought, it was no review that was to take place within the next half-hour!

'All right, Garrett,' he said.

Private Garrett slammed to attention. 'Sir! Then I'll be getting on parade.' He hesitated for a moment, scanning his officer's face. He was a much older man than James Ogilvie and had seen almost twenty years' service with the regiment, at home, in Africa, the West Indies, in Gibraltar, as well as here on the North-West Frontier of India. He said, 'Begging your pardon, sir. You'll do well not to take it too hard, sir. It's the military life when all's said and done and the General had no choice in the matter. You'll know that, sir.'

Again Ogilvie nodded. 'Tell me, Garrett . . . have *you* ever had to see anything like this before?'

Garrett shook his head. 'Never, sir. It's a terrible thing for the regiment. I wish I'd not to see it now and that's God's truth, sir, but what's to be, must be.'

He turned away and left the room; more bugles sounded, stridently calling, and Ogilvie heard the noise from outside, the shouted

4

orders of the drill-sergeants, the tramp of men being moved into their positions. He lingered a while longer, as though steeling himself, guiltily leaving as much as he decently could to Colour-Sergeant Barr, who had been the replacement for Colour-Sergeant MacNaught killed almost a year before during the assault on the peaks beyond Jalalabad. Barr was an efficient soldier, though often enough Ogilvie regretted that the man ruled B Company through ruthlessness and fear. Ogilvie suffered from a nagging knowledge that had it not been for Colour-Sergeant Barr this morning's grim parade would never have taken place at all.

Glancing in the looking-glass on his chest-of-drawers, he adjusted the trim of his helmet and the set of the chinstrap. Then, feeling his hands sticky with sweat, he poured a little water from the jug on the wash-stand into the basin, and rinsed his fingers. He dried them, and left the room. In the bare, green-painted passage outside he was joined by Crampton, one of the new subalterns, a second lieutenant fresh from the Royal Military College at Sandhurst. Crampton was due for a shattering introduction to the regiment and Indian service life. Abruptly Ogilvie said, 'Better cut along, Malcolm. Don't risk being late on parade today or Black'll have your guts.'

'Right you are, James.' Tight-faced, the young officer, too thin in the legs to carry a kilt decently, marched ahead of Ogilvie. Following on behind into the bright sunshine Ogilvie came into the claustrophobic sound of the drum-beats echoing off the buildings, saw the men of the battalion being marched by companies to form up ceremonially. Only the 114th were on parade today; this was to be a strictly domestic occasion. Though naturally this day's work had been, and for some while would continue to be, the talk of the whole garrison at Peshawar, the actual execution was not to be the occasion for any public washing of dirty linen. Today the ranks would be metaphorically closed against all outsiders and although the ceremony was being held on the main garrison parade ground and officially in public there were to be no pure sightseers, no peering ghouls. But for the 114th it was a case of attendance by every man with the sole exceptions of the quarterguard and, of course, the native domestics.

Beneath the early morning sun, now sending streaks of gold and green and crimson across the sky above the far-off snowtopped mountains of the Hindu Kush to the north, and Outer Himalaya to the east, James Ogilvie marched towards his company, trying not to look at the gallows. MacKinlay, his company commander, was already present and was lifting his aristocratic head a little and looking down his nose as Ogilvie came up.

'Good morning, James,' he said. 'Better late than never.'

'I'm sorry,' Ogilvie said. 'What's more, I've no excuse.'

'That's honest enough. Just dragging your feet, what?'

Ogilvie smiled briefly. 'That's right.'

'I can't say I blame you, James. None of us likes it. I can't deny, there's something bloody barbarous about the army at times—' He broke off as Colour-Sergeant Barr approached and slammed to the salute, a hammy brown hand crashing down on the butt of his sloped rifle.

'Yes, Colour-Sarn't?'

'Sir! B Company present and correct, paraded for inspection. Sir!'

'Thank you, Colour-Sarn't. Carry on, please.'

'Sir!' With another crash on the rifle butt and a slam of boots Barr turned about, swinging his kilt around massive thighs, smart, efficient and ebullient. Ogilvie hoped the man wasn't enjoying himself, but he had his doubts. Barr marched away, halted, stood the men at ease, brought them to attention again, turned and faced Captain MacKinlay and his senior subaltern, waiting for them to move across to inspect the ranks. As they approached he fell in behind them. MacKinlay moved along, slowly, hawk-eyed as usual, drawing attention to a badly set helmet, badges that might have been a trifle more shining, boots with traces of parade-ground dust on them. Unlike the

7

Brigade of Guards the Royal Strathspeys did not go to the length of having their men carried on to parade and set down in place so that dust did not settle on them; but they had their standards nevertheless. Colour-Sergeant Barr officiously repeated each admonishment in a loud voice, taking due note of the miscreant's name. At the end of the front rank he halted, took a pace backward, and shouted, 'Front rank, one pace forward—*march!*' The officers moved along the second rank and then along the others. When the inspection was complete the ranks were closed again and Colour-Sergeant Barr marched to the right, took up his dressing with such smartness that Ogilvie could almost fancy he could hear the click of the eyeballs, then stood himself and his men at ease. Ogilvie marched to a central position before the front rank, halted, turned right, and stood at ease himself. All around the parade ground, similar movements were taking place in the other seven companies. On a horse in the centre of the parade, near the gallows, sat Captain Andrew Black, tall, dark, dour, brooding, but with sharp eyes that swept the whole battalion bare. One by one, the company commanders called their companies to attention and made their reports to the adjutant, reports which Black acknowledged with wordless salutes. When all reports were in, Black turned his horse and rode towards Major John Hay, second in command, to whom he in turn reported. Hay rode sedately off parade. He came back within the minute, ahead of a cavalcade of four mounted officers: Ogilvie's father, Lieutenant-General Sir Iain Ogilvie, now appointed General Officer Commanding the Northern Army at Murree; the Divisional Commander, Major-General Francis Fettleworth, D.S.O., riding his charger like a sack of porridge; Colonel Lord Dornoch, commanding the 114th; and Major Morrissey, Brigade Major of the brigade formed by the Royal Strathspeys and the Connaught Rangers, the 88th Foot.

There were more salutes, and more orders passed. Ogilvie, rigid at attention now in front of his company, a little way in rear of Rob MacKinlay, felt the increased beat of his heart, a painful thump in his chest that threatened to choke him. A moment later he heard the solemn beat of crêpe-muffled drums accompanied by the thin, sad wail of the pipes. He looked straight ahead as the sounds came nearer, approaching from the left where a gap had been left in the hollow square of soldiers. Behind him he heard a low murmur from the men, an involuntary ripple of horror. Black heard it, too; there was a shout, a scream almost, from the adjutant: *'Silence in the ranks!'*

There was a sudden crash as a rifle fell, a sound that made Ogilvie start; he didn't look round, and no one else moved. No doubt the man who had fainted would be properly dealt with when all this was over—put on a charge for falling out without permission. The army was a machine and sometimes a soulless one; its parts must be kept working. The muffled drums beat closer and soon Ogilvie could no longer escape the sight of the small, slow-moving procession, except by closing his eyes. He did close them, but because he found his body swaying, he was forced to open them again. He saw Corporal Nichol, or Private Nichol to be precise, since the man had been stripped of his rank by the Court Martial. Nichol, without a helmet, badges and buttons but otherwise decently and smartly turned out and shaved, was marching along ahead of an escort and the drums and pipes, with his wrists handcuffed behind his body; and in rear of the escort came the padre and Surgeon Major Corton, and then six men bearing an empty coffin, Nichol's coffin.

The procession moved on, marched right around the lines of men, turned, and halted in front of the group of mounted officers. Regimental Sergeant-Major Cunningham, behind the coffin, his pace-stick wedged firmly into his arm-pit, turned them into line with something less than his normal authoritative bellow, and then reported to the Colonel.

'Sir! Prisoner and escort present and correct. Sir!'

Lord Dornoch nodded. He took the sheet of

paper handed to him by Black and started reading. He read in a loud, clear, carrying voice, a cool and apparently emotionless voice. The words of the charge, the sentence of the Court Martial, echoed across the otherwise silent parade. Ogilvie heard them only dimly and patchily, through the drumming of the blood in his ears. '... it having been represented ... by Lieutenant James Iain Conal MacGregor Ogilvie of Her Majesty's 114th Regiment, and by Hamish Barr, Colour-Sergeant ... that on the 17th day of May 1895, John Edward Nichol, Corporal ... did kill by shooting Second Lieutenant Philip Harold Westover Adams ...'

Ogilvie shivered.

Yes, Nichol was a murderer all right, and a looter and a raper too. Short of desertion in the face of the enemy, or treason, he had committed the most heinous three crimes in the British Army's book. Killing an officer was a deed that simply had to shake the whole foundation of militarism, all the way from Calcutta to Whitehall and back again; no one was going to quarrel with the G.O.C.'s personal decision to mount a public execution. The army had to know what happened when an officer was murdered—fair enough! But Ogilvie knew that Nichol had never meant to kill that officer. He had aimed at Colour-Sergeant Barr. Barr the bully, Barr the man with the build and mentality of a prize-fighter,

11

Barr the loud-mouthed persecutor of everyone below him. Poor Adams had got in the way, as poor Adams had had a habit of doing ever since he'd arrived from Sandhurst. And Ogilvie was convinced that Nichol would never have used his rifle at all if Colour-Sergeant Barr hadn't asked for trouble by his ranting behaviour ever since he'd got his promotion. Not, of course, that that was any excuse; but it did constitute a reason. Nevertheless, the facts had been all too plain, and Ogilvie had naturally had no option but to back his Colour-Sergeant and make his report accordingly as soon as he had brought his patrol back to cantonments. It had been a simple probe, that patrol, against a village where some Afridi tribesmen, on a sortie from Afghanistan, had been believed, erroneously as it had turned out, to be in hiding; but things had gone wrong, tempers had flared on both sides, Barr himself being far from blameless in this respect, and there had been bloody fighting. In the middle of all this, Corporal Nichol had decided to go on the rampage. He had gone on a looting expedition and had been caught by Adams and Barr in the act of raping a young Shinwari girl and he had used his rifle.

It had been sordid enough and of course Nichol had to die. It was the ceremonial that appalled. This, after all, was the mid-nineties, not pre-Mutiny days.

'. . . found guilty by General Court Martial

and sentenced to die by hanging,' came the Colonel's steady voice, breaking once again into Ogilvie's consciousness. Ogilvie watched as Dornoch folded the sheet of paper and handed it to Black, who saluted punctiliously, his face stiff and formal and solemn. Dornoch went on, 'This sentence has been confirmed by the Commander-in-Chief, India, and by His Excellency the Viceroy and will now be carried out.' He glanced at the Regimental Sergeant-Major. 'Carry on, please, Sarn't-Major.'

'Sir!' Again a salute, and the awesome process, as Cunningham turned about, moved into its final phase. 'Prisoner and escort, into line, left *turn*. Slow . . . *march*. Left . . . right . . . left.' The drums beat out the time. Slow, Ogilvie thought. It was horrible. But it had to be protracted, it had to be given its due weight since a man was going to die within the next few minutes. The small procession wheeled; Ogilvie watched Nichol's face as he passed by B Company. It was dead white and the lips were trembling, but the man seemed composed, dazed perhaps, and was marching smartly, keeping time to the crêpe-draped drums, reacting automatically to his training. It was grotesque. Ogilvie had a feeling that if he were in a similar predicament he would go to his death cursing the army, and the Colonel, and the General, the lot of them. He licked at dust-dry lips, felt a cold sweat pour down inside his tunic. Across the parade ground, in

13

E company's ranks, two more men had fainted and lay stretched out beneath the sun, their rifles lying in the dust.

Cunningham halted the procession in the shadow of the gallows. With Surgeon Major Corton and the padre, Nichol climbed the steps to the platform. He was still hand-cuffed. He looked down at the motionless escort, at his coffin lying open, ready on the ground beside the gallows. Impossible at this stage to guess his thoughts; but Ogilvie saw the eyes widen as the hangman placed the noose around his neck and adjusted the sliding knot. There was a brief and completely pointless examination by Corton, and then the padre began reading his office, very quietly, very privately and personally. Both Corton and the padre looked white and sick. Ogilvie closed his eyes again, and this time kept them closed. He was not looking when the end came for Nichol. He was aware of an utterly indescribable mechanical sound, and then it was all over and done with. He heard orders being shouted in unnatural voices and when he opened his eyes the body was swinging from the rope. There were more orders and the pipes and drums beat strongly to life; the battalion was manoeuvred into column and the scarlet-clad ranks marched around the parade and away, to a lively quickstep, past the dangling corpse on the gallows, back to cantonments.

CHAPTER TWO

The events of that day had not quite ended with the pathetic remains that dangled from the gallows. Later, James Ogilvie was marched into the Colonel's office by the adjutant. Black stood hard-faced and sardonic between him and the door as he stood at attention, carrying his helmet, before Major-General Francis Fettleworth who was sitting behind the Colonel's desk reading, or appearing to read, a batch of papers. The Colonel stood by his side, his face expressionless. Minutes passed before the General looked up and said, 'Now, Mr. Ogilvie, you know, I think, why you're here?'

'Yes, sir.'

'Hrrrmph.' Fettleworth blew through a yellowed moustache, then bared his teeth like a horse; this was a habit of his, a nervous *tic*. It revealed bad teeth, blackened and stumpy. He said, 'If I'd not been going straight to Calcutta from here, young man, you'd have been ordered to Division, naturally. Because you haven't been, you're not to take what I have to say less weightily. Do I make myself clear?'

'Yes, sir.'

'Good.' Fettleworth leaned forward, an action which caused his stomach to bulge across the edge of the desk. 'Now. I don't believe I need go into much detail. You've already heard your Colonel's remarks on the subject of that wretched patrol—what?'

'Yes, sir.'

'You'd have heard mine before now, if it hadn't been considered the official reprimand would sink in more effectively after what you've just witnessed.' Fettleworth stared at Ogilvie from blue pop-eyes the protuberance of which seemed to accentuate the stupidity of his face. 'What did you think of the parade, young man?'

'I think it was abominable, sir.'

'Hold your tongue!' Black snapped from behind.

'All right, Captain Black,' Fettleworth said irritably. 'Mr. Ogilvie, you show a certain courage in saying that to me, though I'm not sure it doesn't verge on impertinence. However. So you think it was abominable, do you? Why?'

Ogilvie said, 'The man deserved his punishment, sir, of course. But to do it ceremonially . . . was sadism.'

'Sadism? Rubbish!' Fettleworth's face grew scarlet. 'Sadism my backside. It seems you need to toughen up, Mr. Ogilvie. Damn little wart. The army, the Queen's service—it isn't a damn bunfight for old ladies! Sooner you realize that, the better it'll be for you.' Fettleworth leaned farther forward and his paunch rose like a flood tide over the Colonel's blotting-pad. 'Murder's murder. The

16

men have to be made to realize that, or we're all liable to be shot in our beds. D'you imagine the lesson would sink home if a murderer was quietly hanged in some civil jail? Hey? What have you to say to that?'

'Nothing, sir.'

'So I should damn well think! Captain Black.'

'Sir?'

'Open a window. Place stinks. If Lord Dornoch doesn't like fresh air, I do.'

'Sir.' Black moved obsequiously and did as he had been told. Dornoch was looking furiously angry at the General's lack of manners. 'Is that wide enough, sir?'

'Yes. Now, Ogilvie. I have a point or two to make.' Fettleworth sucked in air. 'The men are uneducated beasts and must be treated as such! Points must be rigorously and ruthlessly *impressed* upon them. That is the whole point of ceremonial, the whole vital point of today's parade and of the way that blackguard was executed. The men are not as you and I, young man—they are *not gentlemen*. Dammit, there's a world of difference—you know that as well as I do. They don't think like us, they don't react like us, I'd go so far as to say they don't even damn well *feel* like us! They're a separate breed, damn 'em! They're here to do what they're told—by me and ultimately by you, in the name of Her Majesty. It's the only way to run an Empire. Discipline must be maintained

17

by every means available, including hanging when necessary—*public* hanging. Do you understand me, Mr. Ogilvie?'

Ogilvie understood one thing, and that was, why Fettleworth was known to his rank-and-file as Bloody Francis. He found a red mist before his eyes, a mist in the centre of which Fettleworth's face bobbed and gyrated like a blue-veined scarlet balloon; but he managed to say, 'Yes, sir.'

'Good! Then we shall make some progress—make a soldier of you! Now, I have this to say and I don't want to be interrupted while I'm saying it. That man's death today, also the unfortunate end of Mr. Adams, is largely attributable to yourself ... shut your confounded mouth, sir! Did I, or did I not, order you to remain silent?'

Ogilvie, who had started to speak, said once again, 'Yes, sir.'

'Then do as you're told, boy. I repeat, those deaths are largely attributable to you, which leads me to the reason why you're here before me, Mr. Ogilvie. You were responsible for that patrol, were you not? You were supposed to be *in charge* of the patrol? *The patrol was not supposed to be in charge of you?* Looting, rape and murder took place—and why?' A hefty fist crashed down on the desk. 'Dammit, I'll tell you why! Because you had *lost* control and couldn't put a stop to trouble even before it had started—which it was your duty to do! In

18

effect, Mr. Ogilvie, you abrogated that duty and let the men have their will—with the result we all know too well. The Court Martial transcript shows clearly that you believed Nichol to have been aiming for your Colour-Sergeant rather than for Mr. Adams. You were, as I recall myself, insistent upon that point—as though it could make any material difference! But I read into this, that you are not happy with your Colour-Sergeant. You do not, I think, like his methods with the men. Allow me to impress upon you that it is the officers' methods and not an N.C.O.'s that should be reflected in the conduct of the private soldiers in a company. I suggest—I hasten to add this—I suggest no slur upon your company commander—this patrol was in *your* charge directly, not Captain MacKinlay's, and you are his senior subaltern. If you don't like the way your Colour-Sergeant behaves, it is open to you to correct him and lay down the lines within the broader area as set by your adjutant. However, you must not misunderstand me, Mr. Ogilvie. I have not said, and will not say, that I disapprove in any detail of the conduct of Colour-Sergeant Barr. He perhaps realizes, as you so far do not, what material the men are made of. In a word—trash, mostly. He realizes that they must on all occasions be pushed to the limit—and frequently beyond. Nichol behaved as he did because he hadn't the makings of a good

19

soldier in him—and because his officer had failed to exercise full control. For that omission *you* must be punished, Mr. Ogilvie.'

Fettleworth paused expectantly, but Ogilvie was becoming used to the ways of generals so made no response and thus gave no openings. Sharply Fettleworth went on, 'You will not, however, be punished in any ordinary sense. I am told you behaved well in the action against the rebel in Jalalabad a year ago—this has counted in your favour. So your punishment is to be unconventional.' He smiled, coldly. 'You and Colour-Sergeant Barr will continue, contrary to what you may well have expected following upon your remarks to the Court, to serve together in the same company. I have agreed this with your Colonel. It may well be that you have much to learn from Barr. You will learn it well, Mr. Ogilvie. If there should be any further trouble, you will answer for it to me and I shall not be lenient again. That is all. You may go.'

Ogilvie saluted and turned about. As he marched from the room he caught the gleam of satisfaction in Black's cold dark eyes. He had expected that; Black always seemed pleased to see a subaltern in trouble. Ogilvie thrust the adjutant from his mind and later that same day attended an event that had been laid on especially to obliterate from the officers' minds the spectacle they had been forced to witness in the morning: a game of polo, played against the Connaught Rangers. Ogilvie was not one of the regimental team; but he was an enforced spectator—it was expected that all officers not otherwise employed should support such functions. Ogilvie was not especially interested; and found himself a silent member of a group of his fellow subalterns who were giving the 114th's team a vociferous backing.

One of them thumped him violently between the shoulder-blades. 'Give your own side a cheer, can't you?'

Ogilvie snapped, 'Leave me alone!'

'Oh, so you want to be left to cry in the corner, do you, till nanny comes along to dry your tears? My dear chap! One would have thought the memory of past successes would have been enough to see you through a botched patrol—what?' This had been said in a loud voice, and there was a shout of laughter from the others. Ogilvie felt his face flaming; the rest of that game was misery. He hadn't minded the dig about the patrol as much as the sardonic reference to his actions at Jalalabad the year before—the hero's welcome he'd been given after that, when the regiments marched back to Peshawar, had aroused mixed emotions in his contemporaries and one of those emotions had been a degree of jealousy. He had been made to suffer in all kinds of small ways for the enormity of a newly-joined subaltern having the effrontery to distinguish

21

himself before his fellows. Things had been made no easier by his own introverted nature; he knew he was in danger of becoming unpopular with the other subalterns but found himself quite unable to do anything about it. He couldn't break through the reserve implanted by his tutorial upbringing, through an inability to mix on equal terms with other men of his own age. He could get on well enough with older men, and this in itself was another cause of resentment from the younger ones: Ogilvie, if he was not careful, would become looked upon as a currier of favour which, in truth, was very far from being the case. He ached with relief when the polo was finished, his own regiment being the losers. When he got back to his room a messenger came from the Colonel. Mr. Ogilvie's presence was requested as soon as convenient. Fettleworth having by this time departed with much fuss for Calcutta, Ogilvie's interview, he found, was a private one with his Colonel alone.

Dornoch told him to sit down and then asked, 'How's the wound, James?'

'The wound?' Ogilvie was surprised. He had suffered a flesh wound during the fighting in the village, but hadn't thought anything more about it after the doctor had dressed it on his return. 'It's healed, Colonel. It was nothing.'

Dornoch grunted. 'Possibly, possibly. It can flare up again, though. Nasty things

22

sometimes—flesh wounds! It'll do very nicely as an excuse. Major Corton's willing to back that.'

Ogilvie looked even more surprised. 'I don't understand, Colonel. I'm perfectly fit.'

'That may be—in body, James. Oh, it's nothing at all to worry about—it's simply that in my opinion you've been through a pretty nasty experience. The patrol alone . . . and I'm not taking back what I said earlier, nor undermining the General either. You've got to live it down—and I know you will. But today's business, too—and the point the General made about your own indirect responsibility. I don't want you to take that too much to heart, though you can always learn from the moral. I've no doubt you've been blaming yourself in any case. Am I right, James?'

Stiff-faced, Ogilvie nodded.

'I thought as much.' Dornoch drummed his fingers on the arm of his chair. 'Don't, for God's sake, dwell on it. The same sort of thing has happened in the past to more experienced officers than yourself. Ultimately, it hasn't done them any harm. However, to get to the point: I'm sending you up to Simla for a while—and I want a fair excuse, or there'll be talk of medicals. You know what I mean—the army's getting keener and keener on the medicos and their wizardry. We don't want that. The bullet that nicked you is going to be the given reason.' He smiled. 'Any questions?'

'I don't know, Colonel. I . . . didn't expect this. I'm not keen to be away from the regiment. How long shall I be in Simla?'

'Let's say six weeks. You've earned a rest and some leave's due. It'll do you good—give you a chance to take a fresh look at things. Your mother's there, I gather.'

'Yes . . .'

'Well—you'll like to see her, of course. And she'll like to have you for your twenty-first, I know. Your leave'll cover that.' Lord Dornoch reached out for his pipe and filled it. 'Have a word with Silverson at Brigade.' Major Silverson was the Transport Officer. 'The nearest railway station to Simla is at Kalka, that's nearly sixty miles from the town. You'll have to arrange ahead for your onward transport from the railhead.' He added, 'You can push off as soon as Brigade can fix it up for you.'

When he was back in his own quarters Ogilvie told himself what he knew already—that he had a good friend in Lord Dornoch. The Colonel could scarcely have gone further in indicating his disapproval of the way Fettleworth had handled things that day. Ever since Fettleworth had been given the command of their Division, Ogilvie had been aware that he got on with few of his colonels, and Dornoch possibly least of all. Fettleworth had the reputation of a meddler, and worse, a bungling meddler. In a sense he was typical of

24

the senior officers of the day, between whom and the junior officers there was a vast and apparently unbridgeable chasm. Fettleworth's formative years had been passed under the command of veterans from the pre-Mutiny era—men who had fought at Chillianwallah for instance, where one of the brigadier-generals had been so blind from sheer age that not only had he to be hoisted on to his horse before the battle, but had to have the animal pointed towards the enemy in case he should charge in the wrong direction when action commenced. Fettleworth's ideas were those of other days with a vengeance, and mentally he was fighting the campaigns of Lucknow and Delhi and Cawnpore, and of the Crimea as well. Tactical exercises under Francis Fettleworth had been farcical; he had assiduously set his infantry to practise deployment for attack, but always in close formation as at Waterloo; and he had shown his incredible fondness for the good old impregnable British square as well. He was unresilient in mind and body and also he had a total disregard for the welfare of the troops under his command. He was as different from Lord Dornoch as chalk from cheese, but in point of fact he was little worse than a good many other officers of general's rank. This opinion of Fettleworth was not confined to his long-suffering Staff or regimental officers. In different words it found its expression in the mouth of Private Burns in B Company's barrack-room that very night, for Burns, supposedly on some fatigue or other, had been standing spellbound outside the Colonel's office window when Fettleworth had been haranguing Ogilvie; and was now repeating some of the speech to his comrades.

'It's an insult to Scotland to say it,' he was announcing, 'but yon great fat-arsed bugger's as much a sheep's gut as a haggis is. Oh Lord, I've never heard the like of him, rantin' away there about poor bloody Jocks! Trash, that's what we are. Uneducated beasts. His very words, gentlemen. We don't even feel. We're a different breed, d'ye see. We have to be larrupped and flogged along, we can fight only when the skin's hanging off our bloody backsides.' Suddenly, he laughed. 'Does anyone know, has the bastard a daughter? If he has, well, we know a thing or two to do with her, eh?' There was a shout of laughter from his audience; with that day's parade in mind still, they were ready for anything that would lighten their spirits. And when the Orderly Sergeant looked in he was assailed with the chorus:

'Oh, we'll be there, yes we'll be there,
In that little harness room across the square!
When they're blowing up Defaulters
We'll be screwing the General's daughters

26

In that little harness room across the square . . .'

*   *   *

Mary Archdale was brushing her hair in front of her looking-glass when her Indian servant announced that Ogilvie Sahib had called.

She looked pleased. She said, 'Ask Ogilvie Sahib to wait. I shall not be long.'

'Yes, Memsahib.'

The servant withdrew. Mary Archdale finished brushing her hair, dabbed scent behind her ears and on her wrists, and dressed as attractively as she could. She had seen quite a lot of James Ogilvie in the social round and their friendship had progressed a great deal over the year Ogilvie had been in Peshawar. She found she was frequently thinking of him. It was indiscreet of him to call at the bungalow, of course, but she was glad he had done so; and she assumed, with a glint of mischief in her eyes now, that he knew very well that Tom had gone to Calcutta ahead of his Divisional Commander, General Fettleworth. Poor Tom—she always thought of him as poor Tom, though really the adjective was unfitting for that bloodthirsty officer—poor Tom's life was being made a burden by General Fettleworth. After the Jalalabad affair, in which he had scarcely shone, Tom Archdale had ceased to be Brigade Major of the Mahratta Brigade in

27

Sir Iain Ogilvie's Division, and Mary had known quite well that this was Sir Iain's personal doing, since he couldn't stand Tom Archdale. But Tom had had lines out in other directions and Fettleworth had seen to it that he was given a job on his own staff after Sir Iain had been elevated from the Division to the Northern Army Command. But meanwhile, Sir Iain's son was waiting upon her and so she made haste to join him in the drawing-room.

She went towards him, her arms outstretched, as he got up from a chair. 'James,' she said gaily. 'How nice!' Then she saw the look on his face. 'Oh, dear. What *is* the matter, James?' She wanted to embrace him; she felt motherly, but an embrace would never do. Besides, in a curious way, she felt dominated by him at times in spite of the fact that she was seven years the older. Perhaps it was because he was tall, and had a strong and sometimes formidable face; yet there was still that motherly feeling, possibly because of the contrast with Tom, who was nearly thirty years her senior. She knew she didn't look her age, and that James Ogilvie certainly did not regard her as anything approaching a mother, though now and then he did make use of her, to talk to so that he could get things out of his system. This, she could see, was to be one of those times, so she helped him. She said, 'I half expected you, James. That business yesterday morning . . .'

'Yes,' he said, and surprisingly added, 'Damn army life.'

'Dear, dear!' she said lightly. 'James, it's no use damning army life like that! You're in it now.' She turned away towards a sofa, and sat. She patted the seat beside her and when he too had sat she went on, 'Yesterday was horrible I'm sure, and I'm thankful Tom wasn't there. It would have appealed to his blood lust and he'd have been even more impossible afterwards.'

'Why wasn't he there, Mary? I quite expected him to be.'

'He went ahead to Calcutta. You didn't know that?'

He shook his head. 'No. Mary, it . . . it's not just that horrible hanging. It's that patrol and all it's led to. I don't know . . . I'm starting to hate the whole thing, the whole idea of soldiering. I didn't take a commission to be a bastard to the men. And that's what Fettleworth expects an officer to be.'

'Oh, Fettleworth!' she said disdainfully. She smiled at him.

'It's all very well saying that. He has the power to do pretty much as he likes. And honestly, Mary, his mentality makes me sick.'

She smiled again, conspiratorially. 'Not too loud,' she warned. 'Walls have hundreds of ears in Peshawar. I suppose you realize it's quite bad enough we're alone together in Tom's absence—if we should be overheard

29

talking treason as well, we'd both be rushed off to gaol!'

He didn't seem to be listening. He said, 'D'you know, I've a damn good mind to chuck it—send in my papers.'

'Oh, dear,' she said in concern. 'It's as bad as that! I'm sure it isn't really.' She hesitated, then went on crisply, 'Stop being sorry for yourself, James. It never did anyone any good. Think in terms of success. After Jalalabad, everyone knows you have it in you. Don't worry about that old bludgeon Fettleworth. He has a reputation that stretches from Colchester to Hong Kong and back.'

'Yes—and he's still a general! That being the case, I'm not sure my own ambitions haven't taken rather a knock!'

'Oh, fiddlesticks, James. If you become a general, you won't be one like Fettleworth. Tom tells me the army's changing quite fast these days . . . of course, *he* doesn't like that. He likes the old ways. He's old enough to be a general himself if he had the right friends in the right places, and his thinking's much the same as Fettleworth's. But he has enough intelligence to see what's coming. Generals aren't always going to be like Fettleworth. Your time'll come, and when it does, you'll be able to do your bit to speed the process of change. You could regard that as what you owe to the men, couldn't you? But in the meantime, James dear, you can tell me exactly

30

what Fettleworth said that upset you.'

He did; and told her also of his subsequent interview with Lord Dornoch, and of the fact that he was being sent to Simla without the option. She listened to him as she had so often done, without overdoing her sympathy, and chided him out of some of his depression. When he had gone she went back to her bedroom thoughtfully and spent some while in front of her looking-glass, studying herself and thinking about James Ogilvie as she did so. Mary Archdale was no fool and she had a streak of hardness in her of which she was fully aware; and she knew that James wanted far more of her than just a motherly talking-to. She would, indeed, dearly have loved to give him what he wanted, but India was India and the army was the army. No one had a private life unless they were most exceptionally clever. James was far too transparent. If she should have an affair with him his face, when they met socially in company, would give him away. An affair with another officer's wife would be bad, could be disastrous for his career. Mary was fond of him and had no wish to cause him harm; but she liked his company and that streak of hardness made her disregard the possible consequences that could flow from a continuance of their friendship. Despite the social life of Peshawar, her own life was empty and dull; Tom she detested, as James Ogilvie knew well enough—she had never been slow to criticize her husband to him, but she did not feel this to be underhand since she criticized Tom to his face as well. Tom had no money to compensate for his boorishness, either, and as an unhappy young woman married to an elderly boor with no private means she felt a rather desperate need for congenial company whenever possible. The fact that James Ogilvie gave every appearance of having fallen in love with her was a complication and, for him, a shame; but it was also a compliment and quite exciting.

*   *   *

It was a long and uncomfortable journey to Simla, which lay in the foothills of Himalaya some 450 miles south-east of the garrison at Peshawar. Nevertheless Ogilvie, who started the journey three days after his interview with Lord Dornoch, enjoyed the experience of travelling free of regimental cares and duties. At Kalka he was met by a bullock-cart and proceeded at a leisurely pace along a mountain road for Simla, making an overnight stop en route at a so-called hotel that turned out to be little more than a hovel in a smelly village street. He reached Simla through a dense mist that overlay the plain and rolled up around the lower hills, gradually engulfing the peaks. The natural scenery was splendid enough, as he was to see when the mist had cleared—the firs, the

32

multitudinous variety of brilliantly colourful blossoms set against a deep blue sky with the background of snow-covered mountains to the north—but man, it seemed, had done his best to ruin what nature had provided. Simla's public buildings were utterly depressing— nothing more than a conglomeration of terrible architecture, while the private dwellings, thrown across the spurs of the foothills or perched on the hilltops and seeming in constant danger of sliding down into the valleys, were mostly unbeautiful single-storey bungalows of wooden construction and with the most hideous corrugated-iron roofs; even Viceregal Lodge, completed on Observatory Hill by Lord Dufferin back in '88, was little more prepossessing. The roads were excessively narrow and were unable to accommodate carriages, so that while the menfolk rode on horseback the ladies were pulled in four-man rickshaws. The climate, however, was pleasant with the fragrance of the mountain air. In point of fact it was not so very different from that of Peshawar; but Ogilvie could well imagine what a relief it must be to the government officials to shift their place of work, in the summer months, from the steamy heat of Calcutta to this near-English hill station.

His mother, he found, as befitted the wife of the General Officer Commanding at Murree,

33

had a very much more imposing bungalow than the majority of those he had passed on his way in; and she was as delighted to see him as he had known she would be.

'It's so truly wonderful, darling,' Lady Ogilvie said for the tenth time as, soon after his arrival, an Indian servant brought tea to the drawing-room, 'to think I shall have you here for your birthday ... though I've a suspicion you'd sooner have spent it with your regiment all the same! I know quite well what young men are, James.' Her eyebrows lifted at him over her fine, dark eyes. 'Well? Am I right?'

He laughed. 'Good heavens, no, mother! I'm as pleased as punch, honestly I am.'

She nodded, content with the reassurance. 'You shall not be short of people of your own age, James, that's one thing. Half British India seems to be here—plenty of young government men, and any number of daughters of the older ones, of course. You'll have your work cut out to avoid *them*, I can tell you!' He noticed his mother was looking at him curiously. 'Did you know you've grown remarkably good-looking, dear boy?'

'Oh, nonsense, mother,' Ogilvie protested. He was never entirely certain whether or not she was teasing him; and in any case such sentiments embarrassed him.

She said, 'But it's true, James darling. And all the young women are here for one thing above all: husbands!'

'Yes,' he said, 'I've heard that.'

'Well, don't say I didn't warn you.' Lady Ogilvie spoke with a suspicion of asperity. James as a handsome escort for the daughter of a General or a high-ranking Civilian was one thing; he would do his mother great credit. James as a husband was quite another. Lady Ogilvie disapproved of officers marrying young and James was certainly *much* too young; and besides, she wanted him all to herself for a few more years yet. 'More tea?' she asked.

'Thank you.' He got to his feet to pass her the cup, but she waved him back. She said, 'The bell, James. Please ring it.' He walked across the big room and tugged at an embroidered bell-pull and the Indian servant came in, took his cup on a word from Lady Ogilvie, stood while the memsahib refilled it, and then conveyed it back to the young sahib. Ogilvie reflected that he had had to walk farther to the bell-pull than he would have needed to walk to reach the teatable . . . When the servant had withdrawn Lady Ogilvie said, 'I think your father will be coming to Simla soon.'

'Oh—that's good news, mother.' Frankly, he wasn't sure if it was good news or bad; his father was always apt to treat him as a defaulter. 'When's he due?'

Lady Ogilvie shrugged. 'One never quite knows with your father, dear boy. He's terribly busy in his new command and he's all over the place, which is why he prefers me to remain here rather than be with him all the time. I think we can expect him within the next week or so, though. I know he'll want to be here for your birthday if he can.' She smiled, tenderly. 'A twenty-first is a once-and-for-all occasion, after all.'

'Yes.' He drank his tea. He had a strong feeling his mother was keeping off the subject of the patrol and the hanging and he was grateful; he had rather dreaded being questioned, but supposed he needn't have been. His mother was a soldier's daughter and a soldier's wife as well as being a soldier's mother—that must count, though there had been times in the past when she hadn't always been so tactful with his father. There was a somewhat long pause and then Lady Ogilvie said, 'I don't suppose you've heard Anne's coming out?'

'Really?' Anne was James's sister, the Ogilvies' younger married daughter. 'Well, that's jolly good news, I must say—'

'Not really, James—for you, I mean. She won't be here at the same time as you—but I shall hope to bring her to Peshawar, so perhaps you'll see her then. John's managed to get long leave from his regiment and is going on safari in Africa. You remember he always wanted to . . . bag a lion, I think was what he said. He's sending Anne to us while he's out there.' She paused again. 'There's another piece of news

36

as well, James.'

'Something else I don't know?'

'Yes. Hector's out here.'

'Here—in *India*?' Ogilvie looked highly surprised; he could scarcely begin to imagine his neatly-dressed, starchy cousin as part of the Indian scene. Hector Ogilvie was much more suited to his normal habitat, which was Belgravia when away from his duties and, when engaged upon them, the quiet, dark corridors of the India Office overlooking the ordered cleanliness of the Horse Guards. His squeamish soul would surely revolt against the dirt and smells of the sub-continent, the rotting, disease-ridden beggars lying inertly in the Calcutta streets, covered with flies that they had not the strength or the will to disperse from their rag-covered bodies. But then, no doubt, the aristocratic young first-flight Civil Servants of the India Office needed on occasion to come to grips with the territory they so distantly ruled—and in fact it was no bad thing that they should familiarize themselves with the realities of life and the results of their paper work. Ogilvie asked without enthusiasm, 'Where exactly is he—Calcutta?'

'Yes, at the moment. He's attached to the judiciary—don't ask me to be more precise than that, for I can't be—and his department is moving here for the monsoon—'

'Here?'

'Yes—'

'When, mother?'

'Quite soon. He'll be here for your birthday, James.' Lady Ogilvie smiled placatingly. 'I'm sorry, darling, I know you two don't get on, but it really can't be helped.'

'No, mother, of course not.' They sat and talked for a long time of family matters, of life back at the regimental depot at Invermore in Scotland, which Ogilvie was unlikely to see again for the next six years. They talked of home—of Corriecraig Castle left to the cares of the Ogilvies' agent whilst its master and laird was defending the cause of Empire overseas. A servant came in to clear away the remains of tea, returning shortly after to bring in the lamps. Ogilvie sat and watched the shadows grow long over the surrounding hills and valleys—the drawing-room had a magnificent view right into Himalaya—and the sunset colours on the snow-capped peaks in the far distances where they ran back into the mysterious closed land of Tibet and then through to China. They were still talking when the evening drinks were brought in and the curtains drawn. The Indian servant poured sherry for Lady Ogilvie, whisky for the son. After the immense dinner which followed the whisky, Ogilvie went early to bed; he was physically tired from the jolting, lurching ride in the slow bullock-cart, and he was mentally tired as well, his mind still dwelling on the grotesque grimness of that last parade at Peshawar.

The first ten days thereafter passed quickly in a whirl of his mother's social engagements, when Ogilvie was introduced to as many prominent personages as could be fitted into the calendar against a time when they might prove helpful to his career. On the eleventh day he had a surprise, a very pleasant one. Mary Archdale turned up in Simla. The first he knew of this was when a letter came for him. *'My dear James,'* she had written. *'Here I am in Simla!! I can imagine your surprise! Things moved fast after I saw you, Tom seems to think trouble is coming from the tribes north of Peshawar, though I am not supposed to say this, anyway he wanted to get me away in case & decided to pull some strings & send me to Simla for the time being. Do come & see me won't you. Love, Mary.*

With no very precise idea why, Ogilvie said nothing of the letter to his mother, but he went round to Mary's bungalow that very afternoon although he knew he had annoyed and disappointed Lady Ogilvie. She had protested, 'But you can't go out, James. Really you can't! You know the Cuthbertsons are coming to tea, and there are bound to be more callers who will want to meet you.' She saw the obstinate look that came over his face and she sighed. 'What is it you want to *do*, dear boy?'

'Just to—to get away by myself for a while.'

She nodded. 'Simla *is* like that, I know. But *must* it be this afternoon?'

'Yes, mother. I—I have things to think about. I can't explain more than that, honestly.'

She narrowed her eyes, noted the look of strain that had succeeded the obstinacy. Undoubtedly, the immediate past was on his mind, and it was not good that he should brood. She hoped it would not be too long before her husband arrived. Meanwhile, she knew she could do no more than put the best face possible on the present matter. She said a little distantly, 'Oh, very well, James, you know your business best. I'll try to explain to Colonel and Mrs. Cuthbertson . . . but it *is* a pity. Colonel Cuthbertson is such an influential man.'

He couldn't help grinning at that. 'More than father?'

She said, 'Surely I don't need to tell you that an outsider is usually in a better position than a father to help young men?'

'That's true,' he said, 'but I'm not running after influence. I'll work my own way. Sorry, mother, but I really must go out.' He bent and kissed her on the cheek, feeling a rotter. It was thoroughly bad form to run out on his mother when she had a tea-party arranged, and he knew it, and because in addition he had told her an out-and-out lie, if only by way of concealment, for the first time in his life, his

40

conscience was heavier than it would otherwise have been when he presented himself at Mary's bungalow. As the wife of a major on the Staff, Mary had been able to secure a better bungalow than the wives of equivalent regimental officers, but it was still much below the standard of the Ogilvies' accommodation, and looked out to the south of the town, a view which, though pleasant enough, lacked the majesty of the higher ranges to the north. As Ogilvie went up the path between banks of heavily scented flowers, he felt suddenly an acute self-consciousness, as though many eyes were watching him from the windows—almost as though the eyes of Major Tom Archdale were among them, and that the portly figure of the Major would appear, metaphorically with sword drawn, pompously demanding to know what the devil a subaltern from Peshawar was doing, calling unbidden by himself upon his wife . . .

But there was no Tom Archdale, just Mary, in the drawing-room when he was shown in. He took her hand, impulsively, when the servant had left them together. He felt a tremendous longing, an almost overwhelming surge of feeling for her, one that dangerously threatened to overcome all his built-in inhibitions. Had he been sure of her response—had it not been for the fact that always she seemed to keep him as it were at arm's length—he might well have been indiscreet, for it had come into his mind, and he wondered if it had come into hers, that the luxuriantly lazy life of Simla might loosen some of the restraints imposed in distant Peshawar with all its regimental codes and disciplines and trappings.

Mary smiled and said, 'James, you're looking terribly hot and bothered.' She went so far as to lay her cheek very briefly against his; and then at once regretted it. 'No, no,' she said, as his arm went round her waist. 'No, James dear, please, you mustn't make things difficult.'

He flushed. 'I'm awfully sorry.' He stood away from her. Awkwardly he asked, for the sake of something to say, 'How's Peshawar, and the regiment?'

She laughed. 'Oh, James, you don't really want to know that! I thought you'd had enough of the army. So far as I know, they're managing to carry on in your absence, but to be perfectly honest, I'm not in the least concerned just now about Her Majesty's Royal Strathspeys ... except one of them. Come and sit down and tell me about Simla.' They sat, in two chairs facing a big window. 'Have you,' she asked, 'been enjoying yourself, James?'

'I suppose so. It's been—different, and it's been a rest in a way. One can have too many damn tea-parties, though,' he added with a smile. 'Mother loves tea-parties.'

'Yes, mothers do, nobody else does. You

42

needn't tell me! Is that all you've been doing?' She studied his face. 'No young ladies?'

Again he flushed—that hateful habit that he couldn't overcome. 'No.'

'M-h'm. James, you're not *still* brooding?'

'I don't know.'

'Which means you are. That's such a pity. I thought you were going to lead the new army, and see to it that—things such as happened to Corporal Nichol, don't happen any more. Aren't you?'

He said moodily, 'I don't know. Perhaps.' He sat in silence for a while after that, and she didn't break it. At last he said, 'It's a funny thing, Mary, but I begin to feel differently about things when I'm with you, and then when I leave you it all comes back. I think I draw a little courage from you.'

'Oh, dear, you don't need that!' she said gaily, then saw how deadly in earnest he was. In a quiet voice she said, 'You've plenty of your own. I don't think you realize how much. It's been quite a tough battle, tougher than you know. Indian military life isn't life with a private crammer. Sandhurst helped, but you made the transition mostly on your own. If you could do that with credit, there's no limit to what you can do eventually. Don't ever be stupidly blinded to your own achievement or your own potential. I've a feeling you're at a crossroads, James dear. I'd like to give you a good, hard push down the right path.'

43

She meant it; he could see that in her face as he looked into her eyes. But he felt she was wrong, felt that he had already taken the wrong path by joining the army in the first place. What had happened on the parade at Peshawar had affected him too deeply; a man who was born to soldiering would have shrugged it off by now. He said as much to Mary, and her crisp retort was, 'Rubbish. All the subalterns of the 114th will be feeling the same way, but they'll be drowning it in *chota pegs*. When the spirits drain away again, they'll be feeling better. That's what you should be doing.' She added, 'By the way, James, has your mother talked of it at all?'

'No.'

'Has she tried to?'

'No.'

She said, 'I'm glad. Mothers aren't really good for young men—they tend to be over-sympathetic and that's *not* what you want. It's not what you'll get from *me*, my lad!' she added with a mocking glint in her eyes. 'My function in life is to tell you you're behaving like a ninny!'

He started, and looked at her in complete astonishment. 'Do you really mean that?' he asked.

'Yes,' she said flatly.

'I'll bear that in mind.' His tone was stiff.

'You do that, James! And keep on remembering you can give yourself a mission

44

inside the army and the regiment: a mission to do what Nelson did for the navy—humanize it. You know what I mean—"Let humanity, after victory, be the predominant feature in the British Fleet." You're young enough to have a good, long try!'

*   *   *

With a metaphorical fanfare of trumpets to herald him, Sir Iain Ogilvie descended upon Simla four days after his son's visit to Mary Archdale. He meant to spend as long as possible free from the cares and responsibilities of Murree, always provided the disturbing news, as reported by Tom Archdale to Mary, didn't blow up into warfare; which privately he felt it might. Sir Iain would be taking the opportunity of his visit to have some probably lengthy talks with the Commander-in-Chief India, who would also be in Simla with his staff. Sir Iain was accompanied by his nephew Hector, son of Sir Iain's brother Rufus, who, as a rear-admiral in the Queen's Navy, was currently commanding a battle squadron of the Channel Fleet. Hector, who had joined his uncle in Murree from Calcutta, was the very antithesis of Sir Iain—he was pale and slight and pedantic, clerkly—in his lighter moments Sir Iain was given to referring to him in the family circle as the *Munshi* Sahib—liking neither strong language, strong drink, nor any

45

sort of woman (in that sense, at all events). Sir Iain always said, disparagingly for he detested his sister-in-law, that the fellow took after his mother's family and left it thankfully at that. Certainly brother Rufus, who, when he had first been appointed to the indignity of a steam-ship command, had physically and personally and with the accompaniment of the most foul and violent abuse thrown his engineer overboard from the navigating bridge when the man had failed to produce the speed he wanted, had precious little in common with his son . . .

It was not long before Sir Iain tackled his own son about military affairs. He did this bluntly so as to get it over and done with. He said, 'I've no doubt you'll be expecting some words from me, James. As it happens, however, I have *nothing* to say. You've been informed of a certain degree of disapproval, and I happen to know what your Divisional Commander said to you.' Sir Iain, who was in the habit of referring to General Fettleworth among his peers as that bloody old dunderhead, would never have dreamed of voicing such an opinion to anyone under Fettleworth's command. 'All's been said that needs to be said and we'll leave it at that.'

'I want to talk to you about it, sir.'

The General gaped in surprise. 'You *do*—do you?' He seemed unusually irresolute all of a sudden. 'Well, damn it! Don't see why not, I suppose, if that's what you want. Advice—eh?

But I don't come into this as your ultimate commander, James. Father to son—strictly that.'

'I understand that, father.'

Sir Iain blew through his moustache. Then he jerked into action and padded silently on the balls of his feet across the room and opened the door with a sudden sharp pull. He looked out, shut the door, and came back. 'All right,' he grunted. 'Go ahead, boy—before that little bugger comes in. Hector. I'd half a suspicion he might even be listening—*never* know with these damn Civil people from Whitehall, and the feller's as sneaky as a schoolmistress, even if he is my own nephew.'

A gleam came into his eye. 'Don't like him much yourself, do you?'

James grinned. 'No, but—oh, he's not all that bad, father. I think he means well.'

'Do you!' Sir Iain snapped. He took a pinch of snuff, noisily. 'When you're my age and seniority, you'll know better than to trust *any* Civilian. Especially out here—and especially that Whitehall lot! They loathe the army—they only come out to snoop and pry and try to catch us out and cut the estimates.' He became reflective. 'I knew a feller once, colonel in Skinner's Horse, put a major-general's wife to bed. Damn Civilian out here at the time found out about it—hidden under the bed for all I know, wouldn't put it past 'em—probably jealous, bunged in a report—and poor old

47

Benson's career was finished. Died in Cheltenham. What the devil's the matter, boy?'

Protuberant blue eyes—very like Fettleworth's—glared at James, who flushed and said, 'Nothing, father. Shall we talk?'

'What d'you think I've been doing? Still— yes, all right, all right. What's the trouble?'

Summoning his courage James came straight out with it. 'I've been thinking of sending in my papers, father.'

'*What?* Sending in your papers... Why, God bless my soul, boy! Never heard such a thing in all my life. You damn well can't— you're a Royal Strathspey! My God. Officers of the 114th don't resign—they're bloody well kicked out if they want to go! Damn it—damn it, I'll *not* listen—'

'But,' James said loudly, 'I've decided against doing that.'

'What? Oh. Oh.' Sir Iain calmed down, but he still looked gravely upset. 'Well, I'm damned glad to hear it, and God be thanked for giving you a little sense.' He paced the room then stopped in front of his son. 'It's that damn hanging—isn't it?'

'Yes.'

Sir Iain took a deep breath and let it out again, slowly. Then he said, 'In my young day, that wouldn't have disturbed anyone but a few zealous reformers. The damn *missionary* sort. I've seen men similarly hanged for striking

48

their officers! You can't have an army without discipline. Even in civil life ... they used to hang 'em once for stealing a bird's egg, I believe. Still, I admit things are looked at differently these days.' He paused. 'I'll be perfectly frank with you, James. My own stomach doesn't take it as easily as it did when I was your age. I can't say I'm surprised at your reaction, boy.'

Ogilvie certainly had not expected this. In some confusion he said, 'Thank you, father. There's another thing: I'm not sure I'm wise ... in my decision to remain in the regiment. I'd like an impersonal assessment, father—a GOC's assessment, in spite of what you said about this not being official. It's rather important.'

'Assessment—eh? That's your Colonel's job—not mine.'

'But I'd like yours, father.'

Sir Iain saw that his son was in deadly earnest. He walked over to a window, stood staring out for a while, then turned and, with his hands clasped beneath his coat-tails, said, 'This is between ourselves. It's never to be quoted.' He paused; it was damned difficult, he was finding, to give one's own flesh and blood an impartial assessment. 'Take it from me, you're basically a good officer. All you need is experience to enable you to attain your full measure of self-confidence. That, and possibly a more mature and tougher approach to the

49

men. I know very well how your Divisional Commander regards the men, James. I don't disagree with him entirely.' This was as far as he would go on that point. 'They do need a very strong hand. You failed to show that strength on that one patrol, and that may have been because events took you by surprise. You'd never expected British soldiers to loot, pillage, and rape. Am I right?'

'Yes.'

'Well, you know now! Whatever they taught you at Sandhurst, you're learning the hard way that the British private soldier is no different in moments of stress from any other nationality. Not so different from the common people in civil life, either. Frankly, many of them were the dregs of society when they enlisted, and if they hadn't enlisted, they'd have spent their lives in prison. Remember that. Don't be taken by surprise again.'

'No, father. Er . . . there's something else.'

'Well?'

'Suppose there are reprisals for the looting and rape?'

Sir Iain gave his son a long look. 'There may be—there will be. It's in the nature of the hill tribes to take their revenge. *Badal*—revenge— is a Commandment of the Pathans, it is part of *Pukhtunwali*. They are bound to take revenge.'

'If that happens, will I be held to blame?'

Sir Iain hesitated, running a hand over his jaw. 'Did Lord Dornoch, or General

50

Fettleworth, suggest you might be?'

'No.'

'Then don't lose any sleep over it. You've been reprimanded. That's an end of it. We don't punish twice in the army.'

'Not ostensibly. But careers can be blocked, can't they?'

'Oho, so that's the root of the trouble, is it?' Sir Iain went on staring at his son. 'Yes, careers can be blocked. That's something we all fear, from the highest to the lowest. But clouds can be dispersed when you're young, James. If that should ever happen to you, you disperse the clouds by some worthy achievement. And never harbour a sense of injustice—that's a hopeless outlook. That's all. Anything else?'

Ogilvie shook his head.

Sir Iain said, 'Well, since we're having a talk, I've something to say on my own account before your mother comes in.' Sir Iain pulled out his watch and looked at it, then thrust it back into his waistcoat. 'In moments of depression and stress in the army, though of course not in action, a damn good skinful of drink works wonders. Not too often—just now and then when it becomes necessary.'

'Yes, father.'

'So pull that tarted-up bellrope and signify that I'm damn thirsty and don't propose to wait for your mother. One more thing.'

James, on his way across the room, turned. 'Yes, father?'

51

'Get yourself a woman. A good strong one.'

* * *

From next day onwards James Ogilvie was immersed in his mother's arrangements for his forthcoming twenty-first birthday. It was proposed that a ball be given; and after much badgering Sir Iain agreed to approach the Commander-in-Chief for the use of the ballroom at his residence of Snowdon, a gloomy but imposing mansion that would provide a fitting background for the Northern Army Commander's son's coming-of-age celebrations. Sir Iain himself supervised the compiling of the list of guests; all the notables would naturally be invited, and many of the lesser persons both military and civil, together with the rajahs who owed their loyalty to the Queen Empress in British India and some of the princely figures from native India—such of them at any rate who were not hostile. It would be a most glittering occasion. Ogilvie added to the official list by including various friends he had made in Simla, and a handful who had come up from Peshawar on leave.

Sir Iain and Lady Ogilvie went through his additions and approved them formally; only one name caused any query. 'Mrs. Archdale,' Sir Iain said. 'Archdale, Archdale. Not that constipated feller's wife, is she? Brigade Major with the damn mobile commode that he insisted on hauling all the way to Jalalabad?' Sir Iain had never forgotten, or forgiven, that episode.

Ogilvie said, 'Yes, that's the one, father.'

The General pushed irritably at the list, as though it was somehow at fault. 'God, what a fool that man is! How he ever acquired a wife I'll never know. I seem to remember . . . good deal younger than him, isn't she?'

'Yes.'

'Not going to ask him, are you?'

'He's not in Simla.'

'Oh. Oh.' The first 'oh' had carried overtones of relief and gladness, the second carried a subtly different inflexion. 'Grass widow?'

'Yes . . .'

'Hrrrrmph,' Sir Iain said; and that was all. But there was a curious frown of anxiety between Lady Ogilvie's brows as she glanced briefly at her son.

CHAPTER THREE

It was a glittering occasion indeed, almost as colourful with the uniforms and the dresses as the ball in the native ruler's palace outside Peshawar had been, the night before the march through the Khyber Pass to Jalalabad—the night Ogilvie had first met Tom Archdale's

53

wife. Once again the representatives of the British regiments were in the full splendour of their mess dress, as were the brilliantly gilded Staff. All Simla seemed to be present that night at Snowdon—all Simla that mattered. The very air was redolent with the pomp and circumstance of British India. Simla was ever party-minded; there was little else for the ladies, at any rate, to do, except plan for and attend parties and balls, and then to talk about them afterwards, and pull them to pieces, and criticize the style of dressing of Mrs Colonel This and Mrs. Major That; such back-biting and gossip was all part of hill station life and gave spice to days that would otherwise have cloyed with their constant pursuit of pleasure and their total lack of work to be done.

Despite the gaiety there was an element of personal strain about the festivities that gripped Ogilvie as he stood with his father and mother to receive the guests. He felt—and it was no more than imagination—that there was a reserve about some of the officers as they shook his hand. These men would have heard about the patrol, naturally; the bush telegraph was never slow in India, and besides, this was a matter of obvious professional interest, and even officers (and there were all too many such) who took not the least interest in the profession of arms, preferring to concentrate on the career of soldiering with all its social glitter, would have pricked up their ears and sharpened their tongues over that episode. So Ogilvie suffered, and read disapproval into the stiff faces of majors and colonels and generals as they moved past him with their handshakes and nods or brief words with Sir Iain before they plunged into the brilliance of the scene behind.

Ogilvie had his first dance with his mother, while his father gallantly piloted the wife of Snowdon's current tenant. After that James, his programme dutifully filled, for the early dances, with the names of the senior ladies of the district, endured a kind of torture. He had thought it more tactful not to ask Mary Archdale for a dance tonight—he had a feeling she might have refused anyway. He would do better, he had thought, to concentrate on the mothers and the unattached daughters. There was a buffet supper, and endless trays of drinks borne by patient Indian servants with faces held expressionless as they were pushed and jostled and treated as if they did not exist, as though they were mere mobile appendages to the trays they carried. The noise level increased as the military band stepped it up, and officers, and in some cases their ladies, responded to the urgings of a little too much liquor by adding overloud voices to the music. James, at the buffet, found himself the centre of the womenfolk; it was natural enough, of course, as his mother had warned him. But he had not expected to be a magnet for the middle-aged and the old as well as the young. The young, indeed, were not being given a look in; Ogilvie was pressured by the matrons, garrulous and loud-voiced military matrons whom one would have thought from their behaviour hadn't seen a man for months. Ogilvie's natural good manners carried him through, but not without difficulty. One of the ladies, the wife of an Army Service Corps colonel, even pressed her enormous corsage against him continually, which much embarrassed him; it seemed impolite to retreat from it, and indeed when he did so his expensive dress kilt came perilously close to a vast yellow blancmange at the table's edge. He was pinned down and quite unable to reach his objective, which was Mary Archdale, whom from time to time he could see dancing with one or other of the younger officers.

With his tongue he made a kind of conversation with Mrs. Colonel Bates of the A.S.C., but his mind was upon Mary; and mentally he drifted back to the reception at the head of the staircase, and Mary's arrival.

He had introduced her to his mother, who had held herself a little stiffly. 'Oh, so this is Mrs. Archdale,' she had said. 'How d'you do.'

'How d'you do, Lady Ogilvie.'

Lady Ogilvie, without appearing to do so, was looking her over. 'I'm so glad you were able to come, even though your husband could not.'

'I'm very pleased to be here.' Briefly Mary had caught Ogilvie's eye when he was supposed to be concentrating on an arriving bishop; and had then passed on to Sir Iain into whose ear, when Mary had moved away, Lady Ogilvie had whispered something; and a little later, when Ogilvie had happened to be right behind his parents, he had overheard a snatch of conversation.

'Yes, the commode feller,' Sir Iain had been saying. 'Must say I liked the look of *her*.'

'Really? I thought her fast.'

Sir Iain had chuckled. 'You would, Fiona. Must say I wouldn't mind a tumble with her.'

'Don't be so coarse, Iain, you know I detest such talk. That young woman's no better than she should be. I only hope James . . .'

They had been interrupted then and he had never heard what his mother hoped about him, but he could guess well enough. He forced his mind away from Mary now and did his best to concentrate on Colonel Bates's lady, who was asking him if he played polo. 'Yes, I've played,' he told her. 'Not with any distinction, I'm afraid. I'll need a lot more practise, Mrs. Bates.'

'Oh, but really, I'm *sure* you're being much too modest, Mr Ogilvie,' she gushed. She had a big face, over-powdered, with thick lips and big teeth; she repelled him. 'My husband has his own side, of course. I'm sure you've heard of them. Bates's Hell-Raisers.'

He shook his head. 'No, I'm afraid I haven't,' he said. It was an error, as he realized at once; Mrs. Bates was quite clearly offended. She said, 'Oh, but of course you've not been long in India.' She tried again. 'Do you race?'

'Personally? Or—'

'No, no, Mr. Ogilvie. Do you care for *race meetings*?'

'Oh. No, not really.'

'Oh, I *am* surprised. Most young officers . . . and it's *such* fun at Annandale. I simply adore going, but Colonel Bates so seldom has the time to take me, don't you know.' After a brief pause she prattled on again. 'I expect you enjoy pig-sticking. Colonel Bates has quite a reputation at it, you know.' Pride touched her voice, almost reverence. 'Why, he's even known as Piggy Bates in the Corps.'

'Is he?'

'Yes. I'm sure he would be only too pleased to teach you some of the tricks of the sport, Mr. Ogilvie.'

He shook his head; as he did so the corsage came closer. He took a quick look over his shoulder; the blancmange was almost upon him in rear, while to right and left he was hemmed in by gossiping senior ladies. Rather in desperation he said, 'No, thank you, Mrs. Bates, I think pig-sticking is a pretty cruel sport really. Don't you?'

'*Of course* not,' Mrs. Bates answered coldly, and looked around. She caught the eye of a whiskery, bleary major and at once excused herself. Ogilvie realized he had saved himself from boredom and blancmange at the expense of making an enemy, if an A.S.C. wife could be considered harmful. He blew out a long breath; he had spoken no more than the truth. He thought pig-sticking utterly revolting in its senseless cruelty. He had, in fact, taken part in it once because it had been expected of him; but never again. He had always managed to find excuses thereafter, whether or no Captain Andrew Black had liked it. Black was keen himself, very keen, partly because he was a sadistic man anyway and partly because he was a social climber and blood sports were decidedly upper class. What Black's socially doubtful steelmaster background could never give him, horsemanship and bloody sport could in some degree make up for; and Black was a very insecure man basically. To Ogilvie there was something horrible and even insane about a troop of grown officers and gentlemen pounding on horseback after a hapless pig, running for its life from the lowered lances, and something devilish in the glee of those gentlemen when they had driven their weapons into the poor animals' squealing, sweat-lathered bodies. No doubt it was excellent training for the cavalry; Ogilvie was thankful to be an infantryman.

He moved clear of the buffet before he could be hemmed in again. Circulating, he saw

Mrs. Bates now pouring anger into the ear of a small, hunted-looking man in the uniform of an A.S.C. lieutenant-colonel. Ogilvie grinned to himself; poor Colonel Bates! He scarcely had the look of a man whose prowess at pig-sticking had earned him the sobriquet of Piggy ... A high-pitched voice said, 'Hullo there, James. Enjoying yourself, I have no doubt?'

Turning, Ogilvie saw his cousin Hector. Hector was clutching a glass of soda-water, and the pallor of his face, white even in the heat generated by the throngs of guests, was accentuated by the black tails. There was a curious expression on his face; clearly, *he* was not enjoying himself. Ogilvie, answering the question, said, 'Yes, indeed, Hector. Wonderful party. Decent of my people to put all this on. Must be costing a fortune!'

'Indeed it must, yes. Very generous, as you say.' Hector looked around with a supercilious lift to his sandy eyebrows. 'Some of your—ah—cloth seem to be taking the fullest possible advantage, James. Have you noticed?'

'You mean the drinks?'

'Of course I mean the drinks.'

'If I have noticed, I haven't let it worry me too much.'

'Oh? I think it's rather horrid, rather disgusting really, but possible you're used to it in Peshawar.'

Ogilvie felt nettled. 'You sound as though you think we all get blotto every night. We

60

don't. On the other hand . . .'

'Yes?'

'There are times when a man has to let go a little, and in India the best way of doing that is to have a bit of a party.'

'I don't think drink is ever necessary.'

'Don't you? You try a full day out in open country on tactical exercises,' Ogilvie said cheerfully, 'and see if you're satisfied with a glass of soda-water at—'

'James, you wretched military men are all the same. Any excuse will do.' Hector paused, his watery eyes scanning his cousin's face through the thick lenses of his spectacles. 'James, tell me: What do you *do* on these exercises? Isn't it all somewhat old-fashioned stuff?'

Ogilvie nodded. 'A lot of it is. Tactics haven't changed much for a great many years, as a matter of fact. Of course, troops out from home have a devil of a lot to learn about fighting on the North-West Frontier. It's not quite like Colchester or Chatham!'

'Yes,' Hector said. He hadn't appeared to be listening very attentively. 'You know, James, I've not been out here long, but I've kept my eyes open. The impression I have is that Whitehall has no conception of what goes on out here.'

'I expect you're absolutely right, Hector. We—'

'The huge sums of money that are being

61

wasted, simply chucked away. You know what I mean. Grossly over-inflated military staffs, too many servants . . . too many parties—'

'Not at government expense!' Ogilvie snapped, furious at the bad manners his cousin was displaying. 'You've no right to suggest that, Hector, and you know it.'

'Oh, come, James, and please don't lose your temper like a spoilt child. You know as well as I do that there's a very, very thin line between what's paid for by the taxpayer and what's paid for by the officers. To quote just one simple example: military pay for the rank and file—when they're employed on quarters duties if that's the right term—doing work around the house. That's charged to the taxpayer's account, isn't it? It's highly immoral, really.'

'Oh, for heaven's sake,' Ogilvie began, and then, with some gladness, felt a hand come down on his shoulder and allowed the conversation to be interrupted by a Colonel Davenport, who until recently had been Military Secretary to the Viceroy. Hector gave a stiff bow and moved away, wriggling thin shoulders through the crowd. When Davenport had done with him Ogilvie made a determined effort to find Mary Archdale and at last succeeded, drawing her away with a barely perceptible jerk of his head; just as she had done that first time in Peshawar, she came to him at once.

She put her gloved hand in his. 'Oh, James,' she said. 'Thank goodness! I thought I'd never have a chance of a word with you tonight. Some of them are pretty awful, don't you think?'

'Yes,' he said, smiling down at her. 'Mary, we can't talk much now. May I see you tomorrow afternoon?'

'Any special reason?'

'No *special* reason.'

She nodded. 'All right. You know I'm not too keen on bungalow-visiting, though.' She thought for a moment, patting at her dark piled hair, her lower lip pouting. Then she said, 'I'll be in the lounge of the Princess Hotel at two o'clock. I'm lunching there with a friend. I'll shake her off by two o'clock, I promise.'

'And sit alone in the lounge?'

She tapped him with her fan, looking amused. 'Don't be so old-fashioned, James, *I'm* not—not to that extent, anyway. I don't give a damn what people say ... within reason,' she added with mock primness. 'I certainly don't mean to be chaperoned like a girl straight from the schoolroom all the time I'm a grass widow. But don't you keep me waiting James!'

'Of course I won't.'

Before turning away she said, 'I believe your mother disapproves of me.'

'Oh, surely not,' he protested. 'I don't

63

believe that for one moment. She's bound to like you.'

'Is she?' She gave a light laugh. 'You still know *very* little of women, my dear!' Then, without waiting for him to say anything further, she was gone; and was being collected in accordance with her programme by a fat man with an urgent look about him and a fawning smile, a Civilian from Calcutta from whose neck dangled the ribbon and insignia of a Companion of the Star of India—the Order of which Sir Iain, as a result of the Jalalabad action, had been made a Knight Commander, thus adding a knighthood to his baronetcy. Ogilvie danced again with specially selected ladies, including this time some of the daughters, had a few more drinks and conversation with his father's contemporaries, and some of Sir Iain's Staff who were in Simla with him, and then, in the early hours, the festivities ended with a rendering of Auld Lang Syne followed by The Queen; and the guests entered, or were in some cases practically lifted into, the rickshaws whose native crews had been patiently waiting for hours, and were trundled homeward to their bungalows or residences through the narrow streets of sleeping, gossiping, scheming, fornicating Simla.

*　　　*　　　*

In the morning Ogilvie drifted somewhat bleary-eyed down to breakfast at ten-fifteen. Sir Iain and his lady were not yet stirring, but Hector—he was staying at the Ogilvies' bungalow—was; and evidently had been for some while. He had a disapproving look. 'Early to bed and early to rise,' he said pontifically, 'makes a man healthy, wealthy and wise.'

'Oh, for God's sake!' Ogilvie grunted. 'After a twenty-first?'

'I think the occasion makes little difference. I spent my twenty-first birthday with Aunt Agnes in Bath—'

'And not a drink the whole evening, I'll be bound.' Ogilvie sat down with a plate of kedgeree, made of he knew not what Indian fish.

'For me—no. Aunt Agnes took a little sherry before dinner, and a glass of port afterwards.'

'Wicked woman. And what did you have to eat?'

'We had an excellent—' Hector, realizing he was being teased, broke off abruptly and snapped, 'I can't possibly remember. Anyway, dear boy . . . I trust you enjoyed the evening.'

'I did. Immensely.'

'Even though you must be feeling terrible now. That's a thing I never—'

'I'm not. I feel very well indeed, thank you, Hector,' Ogilvie lied.

'Well, I'm delighted to hear it, I must say.'

Hector rustled the pages of the *Times of India*, then put the newspaper down in favour of a four-week-old *Morning Post* which Ogilvie felt sure he must have had sent out specially, since his father seldom bothered with newspapers and his mother made do with the Indian press and the occasional magazine from home. After a while Hector started again; he laid down the *Morning Post* and smiled sourly across the breakfast-table. He said, evidently quoting something or other, 'The night before the dance, Mad Carew seemed in a trance. They chaffed him as they pulled at their cigars.'

'What on earth . . .?'

'Oh, you haven't heard it? Rather a charming little piece of doggerel, which aptly illustrates certain aspects of the Indian military scene.'

'Oh, yes? Do go on.'

'Very well.' Hector smoothed at his heavily oiled hair. 'It's about a colonel's daughter, actually. She was nearly twenty-one and arrangements had begun, to celebrate her birthday with a ball. He wrote and asked what present she would like from Mad Carew . . . I forget some of it just there . . . ta-ti-tum . . . she answered that nothing else would do, but the green eye of the Little Yellow God. Well?'

'Don't see what the devil all this is about,' Ogilvie said testily, pouring coffee.

'Don't you, dear boy? Well, of course it's the other way round, I know, but—what *did* she

66

give you, James?'

'She?' He stared back at his cousin's impudent face. 'Who?'

'Don't act the young innocent, dear boy!' Meticulously Hector spread marmalade on a fragment of thin toast. 'Last night, James, you were having a deep, if short, conversation with a certain lady.'

'Well?'

'I took pains to discover a fact about her, which I pass on to you now. She is a married woman.'

Ogilvie glared. 'I know. What the devil has that got to do with you?'

'Nothing, in a sense, I suppose,' Hector answered, shrugging. 'Except as a member of the family, that is. I don't know what Uncle Iain and Aunt Fiona would think. Or rather . . . I think I *do*.'

His eyes hard Ogilvie said, 'What they think is their own affair, and mine. Not, by any stretch of the imagination, yours.'

'I tend to dispute that, dear boy.' Hector wiped his lips with his napkin and gestured to the Indian servant to bring more coffee. The servant left the room. 'As I said—as a member of the family—our good name *is* my concern.'

'Tripe. Look here, Hector, none of this has anything whatsoever to do with you, and the sooner you realize that the better. Not that there's "anything" anyway, in the sense you mean, so you needn't start having nightmares.

Mrs. Archdale happens to be a friend from Peshawar—that's all. I know her husband. I've served with him, as a matter of fact—in action. And let me assure you, she's perfectly respectable. Even if there were "anything" it wouldn't in any degree sully *your* precious reputation, Hector.'

Hector gave a smooth nod. 'I'm glad to have your reassurances,' he said with a gallant unction, and returned to his short-sighted perusal of the *Morning Post*. Ogilvie was furious, and had it not been necessary to attempt to turn off the heat in the interests of discretion, would never have given his cousin any explanations at all. He considered Hector's probe the most infernal cheek and decided that if this was 'family interest' then he would very much prefer to be without any. He finished his breakfast as soon as he could and left the room. That afternoon, when he met Mary in the Princess Hotel, he was still seething inwardly, and she noticed this, and remarked upon it, but with an effort he put his anger behind him and said it was nothing to worry about. And after chatting for a while Mary suggested they went to Annandale Plain.

'What for?' he asked.

'There's a meeting this afternoon. *Racing*, James.'

'Oh—yes. Would you really like to?'

She smiled and said, 'I simply adore racing, but oh dear, you do sound doubtful! I'm not forcing you if you don't want to go.'

'No,' he said at once. 'Of course I'll take you.' And he did. They went out to Annandale and arrived there just in time for the third race. It was an elegant occasion, a lovely day and a perfect setting. The air was fresh, cool and invigorating and there was quite a lot of excitement in the races; Ogilvie had never cared for it before, but today he did. He really enjoyed it. He lost a handful of rupees on the fourth race, and Mary, plunging a little heavily he thought, made some money on the fifth. That set the seal on the afternoon for them both; he was delighted with her success. He had already gathered that the Archdales had no private means and now, after a year in India, could well appreciate what that meant. Even a major's pay was a pittance; married officers without other resources found life an unending struggle against debt. Ogilvie himself had had a mere fifty pounds a year from a legacy, but now, since yesterday, this was increased to two hundred under the terms of a trust initiated by his grandfather; such a sum would have made all the difference to the Archdales. When he married—if his marriage was pleasing to his parents—he would have a substantial allowance from his father, but Sir Iain did not believe in giving a young officer too much spending power in the meantime.

It was a very pleasant afternoon and it was a pity they had to bump into Mrs. Bates.

'Why—oh, dear me, it's Mr. Ogilvie, I do believe. *Such* a nice party.' The corsage heaved. 'But how funny—you told me *distinctly* you didn't care at all for racing! And who is this, may I ask?'

Tight-lipped, Ogilvie introduced Mary Archdale.

'How do you do. Yes, I remember seeing you last night, now I come to think of it, Mrs. Archdale.' There was just the very faintest emphasis on the Mrs. 'As I was saying—such a nice ball. And your Mr. Ogilvie is *so* charming. Well, I won't keep you, I'm sure you have plenty to do.' Mrs. Bates retreated: and some distance off cast a backward look, full of meaning.

Ogilvie said forcefully, 'Damn.'

'What an extraordinarily ugly woman.'

'That's hardly the point.'

'No, my Mr. Ogilvie, it isn't, is it! What a bitch. But don't worry *too* much, James—that's Simla. Everyone's talking hard about everyone else. Let's forget Mrs Bates.' But it spoiled the afternoon all the same; Mary clearly had the incident on her mind, and as for Ogilvie, taken in conjunction with Hector's impertinent remarks that morning, it worried him badly. In a sense he was almost thankful when, on his arrival back at the bungalow just before dinner, his mother told him a telegram had come for him and, on opening it, he found he had been recalled urgently to Peshawar to

70

rejoin his regiment.

He told his mother the news and she did not appear surprised. He said, 'I wonder what's in the wind, mother.'

'There's some trouble with the tribes. Your father's already started back for Murree.' Lady Ogilvie's tone was severe. 'We had no idea where to look for you. He would have wished to say goodbye before he left. You may be going into action.'

He muttered an apology and asked, 'Did father say anything about this trouble, before he went?'

'Very little. I did gather the tribes north of Peshawar, between there and Chitral, were thought likely to rise against us. That's—'

'Is this to do with—'

'I don't know any more than that, dear boy. Your father would say no more. I'm sure you'll be told when you reach Peshawar.' She hesitated. 'James, where were you this afternoon?'

'I went to Annandale,' he said, fidgeting. 'To the races, mother.'

'I see. I think you could have told us. It's not very fair.'

'I didn't know anything was going to blow up like this, mother. I had no idea father would have to leave so suddenly.'

'No, I realize that, but still.' She was very put out. 'Well, James, I'm not going to ask any more questions. We have little time left

71

together now. Your father's arranged transport for you—you'll be collected from here at nine o'clock this evening and entrain at Kalka for Peshawar. So don't let us spoil things now, darling.'

Just then dinner was announced by the Indian servant and, telling her son not to bother to change, Lady Ogilvie linked her arm in his and they went into the dining-room. Ogilvie picked at his food; he was worried and anxious, his mind split in half. He knew that in a sense this was deliverance from temptation and from a special kind of danger, but he would miss Mary very badly. On the other hand he felt a thrill of real excitement at the recall, at knowing he was wanted to meet a threat of trouble. Deep down—or perhaps not so deep down—there was still the heady feeling of being a Royal Strathspey and he was thankful now that he had not resigned his commission. He couldn't quite make this out; in all the circumstances of his disillusion it was odd that he should welcome action, since action had been the root of his recent troubles. But the period in Simla had helped him more than he fully realized, which was what Lord Dornoch had intended it should do, and he knew that only in further action could he eradicate an unfortunate incident and put himself firmly back on the right road in the esteem of his peers and in his own eyes also. And now here was the chance. But first, there

72

was something to be cleared up. He could not run out of Simla and leave Mary to face the gossip alone, the gossip that was bound to result once Mrs. Colonel Bates had loosed her tongue in a few of the homes—which for a certainty she would have done already.

That had to be put right here and now.

'Mother, there's something I really should tell you,' he said when the servant was out of the room. 'I wasn't alone at Annandale this afternoon.'

'Oh?' Lady Ogilvie looked down at the table, fiddled with some silver.

He plunged. 'I took Mrs. Archdale.'

'I see.'

'I happened to meet her. She has a dull time without her husband.'

'Really? I must say I'm surprised at that. An attractive young woman . . . alone in Simla? She needn't lack distractions, James.'

'No.' He felt himself colouring. 'She has standards of behaviour, mother.'

She crumbled a piece of bread suddenly. 'So I should hope. I hope you have, too. You've been well brought up.'

'Of course. Yes, I have standards.' Under cover of the table, his hands balled into fists. Why should he have to explain like a child? 'I'm sorry, mother. But I thought I ought to tell you . . . for her sake, you see. In case of gossip. That's all.'

His mother gave a short laugh. 'You mean

73

you were seen, I suppose?'

'Yes. There was nothing clandestine about it, anyway.'

'Except that you didn't see fit to tell your father or me.' She looked at him very directly; her fine dark eyes were troubled; she was much upset and hurt. 'Who saw you, James?'

'I dare say, any number of people. I told you—'

'Yes, but who in particular?'

He said, 'Oh, a Mrs. Bates, an A.S.C. wife.'

'Who cannot be simply dismissed as an A.S.C. wife. She's just about the worst woman in all Simla to have seen you,' Lady Ogilvie said crisply. 'Oh, yes, James, you did right to tell me! I would have heard by luncheon tomorrow in any event, though, and it's already too late to put matters right.' She reached out to him, across the table. 'You really mustn't worry, however. I'll put Mrs. Bates in her place when the time comes.'

'Mother,' he said awkwardly, 'I hope you'll think of Mrs. Archdale. It's not just me.'

'But,' she reminded him, 'it *is* you who must come first with me. Any kind of scandal—yes, however baseless in fact—can do only harm to a young man's career. Believe me, James, I *know*. I've seen it happen. I've been an Indian wife long before now! It's worse than at home. Colchester, Portsmouth, Aldershot, Invermore itself, Fort William—oh, dear me! They're *nothing* compared with Simla and Peshawar

74

and Murree and Ootacamund. You must leave this all to me, James, and you must trust me too. Will you?'

Miserably he said, 'Of course, mother.'

She looked at him for a while then said gently, 'Have you any messages? You won't have time to say goodbye, you know.'

He said, 'It's awfully good of you, mother. Will you just say I'm sorry not to say goodbye?'

She nodded; no more was said about Mary Archdale. Immediately after dinner Ogilvie changed his clothes and packed, and sharp at nine the servant announced the arrival of the bullock-cart for Kalka railway station. As the primitive vehicle rumbled uncomfortably out of Simla and down the terrible mountain road leading south, Ogilvie's thoughts were bitter ones. At twenty-one he found no good reason why he should have virtually to account for all his movements to his parents. But his parents were like that, or at any rate his mother was. All the MacGregor women were the same; he remembered his mother's elder sisters, Aunts Catherine and Emily. When staying with them every moment of the day was ruled, supervised, catalogued and commented upon, dissected and perused. No initiative was allowed to youth. Aunt Emily was a spinster, like Aunt Agnes on his father's side of the family; and Aunt Catherine, ostensibly a widow, had lived with her from the time her husband had vanished from the scene after five years of marriage. Uncle Claude had never been mentioned since, word being allowed to drop into youthful ears that he had met with an accident whilst holidaying in Naples. In point of fact he had left her flat, being unable to stand any more of her—this news had emerged via Sir Iain one day, when he had been beside himself with rage over some remark of his wife's. He had referred to the MacGregor family, collectively, as a lot of damn battleaxes—not to his wife but to his son; and had released the truth about Aunt Catherine's husband. He had then remembered the veil of secrecy and had impressed upon his son that he was not to mention his indiscretion to his mother. James, who had been very close to his mother at that time, and had been deeply shocked as well, hadn't wanted to hurt her and had kept his father's confidence. Now the memory tickled him; the MacGregors kept their honour bright by never talking of the ones who fell by the wayside!

*   *   *

Reaching Peshawar three days later Ogilvie found the cantonments placid enough. There were movements in progress on the parade ground, and he heard the shouts of the drill sergeants, but this was mere routine; there seemed to be nothing beyond the ordinary. His boxes were carried to his quarters and he sought out the adjutant to report his return.

Black was busy, and made him wait. After a long delay Black said, 'So you've come back, James.'

'As instructed—yes.'

'You've taken your time.'

'It's a long trip. I came as quickly as I could.'

'I do not like to be answered back, James, as you well know.' Black's sallow face creased into a frown, and the eyes glittered; he saw affront in everything. 'Now, the Colonel is away to Murree for the time being, so you will follow my orders. You may sit down.'

Ogilvie sat in a chair facing Black's desk. Black, whose breath smelt strongly of whisky, lit a short cigar and lay back in his own chair. He said, 'You'll recall that patrol, of course. Well now, it seems there may be repercussions. It is a sorry business, a sorry business indeed.'

'What sort of repercussions?'

'Use your imagination, James. I'm sure you have plenty.' There was a sneer in the tone.

'Reprisals?' This was exactly what he had feared.

'Precisely.' Black sat forward with a jerk, folding his arms on his desk. 'I myself foresaw this at the time. Now it appears likely to come about. The Political Officer from Brigade reports that tribesmen, chiefly Pathans from Afghanistan, are assembling in certain villages on this side of the Frontier—namely, in Sikat, Dera and Mundari. These villages, as no doubt you know, are all situated to the north of us, towards Chitral—in Bajaur.'

'And their intentions?'

Black shrugged. 'Currently not known for certain, but the inference, I would say, of such assemblies, is fairly obvious! They are likely to form the nucleus of a mob that could well try to mount an attack on Peshawar or Nowshera. You will remember, no doubt, that it is not long since the British Agent himself was besieged in Chitral city.'

Ogilvie nodded; he remembered well enough. It had happened in February last, and he had had enviously to watch the column from Nowshera leaving on its march north for Chitral. On 1st January the Mehtar, Nizam-ul-Malik, recognized by the British Raj, had been murdered; and when Lieutenant Gurdon, Agent in Chitral, had failed to extend recognition to the new Mehtar on behalf of Her Majesty, the Mehtar, self-proclaimed, had persuaded Umra Khan, ruler in neighbouring Jandul, to invade Chitral; whereupon Gurdon's superior, Surgeon Major Robertson, joined him from Gilghit and, at the beginning of March, was put under siege by the Chitralis and Jandulis. The British had reacted speedily and the 1st Division of the 1st Army had been mobilized at Nowshera, and a supporting column was made ready to leave Gilghit. The outcome had been brilliantly successful; the siege had been lifted and Chitral garrisoned.

The Raj was intact; and that had been that—or so it had been thought. In fact, there had been a residue of much bitterness.

Ogilvie asked, 'Is there a link between what's happening in these villages and the Chitral business, Andrew?'

'According to the Political people, there could be, but it's doubtful. That is, in my view.' He probably, Ogilvie thought, wished to pin the blame firmly on that patrol. 'No one can say at this moment what is in the wind, except that it is likely to be serious. General Fettleworth is greatly worried, it appears. He is not, however, meaning to mobilize the Frontier for the present. Instead, he has given orders that a token show of strength will be mounted to impress the tribesmen. This show of strength will take the form of a full-scale review of all troops in the district, to be held outside Peshawar at a date yet to be decided. There will be a full muster of all arms—cavalry, infantry, artillery, sappers. We shall, I trust, put on a noteworthy show, James—but you will likely not be present.'

'Oh?' Ogilvie felt a sudden chill, wondering if that wretched patrol was still being held against him. 'What am I to do, then?'

Black said smoothly, 'You will be leading a patrol, James, another patrol . . . and you will make an investigatory probe towards the villages. You will try not to engage the tribes in fighting, you will merely observe, and then return and report upon the whole situation. You will be allowed a maximum of fourteen days in which to bring your patrol back to cantonments. Much will depend on what you report. General Fettleworth will await your return with great interest. You will take twenty men including a piper and a drummer, plus a corporal, and a colour-sergeant. You will enter the villages openly, but, as I have already said, you will avoid any engagements with the tribesmen. This is not to be quite a spying expedition, James, but merely a probe to test the reactions of the tribes to British soldiers. Do you understand?'

'I think I do,' Ogilvie answered. 'May I choose which men I take?'

Black shook his head; there was a vaguely furtive look about him now. 'No, I'm sorry. The men are already detailed and you will find them as experienced a bunch as possible—'

'Isn't this unusual? Surely it's normal for an officer to pick his men?'

'This may be so, but I'll thank you not to question my orders and arrangements. I consider it impertinent. Your corporal will be Corporal Phillips, and—'

'Colour-Sergeant Barr?'

Black nodded. 'Yes.'

'Must I take Barr?'

'You have objections?'

The query was too bland and Ogilvie hesitated, considering his reply very carefully.

Black, naturally, knew the score; he was intentionally making things awkward—taking advantage, obviously, of the Colonel's temporary absence in Murree. Meanwhile Ogilvie could scarcely make particular accusations against Barr, who was a perfectly efficient N.C.O. by current standards, without being able to substantiate them to the hilt and beyond. So all he said, in answer to his adjutant's question, was, 'No, I have no objections.'

'I'm glad to hear that, James. As I recall, General Fettleworth made the particular point that you were to continue in B Company with Barr as your Colour-Sergeant.' Black fiddled with some papers on his desk, not meeting Ogilvie's eye. 'Well—that's all, James. You will be ready to leave with your patrol at first light tomorrow, and this afternoon you will report to Brigade for briefing by the Political Officer.'

'Very well.' Ogilvie hesitated. 'Andrew, may I ask why *I'm* being given this patrol?'

Black smiled. 'Again I ask—you have objections?'

'Of course not.' He said no more; he couldn't bring himself to explain to Black. He got to his feet and moved to the door; as he reached it Black said suddenly, 'One more word, James. You will, I trust, make a *success* of this patrol.'

'I will,' Ogilvie answered shortly, and went out. There had been a very clear threat in

Black's tone.

*   *   *

The briefing by Major Wingate, the Political Officer, which Ogilvie attended with his whole patrol as detailed, was short and to the point and added little to what Black had already told him. He was to make a careful note of all he saw in the villages and the surrounding country—not easy country for a patrol to live and march in—and he was to note the behaviour of the men of the hills and how well they appeared to be armed and supplied. He was to note the condition of the crops. In a sense he was to trail his coat and report the results. The Political people, Wingate said in answer to his question on the point, would deal with the undercover side, the infiltration of spies; and he merely shrugged off the matter when Ogilvie went on to suggest that an efficient infiltration might well have rendered the patrol unnecessary in the first place. Wingate said, 'I feel you've not quite grasped the situation, Ogilvie. Your task is simply to see what comes to a head when you're seen.'

'To act as an irritant, sir?'

'If you care to put it that way, yes. The grain of sand in the oyster that produces the pearl.'

Pearls for adjutants—and Divisional Commanders. That night after dinner in the Mess Ogilvie refused a game of cards,

82

somewhat moodily, with MacKinlay, his company commander, and sat alone over a glass of port and an old *Illustrated London News*. He was joined after a while by another subaltern, Roderick Gray of C Company. Gray dropped a hand on his shoulder. 'Brooding, James—and drinking alone?'

'Any reason why I shouldn't?'

'Not if you like it. It's a bad habit, though.' Gray sat down. 'Worried about this patrol you're taking out?'

Ogilvie laid the *Illustrated London News* aside. He said, 'Well, I think it's a trifle absurd, really. It's not going to serve much purpose.'

'Have you told the adj that?'

'No. Why?'

Gray smiled and yawned. 'A little bird's been spreading the news you cut up a bit rough about going out again with Barr. I don't blame you . . . but it doesn't help to get a reputation for querying orders, you know.'

'When you've been out here a little longer, Roddy, somebody may ask for your advice. Just at the moment, I'm not in need of it.'

'All right, no need to get hot under the collar.' Gray was a plump young man, easygoing and unruffleable. He smiled again, comfortably, and said, 'Don't bash your head against too many brick walls. I *have* been in the army a little longer than you, James my boy, after all. Things don't run smoothly all the time, you know. Did you hear about young

Bruce, by the way?'

Ogilvie shook his head. Bruce was one of the second lieutenants who had only fairly recently joined the regiment from Sandhurst, and Ogilvie had no great opinion of his abilities. Gray said, 'He took a patrol out while you were in Simla, just a routine job, with Corporal Simmons. Between them, they made a balls of the commissariat and there wasn't half enough water. They all came back with their tongues hanging out, just about at their last gasp. Bruce made a report that one of the privates had abused him over it. Well, of course, one can't condone insubordination, but damn it, the man was half mad with thirst and young Bruce had only his own bloody silly incompetence to blame.'

'And?' Ogilvie asked.

'Black gave the man fourteen days cells. The Colonel had already left for Murree and the Major was on the sick list as it so happened. So Black laid into Bruce as well—gave him a month's stoppage of leave. If Bruce had had any sense, he'd have settled with the man privately. My father's told me he's known officers before now who've fought it out behind their bungalows and made a firm friend of the man afterwards. But the point I'm trying to make is this: you're not Black's one and only target, James. He just doesn't like his fellow-men.'

Ogilvie grinned. 'It looks as though he did

the right thing this time, doesn't it? After all, Bruce could have killed some of his patrol by sheer drought, from what you've told me. Whereas the poor, thirsty, insubordinate private ... *that*'s where Black slipped up!' He looked around the room, at the semi-somnolent officers in their mess dress, at the quietly-moving servants, at the comfortable furnishings and the silver and the glasses of port, brandy and whisky, with cigar smoke wreathing over all. Abruptly he said, 'I wonder the men put up with it, really.'

'It's a man's life.'

'You need to be a man to stand it, certainly!'

'That's what they like about it—that, and the adventure. The people at home know they're leading a man's life, and that does their ego good when they're on leave. They get the girls, James ... don't we all! Besides, think of the alternatives outside—unemployment, slums, semi-starvation even, in a good many cases. Hard taskmasters when they get a job, and always the threat of the sack.'

'What about their officers, Roddy?'

Gray laughed. 'Black again?'

'Yes. But not only him. Fettleworth.'

'Fettleworth, eh?' Gray rubbed at the side of his nose, reflectively. 'He's not so bad. My father served under him some years ago. A little bigoted, perhaps, a little set in his views, but he's a fighter, James. He's no headquarters general. He's really quite a brave old boy, I've

85

heard. Personally dragged a wounded man out of the line of fire in Zululand. I wouldn't be too bitter about men like Fettleworth. They've done well in their time.'

'That's just it,' Ogilvie said. 'In their time! We have to suffer them in the present—and their time's in the past! That's what worries me.'

'Well, we'll see how things shape if the Frontier blows up,' Gray said, 'which doesn't seem all that unlikely to me. But if you want another word of advice, and I don't suppose you do, it's this: stop being so damn morose and stand-offish. That's not the way to win friends and influence people!' He got to his feet and went off before Ogilvie had had a chance to make any reply. Ogilvie finished his port and left the Mess and, walking along towards his own room, he passed MacKinlay's. The company commander's light was on; it seemed he had not found another card player. On an impulse Ogilvie knocked and went in. MacKinlay was sprawled on his bed with his pipe in his mouth, re-reading a letter from home. He sat up. 'Come along in, James.'

'Aren't I disturbing you?'

'Not a bit. What's the trouble?' He waved Ogilvie to a chair.

Ogilvie said hesitantly, 'I just wanted a bit of a talk, that's all, Rob. About that patrol.'

'Yes,' MacKinlay said quietly. 'Yes, I thought as much. I did try my best to pull you clear of that, as a matter of fact, but you know what Black is. He and Barr are two of a sort, I'm afraid.'

'Why did he choose me in particular?'

'You mean because of what happened last time?'

'Yes.'

MacKinlay got up and walked across the room, frowning. Coming back, he stood in front of Ogilvie and looked down at him seriously. 'No reason why he shouldn't choose you,' he said. 'You must never doubt your own competence, old boy.'

'I didn't mean that.'

'No. No, I know you didn't. All right, I won't dodge the issue, James. You think Black hopes you'll make a balls, isn't that it?'

Ogilvie nodded. 'Something like that.'

'Face it, then. Don't try to dodge the undoubted possibilities of his devious mind.' Frowning still, he added, 'All you have to do is to concentrate on making a damn big success of it—that'll not only confound Black, but leave him powerless as well. I can't say more than that, old boy. I'm sure you understand. Personally, I have every confidence you'll bring that patrol off brilliantly. There's just one other thing. I'm glad you looked in, James, because I was meaning to have a word with you—a word of warning.'

'About the patrol?'

'About Colour-Sarn't Barr in particular. I

87

know Barr. He's a good soldier—a very good soldier—but he has a bad side to him. You'll agree on that, James, of course. Now, I believe you'll be finding him exceptionally difficult during the next two weeks, because, you see, he knows you know he was at fault during that last patrol. Also, you weren't slow to show your feelings to the Court, even though you did your duty and backed Barr formally. He'll not forget that. He's far too clever a man to give a foolproof opening, but he'll go as far as he can short of that point. Watch it, James. And unless he *does* overstep the mark really seriously, don't make any reports you can't substantiate afterwards or you're in for big trouble. Barr will get to know and he'll also know Black will be reading your own personal dislikes into your reports. Just wait your time, James. Given the rope, sure as fate, Barr will hang himself in the end. Remember that and suffer him till that happens.' He brought out his watch. 'Since you've an early start and need the clearest head you've ever had, I suggest you cut along to bed.'

*　　　*　　　*

In the morning Ogilvie's servant called him just before dawn. He got up at once, and washed, shaved and dressed. He strode out to the parade ground, where his patrol had assembled and was standing easy awaiting his arrival. Furious with himself, Ogilvie understood from Colour-Sergeant Barr's face that he was a little late; he wondered if Barr had intentionally ordered the men on parade five minutes early. But there was nothing wrong with Barr's manner that morning. He brought the men to attention with a shout that echoed clear across the cantonments, probably awakening the whole battalion quite unnecessarily, and slammed to the salute in front of Ogilvie.

'Patrol present and correct. Sir!'

'Thank you, Colour-Sergeant. Stand them at ease, if you please.'

'Sir!' Barr turned about, swinging his kilt around his knees, and shouted the order. There was a jingle of equipment. Ogilvie went towards the men; he had a brief word with each of them. He knew they appreciated that; Barr's heavy breathing behind him announced that the Colour-Sergeant disapproved. When he had finished Ogilvie took up his position ahead of the men and gave the order to march. They left the cantonment with the pipes silent, keeping step to the beat of the drum, marching north-east for the Frontier villages, not taking it too fast, conserving their energies for whatever might lie ahead of them on the march as, in the name of the Empress of India and the might of a far-flung Empire, they set out to probe the strongholds of that Empire's likely foes.

CHAPTER FOUR

In the village of Sikat a young Pathan, lately arrived from Afghanistan by way of the Khyber Pass, rode along rutted tracks between the hovels of the villagers. Men, women and children grovelled in the dirt beneath a hot sun as this man passed by, riding a big black stallion. The young man had the hawklike features of his race; and his expression was commanding and autocratic. Dark eyes roved over the bent backs, the bowed heads, but he gave no acknowledgement of the obeisances. He seemed preoccupied as he rode out from the other side of the village, making for a walled fort, known along the frontier as the Black Fort, that stood guard along the terrible track running through from Abazai, through the almost inaccessible tangle of mountains that reached heavenward, stretching as far as the eye could see and shimmering beneath the great heat of the day. His approach was under observation from the fort, and as he came up to the gates they were opened from within to admit him. He rode past a quarterguard of four tallish men with their scimitar-shaped swords drawn; and on across a courtyard towards a doorway set in a square tower that cast its shadow, grotesquely large, over the sand-coloured walls and ground. Outside the doorway the rider stopped and dismounted, handing his horse over to a young boy who salaamed deeply.

In a cool, disdainful voice the Pathan said, 'Your master expects me.'

'Yes, Highness.'

'Why is he not here to greet me, boy?'

'Highness, I cannot say.'

The Pathan grunted irritably. 'Look well after the horse,' he said with a dismissive gesture, 'or I shall slit your throat.'

He looked quite capable of it; the boy cringed a little and said, 'Yes, Highness.' The man from Afghanistan turned away and walked into the doorway. Inside he was met by a terrified old man, white-haired and bent, abject in his apologies for not having personally met his visitor at the gates of the fort. The Pathan cut him short. 'Hold your stupid old tongue, Masrullah Sahib. You were not there to pay the proper courtesies, and excuses are useless, and powerless to alter the facts. On this occasion I shall overlook your slackness.' He strode ahead along a bare stone passage, knowing his way well, and turned into a square apartment with a single window and its walls draped with dirty, torn tapestries. The air smelt stale and foul; two middle-aged women and a young girl sat on cushions. The Pathan—his name was Shuja Khan and he was a descendant of the Shah Shuja who had been set upon the throne in Kabul by the British in

91

1839—swung round on the fort's aged master. Roughly he said, 'Get rid of the women, Masrullah Sahib. Our business has nothing to do with female ears.'

'Yes, Highness.' Waving his arms, the old man despatched the women, who bobbed and grinned obsequiously at Shuja Khan as they passed by him in an aroma of unwashed flesh.

When they had gone the princeling, without waiting for the invitation to do so, sat himself on one of the cushions and gestured his host to do likewise. He said, 'You know what I have come to discuss.'

'Indeed, Highness.'

'I believe matters will come to a head sooner than we expected, Masrullah Sahib. This is why my father has sent me into India.' The dark eyes stared intently into the old man's face. 'Already, since I have been in India—in the village of Dera, as you should know—I have heard that the British are moving. Not in strength, but they are probing. A small force, no more than a patrol, has been observed in the hills, having presumably moved out from the British base at Peshawar ... the men who dress like women, in skirts, the most bloodthirsty and savage of them all. Do you know anything of this, Masrullah?'

'I, too, have heard the tidings, Highness.'

'Do you know any more than I have told you?'

'No, Highness, nothing more.'

Shuja Khan went on staring, broodingly, a slim brown hand stroking his jaw. Then he asked, 'What action have you taken, as a result of these tidings, Masrullah Sahib?'

The old man bowed his head. 'Highness, I have given orders to my Captain of the Guard that at all times a most wakeful watch is to be kept for these skirted British soldiers and that I am to be informed the moment they are seen, if they are seen.'

'Yet it seems your guard was not alert enough to report my own coming to you, in time for you to meet me decently.'

The old man bowed his head once again. 'This was due to my own slowness of body, Highness. Alas, I am no longer young.'

'The slowness of body must not be transmitted into slowness of mind also, Masrullah Sahib. What else have you done, what other action have you taken?'

'I have ordered no firing, Highness, it being my understanding that such was your father's wish.'

The Pathan smiled, coldly. 'Masrullah Sahib ... what would have been your action, had your men reported seeing British soldiers in strength?'

'Highness, I would at once have sent word to the village, and a runner would have been despatched to inform His Highness your father in Afghanistan. I did not consider the movement of a mere patrol of sufficient importance to send word to your father. Patrols are often observed.'

'Yes. But this business of sending word . . . it is slow.'

'The best that can be done, Highness.'

'Until now, yes.' Shuja Khan stretched his long limbs and yawned. 'I have been sent into India for two reasons, Masrullah Sahib. One, to take personal charge of the rising of the tribes on my father's behalf. Two, to inform you, and all others, that my father's wishes have changed. Since the time for action is now very near, my father commands that all British troops seen in the vicinity shall be killed. He wishes to take no risks of the British finding out our plans.' He gave Masrullah a close look. 'What is the matter, old man?'

Masrullah said humbly, 'If British soldiers are killed, and if the main rising does not come very quickly, I fear reprisals on the village, Highness.'

'Then you fear unnecessarily, Masrullah Sahib. If you do your work well, the British will not know whereabouts in the hills their soldiers died. For you will see to it that you kill them all, and that you leave no traces of what has happened. Is this understood, Masrullah Sahib?'

The old man bowed low. 'It is understood, Highness.'

'Good. Let me tell you this, old one. It is

94

well known to my father that you have always maintained good relations with the British invader and that there has been no blood shed in Sikat for many years past. This does not speak well for your loyalty to our cause—'

'Highness, I have thought only of the welfare of my people, and of the advantages of peace, and of a turning of the other cheek—'

'Then you will think no more of such things,' Shuja Khan said roughly. 'Your people's welfare and your own will be much better served by driving the British from the Frontier. We have allowed you to remain here in the Black Fort because there was no other suitable person available to put in your place without questions being asked by the British, and also because you are known to have your people under good control. This happy state of affairs may not always prevail, Masrullah Sahib, and will assuredly not prevail if you do not follow my father's wishes to the letter. I am empowered to inform you that if you fail us, in the smallest degree, your village of Sikat will be razed to the ground, also this fort, and your men slaughtered, and your women delivered to our men to use as they please. When you have witnessed all this, then you also will die, but slowly. Thus, old man, you will kill any British soldiers who approach Sikat, for that is the one path along which lies your own safety. If you play your part well it will not be the women of Sikat who will be delivered to our men—but the British women in Fort Gazai beyond Chitral! You will do well to bear in mind one other thing: your known friendliness towards the British will be of much help to you in luring any soldiers into the paths of your artillery and rifles.' He paused. 'Now, Masrullah Sahib, I wish to speak personally to the British gunner, Makepeace.'

*   *   *

By this time Ogilvie's patrol, sweat-streaked and covered with dust, had already passed through the village of Mundari and the men were now climbing through the hills beyond. In Mundari they had all been aware of the strong undercurrent of hostility as they had marched behind their piper and drummer through the village. There had been nothing overt; indeed, the inhabitants had appeared lethargic, almost apathetic, but Ogilvie's impression had been that the apathy was a studied, contemptuous expression. Even the children of the village had been subdued and somehow disdainful. There had not been so much as a stone thrown, not so much as a single stream of saliva directed at the marching men, actions which might have been expected following upon the comparatively recent beastliness of the late Corporal Nichol in raping a native girl. Ogilvie had felt that he had been taking part almost in a stage farce. The swinging kilts, the

96

smart step, the raucous voice of Colour-Sergeant Barr, the martial sound of the pipes and the beat of the drum as they passed by the mud walls had struck a note so odd as to bring a sinister feeling to the very air. Ogilvie was seriously worried about the implications; all along, the country had seemed unnaturally quiet. From time to time they had passed men of the tribes tending flocks of goats or mountain sheep, or hunting the occasional gooral that had strayed down from the higher peaks of Himalaya, or digging in the rough fields in the lower-lying areas before the hills; and now and again they had been aware of eyes upon them and had seen furtive men with long-barrelled rifles lurking on the high peaks as they had pushed on into the hills. Those men had the look of Afghanistan about them and Ogilvie had mentioned this to Barr.

The Colour-Sergeant had said, 'That may be so, sir. And then again it might not. I'm thinking there's a deal of Pathan blood amongst the tribes this side of the border too.'

Ogilvie nodded, shielding his eyes against a high sun. 'True enough. But there's something in the air. Don't you feel it, Colour-Sarn't?'

Barr scoffed. 'Och, ye've no' but a touch of the ghosties an' bogles,' he said in an infuriatingly familiar way. 'Ye've no' been out here long, Mr. Ogilvie. Myself, I had five years on the Frontier wi' the Black Watch.'

That was another thing about Barr: he

couldn't forget he had served with the Black Watch, which he seemed to think a cut above the Royal Strathspey, and he brought his old regiment into every conversation if he could manage it. Barr had been one of those time-expired seven-year men who had opted for the reserve and then found he couldn't settle to civil life. He had re-enlisted, this time in the 114th where he had seen more chances of promotion, and had worked his way up again, past his old rank of Corporal, to Colour-Sergeant. He couldn't have done that if he hadn't been an excellent soldier, but his manner grated nonetheless. Fighting down his irritation Ogilvie said, 'It's not imagination, Colour-Sarn't. Far from it. There's something brewing.'

Barr shrugged his wrestler's shoulders. 'I've never known the North-West Frontier when there has *not* been, Mr. Ogilvie.'

They had marched on, and from time to time had seen more men who looked like Pathans or Afridis from beyond the Afghan passes. Despite Barr, Ogilvie felt certain that was where they were from; after all, it was known in Peshawar, according to Black and Major Wingate, that Afghans had been infiltrating and assembling in this area. They made camp each nightfall with vigilant sentries posted. In the evenings, after the day's march, a rum ration was issued to each man, neat spirit which had to be drunk in the presence of the officer to ensure that none was kept back for a subsequent binge. Ogilvie, disinclined for disciplinary reasons to supervise his Colour-Sergeant, felt convinced Barr was in fact keeping back some of his own issue and bottling it, though Barr would have been the first to put on a charge any of the rank and file caught doing the same thing. Ogilvie's general apprehensions grew as the patrol progressed, and, after they had passed on through Dera, finding a similar atmosphere to that in Mundari, and were heading up for Sikat, three days out now from Peshawar, he took Barr aside during one of the halts on the march when the men fell out to ease sore feet and aching legs.

'That village confirms it,' he said. 'They're definitely up to something, Colour-Sarn't. I've a feeling we don't need to go any further than this.'

'The orders said a fortnight, sir.'

'Fortnight maximum. I'm aware of that, Colour-Sarn't. But my report was wanted urgently. If we're satisfied with what we've already seen, then it could be better to go back fast before anything blows up.'

Barr looked obstinate; he twirled his waxed moustache. 'The orders, sir, were for a fourteen day patrol.'

'I don't think you've got the point, Colour-Sarn't.'

'No, Mr. Ogilvie, I don't believe I have.'

'Then I'll say it again. Speed in making the report may be the most important aspect of the patrol.'

'It may be, sir, and again it may not. Accuracy is also important. I have no doubt Captain Black and Major Wingate specified a probe into Sikat because they meant us to carry out the order. We have not yet reached Sikat, which is well north of here and therefore in a possibly different position from Mundari and Dera. I have no doubt the officers will be asking for my observations as well as your own, Mr. Ogilvie. With respect. I feel I could scarcely give these gentlemen a decent view on the strength of having passed through only two villages of the three ordered.'

Barr looked Ogilvie full in the face, with a hint of a smile twisting the corners of his thin mouth, lifting the heavy moustache in an arrogant, irritating smirk. MacKinlay had been right; Barr was going to be difficult, and his difficultness was going to take the form of a near-the-mark insolence. Ogilvie breathed hard, then swung away and walked up and down for a while, thinking furiously, giving himself time to cool down. It would never do, now, to get up against Barr, and it would be disastrous if he were to be seen by the men in open disagreement with his Colour-Sergeant. Not that he would have allowed himself to be swayed by that consideration if he should decide to return to cantonments; he would give the order and that would be that. Barr, as a good and experienced N.C.O., would obey. But there was a strong possibility that Barr was right. Two in three was not one hundred per cent and might not be good enough to satisfy either Black or Wingate, and if anything should go wrong subsequently, Black would undoubtedly remember that he, Ogilvie, had brought his patrol back ahead of time, with his mission uncompleted—in face of the expressed contrary advice from his Colour-Sergeant . . .

Ogilvie, stiff-faced, halted in front of Barr. 'Very well, Colour-Sarn't,' he said. 'You may be right. Thank you for your advice.'

'Then the patrol continues, Mr. Ogilvie?'

'Yes, Colour-Sarn't, the patrol continues.'

'Very good, sir.'

'Fall the men in, please.'

'Sir!' Barr saluted and turned about and began shouting the men back on their feet. Once more they moved off into the day's mounting heat. It was only 10 a.m. but there had undoubtedly been a smell of rum on the Colour-Sergeant's breath. If the men smelt that, there might be trouble. They were not fools; they would know well enough that the officer must have smelt it too.

*   *   *

When Lord Dornoch returned to cantonments in Peshawar he had a word with his adjutant.

In the privacy of his own quarters, over whisky and cigars, he raised the question of Ogilvie's patrol. 'A trifle unnecessary, I'd have thought, Andrew, to recall young Ogilvie from leave?'

Black pulled at his cigar. 'I'm sorry, Colonel.'

'There are plenty of other subalterns readily available.'

'True, true. But I fancied Ogilvie could do with the experience—'

'Some of the newer ones could do with it more.'

'Ah, yes, Colonel, but I felt they would not be experienced *enough*. It is an important patrol, you'll agree.'

'It's open to question, but I'm not criticizing the fact that you had to meet the wishes of the Political people, Andrew. My real point is this: why send Ogilvie and Barr together again?'

Black shrugged and failed to meet the Colonel's eye. 'It was the General's expressed wish that they should continue to serve together, Colonel.'

'I know that.' Dornoch shifted irritably in his chair. 'There's still no need to stick rigidly to what the General said—don't misunderstand me—no need to *deliberately* send those two off together. In my view it's asking for trouble. And I'll tell you this: I would be sorry, most sorry, to think that my adjutant was acting from any kind of personal spite. I shall say no more than that, but I ask you very earnestly to keep your position as adjutant very well in mind, Andrew, in the future. I think you will understand me.'

When his cigar was finished Andrew Black stalked back to his quarters, scowling his way across the dark parade ground. The Colonel's tone had been undeniably sharp during that particular discussion.

* * *

'That's the Black Fort, Mr. Ogilvie,' Barr said three days later. 'On the other side is Sikat village. The Black Fort is friendly.'

'So it's said.' Ogilvie halted his patrol. He focused his field glasses on the mud-walled fort commanding the valley along which they had been advancing. The walls were thick, very thick he fancied, with a wide platform behind the battlements. Ogilvie could see armed men through the embrasures between the merlons, and a moment later he could hear the tinny note of some native wind instrument. He said, 'We've been spotted, Colour-Sarn't.'

'I should think we would have been by now, sir. We've not been in much cover just lately.'

Ogilvie went on looking through the glasses. 'I'd give a lot to know their intentions. They don't look all that peaceful or friendly to me.'

'We'll not know for sure till we approach closer, Mr. Ogilvie, but I don't believe myself they'll open on a British patrol, if that's what

103

you fear.'

There was an inflexion in the man's voice that Ogilvie didn't like. Sharply, as he lowered the glasses, he said, 'It's not a case of fearing anything, Colour-Sarn't, but we happen to be under orders to avoid any engagements.'

'Aye, sir, that's right, I know it, but we still have orders to march through Sikat.' He waved an arm around the enclosing light-brown hills. 'The one way into the village lies past the Black Fort, sir.'

'No deviations anywhere?'

'None at all, sir, short of climbing into the hills and then turning back to the track again farther along, to approach from the north. But I'd not be wanting to give the buggers the idea we were scared of marching past their guns. Sir!'

Ogilvie compressed his lips. Nettled by the man's tone as usual, he ordered curtly, 'Move the men on, Colour-Sarn't. March at attention.'

'Sir!' Barr marched smartly towards the soldiers. 'Patrol, atten—*tion*. Slope—*arms*. By the right, quick—*march*! That's it, step smart now. Left-right-left . . . left—left—left. Shoulders back, Mathieson, you're a soldier, you scraggy bugger, you, not a skivvy, and this is hostile territory, not Sauchiehall Street on a Saturday night. Left—left—left, right, left. Do we march past in proper order, sir, or do we not?'

By 'proper order' Barr meant the pipes. Ogilvie said, 'With the pipes, please, Colour-Sarn't,' and Barr yelled again and a moment later wind was blown into the pipes and they advanced along the terrible track to the sound of the highland music and the beat of the solitary drummer. The pipes were playing 'Cock O' The North', the notes beating defiantly off the hillsides, bringing the sound of Empire and glory to the wild Frontier hills. The gap closed, the Black Fort loomed nearer, forbidding, lonely in its grim surround. As the British soldiers came on the tribesmen stared down from the battlements, brooding but immobile, seemingly not meaning to open fire, their long-barrelled pieces slung across their backs. Slowly overhead, vultures wheeled and called. Ogilvie detested the vultures; they seemed, he felt, to sense death before it came. There was always premonition in their very presence, as though they could see, and interpret, what lay beyond the next hill, the next bend in the track.

Perhaps it was those vultures that made him extra wary and suspicious, despite those peacefully slung rifles, as they neared the fort. Whatever it was, he reacted instantly and almost without conscious thought when suddenly, just as the piper changed his tune to 'Blue Bonnets Over The Border', the gates of the Black Fort were thrown wide open. He yelled out, 'Barr, scatter the men—quickly!'

Barr stared. 'What's the panic, Mr. Ogilvie? There's no' but an open gateway—'

'*Do as I say!*'

Barr shrugged, but obeyed. Within seconds the patrol was widely dispersed to the right of the track, hidden from view by boulders and in the *nullahs*. Ogilvie touched his Corporal on the shoulder. 'Keep under cover, Phillips,' he said, 'but go among the men. Tell them, no firing unless I shout and give them a target. They're just to stay out of sight.'

'Aye, sir.' Corporal Phillips crawled away. Ogilvie watched the fort. Barr was crawling towards him, blaspheming. From out of the gates six elephants were now trundling, each of them hauling a heavy piece of artillery. 'Ten-pounders,' Barr said in a harsh whisper, 'and by the look of 'em, well maintained.' Once again Ogilvie smelt rum. 'The dirty, treacherous buggers . . .'

Ogilvie couldn't help saying, 'They didn't ask us to come here, you know. Treachery's not quite the word.'

'Old Masrullah makes out he's a friend.' Suddenly, Barr spat; Ogilvie was in some doubt as to whether the act was directed at Masrullah or at himself. He said, 'It looks as though we've met the trouble all right, Colour-Sarn't. If we come out of this, it's back to cantonments without a doubt this time.'

'As you say, Mr. Ogilvie.'

They watched and waited as the elephants

106

were moved into position. They were within easy range of those guns, but the enemy gunners were not all that well placed. They would need to aim upwards, and they would need to find their targets. With the men well hidden, they had the whole hillside to choose from, even though they would have some idea of the general whereabouts of the British. Meanwhile, a cool fire from the patrol might be able to make mincemeat of the gunners, even though the range was too great to have much effect on the tough hides of the elephants. 'Spread the men out in line, Colour-Sarn't,' Ogilvie ordered. 'I want as wide a spread laterally as possible. Report when ready—and tell each man he's to open fire on the gunners the moment he hears me shout.'

'Very good then.' Barr moved away on his stomach. A few minutes after he had gone the fort's artillery opened. There was a ripple of flame and a lot of smoke, and a roar of sound. There were whistles overhead, and Ogilvie pressed his body into the ground in the lee of his covering boulder. The explosions of the shells came from their rear, and debris hurtled down around them. The gunners had overshot, but had been lucky in their bearing. The next salvo was even farther over, and, this time, well to their left.

Ogilvie grinned to himself. They were pretty poor shots; he felt reasonably confident of being able to pick off the gunners quickly when he was ready, even though the fire from the hillside would give the artillery a nice point of aim. The bombardment was kept up as ineffectively as before, and beneath the rain of debris as the odd shell smacked into the hill above their heads, Colour-Sergeant Barr came crawling and sliding back, covered with dust and muck and with his khaki-drill tunic ripped in several places. He said breathlessly, 'Orders passed, Mr. Ogilvie, and I'm thinking the sooner you give the word to open fire, the better it'll be.'

'We may as well let 'em go on wasting ammunition,' Ogilvie said, then he stiffened in sheer astonishment. He said 'What the hell!' He lifted his glasses and studied the scene below. A strange procession was coming from the gateway now, a procession that looked for all the world like some sort of royal progress. In the centre of two lines of scruffy native infantry, a solitary and dignified figure walked. A tall brown man with an upright bearing, broad-shouldered once but shrunken now with age, white-haired and white moustached with a cleanshaven chin—and wearing a blue tunic with polished brass buttons and blue trousers with a broad red stripe down the seams. And on his arm the three gold chevrons of a sergeant of the British Army.

Ogilvie said, 'My God.'

'May I have the glasses, please, Mr. Ogilvie.'

Wordlessly Ogilvie handed Barr his field

108

glasses. Barr looked. In a scandalized tone he said, 'The man's wearing the uniform of the Royal Field Artillery, sir. An old style one, but still the Royal Field Artillery. I don't understand, sir.'

'No more do I,' Ogilvie said, 'but it's a fair assumption that somebody, some time, lost his uniform and probably his life as well.'

They watched.

The strange figure stalked towards the guns and took up a position in rear of the battery. He seemed to be haranguing the men, then he went individually to each gun and spoke briefly to its native crew, after which he brought up a pair of field glasses and intently studied the hillside. Then Barr came to life again and said urgently, 'Mr. Ogilvie, are you not going to give the order to open fire, for heaven's sake?'

Ogilvie nodded. *'Open fire!'* he shouted. Immediately the rifles crashed out, a line of smoke puffs from the hillside. Spurts of dust were seen around the guns and three of the gunners keeled over. They were left to lie where they had fallen and the man in the sergeant's tunic himself leapt forward to the guns as the elephants started squealing under the sustained rifle fire. A moment after that the battery opened again, no longer firing as one, but firing with devilish accuracy all the same. It was almost uncanny; those guns were now laid slap on target, right in the centre of the concealed British line. The earth seemed to erupt alongside Ogilvie; he was thrown into the air, to land with a crash back on bare earth while half the hillside dropped upon him. There were yells, cries, oaths. The rifles crashed out still, less of them now, and down below more gunners were hit. But no one seemed able to hit that blue Field Artillery tunic, though its wearer didn't appear to be worrying about taking cover. As his gunners died or lay wounded, and no replacements were sent in, he was everywhere at once, laying the guns, firing them, and still firing them with that ferocious accuracy of aim. The man was an expert, a master gunlayer. Ogilvie did the one thing he could do in the circumstances and passed the word for a general retreat up the hillside for re-grouping and the planning of some sort of counter-attack before the fort's riflemen could move into action. As the men withdrew towards the crest of the hills, the sporadic artillery fire was kept up as accurately as ever, only one gun firing at a time, but reasonably fast as the ancient white-haired gunlayer galloped from gun to gun. Breathlessly what was left of the patrol came over the crest and slid down the far side. Ogilvie counted heads. They had left seven men behind, dead or wounded. Corporal Phillips was one of them. All the others were in a dishevelled state and four were bleeding; one had a broken arm. Barr was intact except for a nasty lump on his head and Ogilvie himself was merely shaken and bruised. He asked, 'What do you make of all that, Colour-Sarn't?'

'What do I make of it, Mr. Ogilvie?' Barr shook dust off his immense body. 'I'd say we're bloody well outgunned and all we can do is beat it back to cantonments and report.'

It was a change of tune with a vengeance; Ogilvie felt like rubbing it in, but all he said was, 'Thank you, Colour-Sarn't, that's what we're going to do if we can—after we've had a look for any wounded over there. But what I meant was, what do you make of that gunlayer?'

'He's good, sir. Bloody good. Better than any bugger of a native is ever going to be.'

'That's what I thought.'

Their eyes met and Barr said, 'An' I believe he's no native, Mr. Ogilvie. He's an Englishman.' Once again, he spat. 'An English bugger that's deserted from Her Majesty's forces and is dirty enough to fire on his own kith an' kin. That's what I think.'

'Once again, we agree, Colour-Sarn't. I fancy his skin's sunburn and not birth, somehow—and there was that bearing. Very regimental. It's a dirty business, all right!'

'And one that the regiment'll put right in double quick time, Mr. Ogilvie, if I know the Colonel. Let's march, sir, and not waste a minute longer!'

'First, the wounded. I'll take a look myself, with two men. The fittest—you, Kinnear, and

111

Lochen.'

'Aye, sir.' Kinnear and Lochen came towards Ogilvie. Together, keeping low as they neared the crest, they moved back in the direction of the Black Fort. Watching from cover, Ogilvie saw that the guns were being withdrawn, but men were forming up in the fort's courtyard, ready, no doubt, for the pursuit. All at once he felt doubtful that his men could ever make the journey back to Peshawar. Barr knew this territory well, but its inhabitants must know it better; and it was six days' march to Peshawar, maybe a little less if they could find a direct route; in the meantime no one in Peshawar would be worried about them for another eight days yet at least. Ogilvie shrugged away his anxieties and concentrated on the task in hand. With Privates Kinnear and Lochen behind him he crawled over the top and made his way down the hillside. So far at any rate, he had not been seen, but that immunity couldn't last long. Reaching the vicinity of what had been the British line, Ogilvie and the two men hunted around. They found five men dead, and two others seriously wounded and unconscious, but breathing. One was bleeding profusely from a stomach wound—it looked as though a jag of rock had taken off the man's belly covering—while the other had a completely smashed hip and pelvis. Neither of them would make it back to Peshawar, but along the North-West Frontier a regiment never left its wounded behind. Ogilvie and the privates collected all the rifles, then bent to the wounded. As the men were lifted pain broke through to their consciousness and they screamed in agony, but Ogilvie and the others shut their ears to the dreadful sounds as best they were able and began staggering up the hillside with their burdens. That was when they were seen. There was a long-drawn cry from below and a rifle crashed out, its bullet going wide. More shots followed, and then Ogilvie saw the men running from the open gates. He came over the crest of the hill with Kinnear and Lochen, and men ran up to help them. With two soldiers carrying each of the wounded, the remnants of the patrol made their way as fast as possible down into the next valley, accompanied by the continuing cries of the wounded as the tortured bodies were jogged and twisted in the fast descent. The party had scarcely reached the valley when the tribesmen came over the crest of the hill and the firing began again. A soldier fell with a bullet through his head; the remainder dropped behind the boulders and brought their rifles up. They fired back steadily, began to pick off the advancing, yelling tribesmen. The British held the advantage and they made the fullest use of it. They scarcely wasted a shot; before the gap was half closed, the natives wavered, halted, and then retreated, scrambling back towards the crest, chased by the British fire. Ogilvie's patrol had suffered no further losses beyond the man shot through the head. Once again, for a spell, they breathed easy. But Colour-Sergeant Hamish Barr voiced the fears of them all when he said, 'From now on, lads, we'll have them on our backs till we're within shouting distance of Peshawar, and we'll not be able to let up for a single instant.'

*   *   *

The tribesmen would be back soon, but they hadn't returned just yet. The small British patrol struggled on, along the parallel valley now, the valley that led south for a little way, according to the maps, the evidence of which was supported by Barr, and then took a turn to the south-eastward. It ran more or less parallel with the course of the Panjkora River to Abazai and Nowshera. When they reached Abazai, they would find safety and communication with Peshawar. If only, Ogilvie thought, some more of that money that cousin Hector was so niggardly about had been allocated by the Treasury to the army, more progress might have been made by now with the new wireless telegraphy, and then he could have been in communication throughout; the army's current equipment, the cumbersome field telegraph, with its drums of insulated wire, was utterly unsuitable for maintaining

114

communication whilst on extended patrol. It was all right for a straightforward line of march, or for use when in action to maintain touch with base, but that was all. And meanwhile, burdened as they were with the wounded, Abazai was, at a rough estimate, three days' march away. On the face of it, it was a sheerly impossible task to reach that far. At best they faced a slow whittling away of their number until the last man fell. Responsibility lay heavily on Ogilvie's shoulders; this was yet one more patrol messed up, though this time he felt it to be through no fault of his own. He had had no orders to refuse to return fire if attacked, and he had had no option but to pass the Black Fort if he were to advance at all in execution of his orders. But he wished, now, that he had returned to cantonments after passing through Dera . . .

He wondered what he should do about the wounded; they were indisputably a drag on weary men and they were slowing the retreat disastrously. Ogilvie would have liked to discuss them with Colour-Sergeant Barr, but this he refused to do, knowing that he couldn't shift the responsibility and knowing he would get little help from Barr in any case. If only he had old Bosom Cunningham, the Regimental Sergeant-Major, with him! Everything would have been quite different. None of the ultimate responsibility would have been shifted, but Cunningham, with his firm and kindly wisdom, would have eased the load tremendously. Cunningham was a fine soldier and a fine R.S.M., respected and liked throughout the regiment, with which he had his own family connections; a very different kettle of fish from Barr. And what would Cunningham have said about the wounded? That they were a threat to other men, a danger to life when their own lives were obviously worth nothing now unless they could be got to a doctor within hours, and that their sufferings were a misery to them anyway? Or that the wounded were a first charge and fit men had to bear the burden whatever happened?

In any case, a British regiment still never left its wounded behind along the Frontier.

That left only the merciful bullet, fired from a friendly hand close to the ear. Ogilvie's problem was resolved. He knew he could never bring himself to despatch the wounded, even if to be unable to do so was cowardice in a commander of men. The fit must simply carry their burdens and march.

*   *   *

The next attack came within the hour, and this time it was a larger and much more co-ordinated manoeuvre. Tribesmen poured down the hillside on the flank of the retreating men, and others came along the valley behind.

With two men acting as rearguard and keeping up the fire, Ogilvie and Barr shouted for all the speed they could produce in an attempt to get ahead of the descending tribesmen before the valley was cut in front of them. But very soon they all realized their situation was hopeless and that they would have to stand and fight it out. Inevitably, then, they would go down, and be written off the War Office lists as just another brave patrol that had joined the numbers of earlier Britons who had never come back from the North-West Frontier, who had fought and died but who, in dying, had held the line in the name of the Queen Empress and had planted the flag of Empire firmer yet.

Ogilvie, his face white beneath its tan and a thick coating of dust, halted the patrol. He said, 'This is it, men. We'll get as many of them as we can, and God be with us all.' That was when he noticed, as he looked round for the best position from which to fight, the fissure in the rocky face of the hill. It was half hidden with scrubby, parched growth. He said, 'Hold on a minute.' He went and had a look and found that the fissure extended inwards some twenty feet. Running back towards the men he called, 'Over here . . . we'll get inside and turn it into a strongpoint. We'll see what they make of that!'

*   *   *

There had been silence outside for a while but then the concealed soldiers heard weird, wailing cries as the tribesmen, widely dispersed, called out to their compatriots. Soon there was movement visible in the valley as the dark-skinned figures came down the opposite hillside.

Ogilvie, thinking of the food and water, said, 'We're going to have to withstand a siege. Colour-Sarn't.'

'So it seems. I think we all expected no less, Mr. Ogilvie. Well—we have our provisions, which must be strictly rationed, and we have rifles and ammunition. We'll give a good account of ourselves, sir, and take plenty of those bastards with us before the end.'

'We won't think in terms of the end just yet, Colour-Sarn't! We shall be noted as overdue in cantonments eventually.'

'Eventually, Mr. Ogilvie, yes. But not inside six days. And action will not be taken right away, you may be sure.' Barr eased the collar of his tunic; it was a band of sweat. 'It'll take time for a relief force to reach us, too. Added to which, they do not know where we are.'

'Oh, come! They know the area we're operating in!'

'But we're off the track, Mr. Ogilvie, do you not see? Besides . . . they'll not be wanting to light any more fuses along the Frontier just now, not until Division is ready for it.'

'You mean you actually think they'll leave us to it?'

'I'd not be surprised; not at all.'

Ogilvie felt a surge of anger, but fought it down with an effort. All the time he had been talking to Barr he had been keeping a watchful eye on the tribesmen. The circle had halted some distance off, currently out of range of the rifles. There seemed to be a consultation in progress, so far as could be seen at such a distance, and soon after this the hillmen melted away. Once again there was silence; it was unnerving while it lasted. Again Ogilvie saw the foul vultures hovering, descending now and again to sweep past the fissure's entry as though impatient for their meal. Then the silence was shattered and the carrion birds rose, screaming hoarsely. Bullets smacked into the rock around Ogilvie, and he ducked, Barr doing likewise behind him and cursing viciously as he did so. No one had been hit. Ogilvie was ready with his revolver and when he saw a movement in some bushes close at hand he fired. There was no reaction. Tensely, he waited. For a while there was no further movement and then, as if from nowhere, three figures emerged into the open and rushed the entry, firing as they came. Bullets sang over Ogilvie's head, and he squeezed the trigger of his revolver; at the same moment two rifles crashed out from behind him. Two of the tribesmen fell, writhing in agony on the

119

ground, and the third turned and fled. The rifles got him before he had gone a dozen feet and he, too, fell. Again the besieged men waited; within half an hour there was another attack, with a similar result, except that this time five tribesmen died together with one British soldier, shot clean through the heart right beside Ogilvie. By nightfall there were seventeen native bodies lying on the ground outside; Ogilvie had spent the remainder of the daylight hours watching them die, and during that time one more of his men had also died—one of the wounded, the man whose stomach had been so badly lacerated by the fall of shell from the artillery earlier. By now the vultures were at work, satisfying themselves on the corpses in the open. In the fading light Ogilvie had watched with revulsion as the sharp beaks tore and ripped at human flesh. By the time the light went the bones were mostly bare.

During that night there were three more attacks, all of them repulsed with heavy losses to the enemy—and three more of the 114th dead, including the second of the badly wounded men.

By daybreak Ogilvie's force consisted of nine fit men and one wounded, plus Colour-Sergeant Barr. At this rate, they could scarcely hold out for the full six days—five now—let alone until a relief force could march to their assistance and locate them. It helped them little that the enemy's losses were greater; the Black Fort must obviously hold an overwhelmingly larger number. Nevertheless, the tribesmen didn't appear anxious for any more losses, at any rate for the time being, for the morning passed without further attack, though Ogilvie could see that the fissure was under distant observation throughout.

Barr said, 'They'll hope to starve us out, Mr. Ogilvie.'

'I doubt if they'll let it go at that, Colour-Sarn't.' He rubbed at his eyes, which were red-rimmed now and filled with harsh dust. 'They'll have a relief force in mind, and they'll know we're provisioned for a long patrol.'

'Aye, maybe, sir, but ye'll bear in mind what I said about the unlikelihood of a relief.'

Ogilvie shrugged. 'Whether or not you're right about that—and I don't think you are—those natives won't believe the Raj will leave us to be cut up! There'll be another attack before much longer. We must keep on the alert, Colour-Sarn't.'

'I never suggested we shouldn't be doing that, Mr. Ogilvie.'

'Very well, Colour-Sarn't.'

They kept up the watch but in fact nothing happened all that day nor during the succeeding night. Men grew lethargic, even careless of the watch; Ogilvie had constantly to chase them. Hamish Barr seemed in a sardonic mood; his churlishness, his basic enmity, was

121

increasing under stress. He and Ogilvie were taking turns at sleeping, one of them always on the alert, to watch and to supervise the niggardly rationing of their dwindling food and water—especially water. As Ogilvie relieved his Colour-Sergeant at the next dawn, Barr said, 'I've been thinking, Mr. Ogilvie. It seems to me we should try to break out.'

'No,' Ogilvie said at once.

'Why not, Mr. Ogilvie? It would be the way of the Black Watch, to do that.'

Ogilvie compressed his lips; officers were not normally questioned as to their decisions by N.C.O.s or even by Warrant Officers such as the R.S.M., though in the present circumstances the query was possibly natural enough—would have been, in the case of Cunningham for instance. But Barr's question had the ring of impertinence, which was a different thing; besides which, the Black Watch was beginning to irritate. However, Ogilvie answered the question. He said, 'Because the moment we show our noses outside, we'll be mown down. That's why, Colour-Sarn't.'

'Aye,' Barr said in a considering way. 'No one likes to be shot at.'

'What do you mean by that?'

Barr shrugged, and twirled his heavy moustache. 'Oh, nothing at all. Only I'm willing to take a chance, myself, and see if the buggers'll shoot—'

'You'll do no such thing.'

Barr's face was grim. 'As you say, Mr. Ogilvie. But I'm informing you officially that the men are becoming restive and I'll not be answering for what they may do.'

'Don't worry, I'm taking full responsibility. I'm as close to the men as you are, Colour-Sarn't. I know as well as you how they're feeling. The answer's still no.'

'Very good, Mr. Ogilvie. You're the officer.' Barr looked him up and down, insolently. 'But you'll be remembering I spoke, will you not?'

'Of course I will!' Ogilvie snapped.

'Then that's all right.'

Ogilvie opened his mouth, then shut it again. He was trembling with anger and frustration, but knew that the worst possible thing for them all in this situation would be for open hostility to develop between the officer and the Colour-Sergeant; such could prove fatal. Ogilvie's one duty was to bring the remnants of his command through this in as good order as lay within his capabilities; everything, all personal feeling, must be subordinated to that. He knew it would be suicide to attempt any dash into the open; quite clearly, though they could pinpoint no movement anywhere, they were still being very closely watched. After a while, however, Ogilvie heard some of the mutterings of the men. They were taking their tune from Hamish Barr, it seemed, and the officer's stomach for a fight, for lead, was being called into question.

His face burned but he could do nothing but pretend he hadn't heard.

Four days at the very least to go now. Ogilvie was wishing his life away, hard.

He had half a mind, he told himself, to put an end once and for all to the whispers, and show Barr up before the men. It could be done easily enough; all he had to do was to walk out of the fissure, himself, alone, and draw the fire he knew would come. He might be lucky enough to get away with a whole skin, dash back in safety to the fissure, and look at Barr's red face. That would cover Colour-Sergeant Barr in the greatest possible confusion! At the same time it would establish that he was no coward, which was important. But afterwards, if they got back safely to cantonments, he would incur official displeasure for having pointlessly risked his life knowing the odds against him; if he had been unable to assess those odds he would be adjudged unfit for leadership, and if he was known to have gone out regardless, he would be criticized for not having the strength of character to resist a display of useless personal bravery. That would be how the official mind would work—Black's kind of mind, cousin Hector's kind of mind. It was not unknown for Whitehall clerks to assess the field reports on officers whose military skills they knew nothing of, and then make their own reports thereon to higher authority. Ogilvie was beginning to learn that in the

British Army two things counted above all: total success, which forgave everything; and enough luck to ensure that one's errors of judgment remained undiscovered until one reached high rank, when one could do no wrong. Generals were allowed to make the most colossal blunders and get away with them. In this current situation there was another point to be considered: Ogilvie felt he had no right to risk leaving the men leaderless if he should be killed on some useless endeavour. Barr was an excellent soldier, a first-rate N.C.O. on the parade, a faultless drill instructor, smart and loud-voiced and full of bounce. But out here on patrol, Ogilvie felt that such attributes were not of themselves enough and that Colour-Sergeant Barr lacked the capacity for real leadership and self-discipline. He would never make Regimental Sergeant-Major. And Ogilvie would never trust him to take the patrol back to Peshawar.

*　　*　　*

Outside Peshawar Major-General Fettleworth's gigantic show of strength had been held and Bloody Francis himself, with his Staff, had personally, pompously and with a protuberant eagle eye inspected every man, riding on his charger along the endless lines of the great military review. As each colonel had attached himself to the procession on his regiment being reached, General Fettleworth had delivered a little homily.

'Colonel, I trust I shall find your men fighting fit in every respect, ready for battle should they be required. We hold much in trust, much in trust for Her Majesty and the Empire. We must all carry that trust efficiently.'

The colonels had mostly reacted as they were expected to react to General Fettleworth: obsequiously. Lord Dornoch, however, had not. The noble Earl commanding the 114th Highlanders was not an obsequious man; nor was he particularly good at pretence, even an expedient pretence, considering such to be beneath him. Polite, yes, deferential when he wished to be towards those for whom he had respect, but never obsequious. He had looked the Divisional Commander straight in the eye and said in a loud, clear voice, 'Her Majesty's 114th Regiment, sir, carry *everything* efficiently.'

General Fettleworth had already started to turn away, expecting no such speech. His face grew scarlet as he reined in his charger. He bared his teeth, giving his horse-like nervous grin. He turned to his Chief of Staff. 'What did he say?' he demanded.

Without waiting for the Chief of Staff, Dornoch repeated his words.

'Oh. Oh, very well,' Fettleworth said distantly, making a mental note that the

Colonel of the 114th was a talkative and upstartish fellow like so many of the damn clansmen. Disagreeably, he rode down the line of the 114th Highlanders. He spoke to none of them; he was too put out. He glared at the Scots. Kilts and sporrans and *skean dhus*, coloured wool stockings when ordinary soldiers wore trousers—ridiculous! Messy and fussy. Fettleworth found fault endlessly, addressing not the Colonel or his adjutant, but his own Chief of Staff, with his querulous complaints. These complaints, which Lord Dornoch had heard perfectly well, would now be passed time-wastingly down the chain of command until they reached him once again in very official form. Dornoch smiled to himself; they would not be acted upon. None of them were genuine and he had much more weighty matters on his mind. He could easily put General Fettleworth in his place at some suitable time; there were solid advantages in having a seat in the House of Lords, and Dornoch, who would never in fact have dreamed of abusing his privileges to the extent of using them for his own ends, was regretful that the army was moving away from aristocracy. He saw many dangers ahead; when Colonels of regiments were no longer men of private wealth or import, they would need to be much more attentive to the whims of men like Fettleworth. Dornoch, proud of his regiment as he was, was not dependent on the army for his livelihood; in that lay much strength, and the strength was used on behalf of his men. He was a very effective buffer between them and the more peculiar manifestations of incompetence in the high command. Dornoch's mind went back to those more weighty matters that were absorbing his attention. Trouble was undoubtedly stirring along the Frontier. His own *Munshi* Sahib had spoken to him privately, indicating that not all was well with the British Raj, and mourning the almost unmentionable fact that his own youngest son was one of those who wished to see the end come for British India. That had shaken Lord Dornoch considerably. If the venerable old regimental *Munshi* was unable to impart his loyalty to his own son, then things were coming to a sorry state indeed. And reports had reached Murree, as it now appeared, that some threat was developing to Fort Gazai near Chitral city—a threat which not even the astute and devious Political Officers fully understood the reasons for. There were British women and children in Fort Gazai and only a comparatively small garrison; and it seemed likely that the 114th would soon find themselves marching north to their relief, along with most of the Peshawar garrison (and on that march it would matter to no one except, presumably, General Fettleworth if a sporran was hanging crooked here, or a kilt-pin was wrongly angled there, or a highlander's buttocks leered at the man behind him because of an over-short kilt). It might be some while before this present spectacle of military power would be repeated in the formal surroundings of Peshawar; Peshawar could soon be an empty place, with all its sons away. Dornoch, moving slowly on his horse behind General Fettleworth, looked out at the regimental colours with their battle honours, at the guidons of the cavalry squadrons fluttering from the lances above the gilded uniforms and the magnificent shabraques of the horses, at the massed guns of the artillery, the colourful native troops, the support corps—Engineers, medical columns, A.S.C., Signals. It was really a most imposing array, but privately Lord Dornoch doubted if it would deter the Empire's foes from their set courses. The tribes were not like that, in his experience. They already knew the strength of British India; *they* were not fools! They did not back down under such arrogant displays of the mailed fist. Their leaders worked in other ways—largely with talk, talk that inflamed the warriors and emboldened them. No, they were not fools ... thinking of fools, Dornoch thought again of the thick-backed figure in front of him, dumped solid on his horse as though nothing would prise him loose. Fettleworth was a fool, all right. Brave enough—he'd fought in the Ambela campaign of '63 as an ensign, and with distinction so it was said. He had been among the earliest officers to be awarded the Distinguished Service Order on its institution in 1886. And in today's army there were not so many men left with, for instance, the Abyssinia 1867–8 Medal. The holders were either dead, or retired into a doddery old age—or, of course, were generals . . . a clean sweep was needed. Fettleworth was years and years out of date, even stood out among his contemporaries on that score, which was a feat in itself. Fettleworth had a fetish, not entirely uncommon among the senior officers of his younger days: infantry and cavalry won all the battles, all on their own. Guns were an interruption—like surgery to the physician, they were a last resort and their indiscriminate use reflected upon the tactical skill of the General Officer Commanding. Dornoch had no quarrel with Fettleworth's love of infantry, of course; but he did feel a shade more confident of winning his battles if the artillery were somewhere at hand, even though they undeniably had an unnerving propensity on occasions to lay their guns on the wrong target—which was one of the points Fettleworth was in the habit of making, Dornoch remembered. By the same token, however, it had not been unknown for a battalion of infantry to be directed by the high command to attack the wrong hill, or fort, or troop concentration. . . Dornoch hoped that day, as finally he saluted his Divisional

Commander's frosty face when the procession left the Highland ranks, that not too many mistakes would be made in the campaign that he felt certain lay before them. When the whole review was over and the men had marched proudly and with a crash of martial music back to cantonments, Dornoch called a conference of his company commanders. Major Hay, second-in-command, and Black, were also present, as were Surgeon Major Corton and the Quartermaster, Lieutenant MacCrum, along with Mr. Cunningham, Regimental Sergeant-Major.

'I think it all went off well enough,' Dornoch said with a touch of weariness.

'Apart from the complaints, Colonel.'

Dornoch glanced at the speaker, who was Black. 'Oh, I'll not let the complaints worry me,' he said. '*I* had none! The turn-out of the men was a credit to all of you, gentlemen.'

There was a murmur of thanks. Dornoch went on, 'I've called you here to tell you one thing: I want the battalion brought to instant readiness to march.'

Black lifted an eyebrow. 'This is the General's wish, Colonel?'

'No, it isn't, Andrew, it's mine.' Dornoch's tone was brisk. 'But it'll very soon be followed up by our General's wish as well, believe me. The Frontier's not healthy—we all know that. Without any positive order having been received, or even a hint of an order, I'm

131

expecting to be told to march quite soon, gentlemen. Call it intuition ... no, it's more than that. If I may say so, it's an intelligent appraisal of a fairly obvious situation.'

'In that case,' the adjutant observed, 'I'm really somewhat surprised the General has not already given the necessary order.'

Dornoch lifted an eyebrow. 'Are you?' he asked innocently. 'I really can't say I am.' He turned away towards a window overlooking the Royal Strathspeys' parade ground. Orders were being shouted; a defaulters' squad was being put through it by a drill-sergeant. Full kit, full packs, under a blinding sun. There was something childish about it. Dornoch turned away again, and faced his officers. 'I want full sick and light duty lists,' he said. 'I want to be informed each time the lists alter—at once. I want all stores, weapons, ammunition, horses and pack animals made ready as soon as possible, boots inspected, active-service kit brought up to date—but you all know what you have to do without my telling you, gentlemen. Tomorrow morning a full training programme will be put into effect, and it's the details of that I want to discuss with you. You especially, of course, Andrew, and you, Sarn't-Major. There's one other thing. Social life will have to go hang for the time being. I think you'll all understand. All officers will be required for duty continuously until further orders. Andrew, when is young Ogilvie due back from patrol?'

Black screwed up his face in thought. 'In four days' time, Colonel, at the latest.'

'H'm . . .' Dornoch frowned. 'I hope he gets back before things blow up in our faces, Andrew. If the Frontier rises, he's not going to be at all well placed . . .'

*   *   *

In the fissure, Ogilvie's nerves were at full stretch; Barr seemed to have forgotten his wish to break out by now, but Ogilvie found him of little help, and was angered by the way his Colour-Sergeant spoke to the men. Blasphemies were always on his lips, and every man in his turn became a bloody bastard. If this went on, someone was going to be goaded into answering back, possibly even into striking Barr; upon which it would be Ogilvie's duty to have the man concerned put on a charge as soon as they reached cantonments. And then, if Black had anything to do with it, the extenuating circumstances which Ogilvie would plead on the man's behalf would have but little effect upon the punishment. Discipline, especially in the field, must be upheld. This was true, and proper enough also. Ogilvie felt his own shortcomings keenly; he should be able to deal effectively with Barr. The trouble was, he couldn't do so in the men's hearing, and was physically prevented from doing so out of it. But an officer should by his bearing and his tone and the exercise of his personality be able to control an N.C.O. The impossibility of the situation weighed upon him, the more so in the tenseness of waiting for the enemy to strike again. His thoughts were turning in upon themselves.

In the end he was driven to some sort of remonstrance, after Barr, currently off watch duty, had lost his temper with a private named Rennie and had called him, in insulting tones, a bitch's whelp. Rennie, his face white, had clenched his fists; for a moment there was murder in his eyes, but he controlled himself; Ogilvie didn't know how he'd done it, but was thoroughly relieved. And he realized the time had come for a heart-to-heart talk with Barr.

From his place at the entry to the fissure he said quietly, 'A word in your ear, Colour-Sarn't.'

'What is it, Mr. Ogilvie?'

'Come to the entry, please, Colour-Sarn't.'

Slowly, watched by interested faces, Barr lounged across. In a low voice Ogilvie said, 'I heard that, Colour-Sarn't. That man very nearly struck you. I suppose you realize that?'

'I realize that, yes. Thank you for your concern, Mr. Ogilvie.'

Ogilvie disregarded the last sentence. He said, 'Then you must also realize the implications.'

'That's a long word, Mr. Ogilvie.' Barr

134

paused, then, with his hands on his hips and a smell of rum on his breath, he said insolently, 'I realize the *consequences* to Private Rennie if he should strike a superior officer.'

'I wasn't thinking so much of that, although it would be damned unfair, but of the consequences to yourself, Colour-Sarn't.'

'To *me*? Were you now? That's very kind, Mr. Ogilvie. Very kind indeed.' Barr's tongue came out and he licked his lips. 'Now, what would be the consequences to *me*, may I ask?'

'Serious, Colour-Sarn't. I would report on our return that you had deliberately provoked Rennie and that he had every moral justification for striking you.'

'Moral!' Barr sneered openly now, but pulled himself together as he saw the look on Ogilvie's face. 'Who would you make this report to, Mr. Ogilvie? To the adjutant?'

'Oh, no,' Ogilvie answered. 'Direct to the Colonel, Colour-Sarn't. And if necessary— which it wouldn't be—to Brigade.'

There was a silence; the two men's eyes held each other's for the best part of a minute. It was a strain, but it was Barr who looked away first. He muttered, 'So be it, then. Oh, I'll do my best not to sully the dainty ears of these *gentlemen* with barrack-room talk! But they're no' men, if they can't take that. It was different, in the Black Watch.'

It was victory, and Ogilvie let the insolence pass. There was quite enough trouble around

135

already; all he could do now was to watch Barr as carefully as he watched for the enemy, and try to stop anything else developing. And in the meantime he hoped the men, who must have taken in the sense of all he had been saying even if they hadn't caught all the words, would have the common sense not to show any consequent disrespect towards the Colour-Sergeant. Apart from the immediate difficulties that would ensue from that, it would lead, as so many things could, to a black mark for an officer who had reprimanded a senior N.C.O. in the men's presence. There was no end to the permutations of error. But soon after this episode domestic details passed right out of Ogilvie's mind, for, at long last, the enemy showed himself.

The first intimation came with a strange, still distant sound, as of enormous feet trampling on undergrowth and stunted trees, and then the rattle of equipment and the squeal of what sounded like oil-starved wheels. Ogilvie, on watch still, hastily awoke such men as were sleeping and called Barr to his side. 'What is it?' Barr asked.

'I don't know yet. Just listen.'

Both men listened. Barr said, 'Elephants.' Then, a few minutes later, they were able to see that he was right. Some two hundred yards away and coming along the valley from the right, was an elephant. As the animal plodded on, they saw the gun coming on behind. Beside the animal, a small crowd of tribesmen came along warily while a *mahout* sat behind the elephant's ears.

'So that's it!' Barr said. 'I told you, you should have got us out before this. Man, they're going to send a shell into the fissure and we'll all be roasted!'

Ogilvie didn't answer; he called to the men to stand ready with their rifles. As the elephant turned a broad bottom towards the fissure, and, behind it, the gun began to turn on to the bearing, he ordered the rifles to fire. There was a series of cracks and the natives dodged behind the gunshield; the elephant angrily waved its tail. Then Ogilvie saw the tall, white-haired figure in its dark blue artillery tunic. Barr saw him as well and let out a string of oaths. Instinctively, as the old man bent towards the gun, he and Ogilvie pressed back from the entry; men fell away behind them. Then a surprising thing happened. They heard an explosion some little way off—a big one, but no shell-burst followed it. Ogilvie turned back to the entry and looked out; he saw the hillmen running in disorder and the shattered remains of the gun trundling away down the valley in rear of the terrified elephant, which was squealing like a stuck pig, trumpeting madly with its trunk lifted high above its ears; and, coming towards the fissure at a speed dangerous for his age, the white-haired old man.

Barr spoke from behind Ogilvie. 'I'm going to get the bugger,' he said, and lifted his rifle.

Ogilvie snapped, 'Leave him—can't you see, he's coming to join us?'

'The bugger's going to get a bullet smack between the eyes no matter what you—' Barr broke off; he was livid. Ogilvie had knocked his rifle up with a sudden movement of his fist. As the bullet whistled away into emptiness the old man reached the fissure. He pushed his way inside, panting and almost spent. But with a colossal effort he dragged himself upright, slammed a veined hand to the salute, and said, 'Sir! Sergeant Makepeace, Royal Regiment of Artillery . . . reporting after twenty-eight years' absence from duty. Sir!'

CHAPTER FIVE

The old sergeant had set a charge and, as he put it himself, 'blown up the bloody gun, praise God'. They got his story later. Sergeant Makepeace had been captured twenty-eight years before, along with his wife Ellen and their three young children, two girls and a boy, during a raid on Peshawar itself. The family had been carried off into the hills and thence through the Bolan Pass into Afghanistan and incarcerated in the fort at Kabul. It appeared that one of the objectives of the raid had been

Makepeace himself, who had had a brilliant reputation as an artilleryman and gunlayer. He'd had no equal, it had been said, in all the army in India in those days, and the hill tribes had known of this reputation and wanted him so that he could lay their guns for them, against the British.

Stoutly enough, naturally enough, Makepeace had refused.

He had gone on refusing (he said) even when they threatened to murder his wife and children. He had even refused when first of all they flogged himself, and then his wife. 'Ellen died under the lash, sir,' he said simply. 'They flogged her naked, sir, before a crowd of filthy natives, sir, and then, praise be to God, she died. And after that, sir, I still refused, and I went on refusing, although they flogged me again and again—me, a sergeant in Her Majesty's Royal Regiment of Artillery—and I refused until they took my son and spitted him upon a lance, and let him die slowly in the sun. To my shame, sir, I could take no more, and knew I must now consider my young daughters. So I laid the guns, sir, upon a British column under General Horace Fisher . . . the column consisting of the 32nd and 46th Foot, the 9th Lancers, and the 33rd Bengal Infantry as I recall. Sir, I laid the guns badly, though such went against my nature, and the shells landed very far behind the column. So they pegged my younger daughter out in the courtyard with tent pegs, and they smothered her body with honey, and they allowed the ants to consume her flesh. She died in torment, sir, as I was made to watch. When next called upon to fire, sir, I fired, and I fired truly. After that, they kept my elder girl alive to encourage me ... until she died of the cholera, and I was spared, though I wished every moment to die too.'

Ogilvie found he was trembling as this terrible story was told. In a hushed voice he asked, 'And after that?'

Sergeant Makepeace said, 'I have continued to fire when ordered, sir, though hoping always to be able to rejoin my comrades. That is why I always wear my uniform, sir. I hoped always to be seen, and rescued, though I knew what must happen when I rejoined my battery. I fooled the natives, sir. They are simple enough. I gave them to understand, sir, that I was lost without my tunic ... that I must always wear it in action. But until now, no one has noticed my presence, either in Afghanistan or in India. I have only recently been brought back into India,' he added.

Harshly Barr asked, 'What made you go on laying the guns, after the last of your family was dead?'

'The lash, Colour-Sergeant. My strength dwindled, and I became sick, and I could no longer take the flogging. On many occasions I have received one hundred lashes, sometimes two hundred or more. It is more than an ageing man can take. So, you see, gentlemen, I fired when ordered.'

'Why should we believe any of what you said about your family?' Barr demanded. 'Why should we believe you're any more than a common deserter and a traitor?'

With dignity Sergeant Makepeace said, 'I cannot make you believe me, and I do not seek to be excused for the wrong I have done. I am ready to take my punishment and it matters little whether or not you believe me so far as that is concerned. But I assure you, I speak the truth.'

'Let's see your back,' Barr said arrogantly.

Ogilvie tried to intervene but Makepeace would have none of that. He said, 'Sir, the Colour-Sergeant is right to insist. Even I offer no defence for my actions.' He lifted his arms; they were thin and withered. Barr snatched the tunic off. They looked down on the bared back. The flesh was brown, but corrugated with deep whitened furrows from the base of the neck to the buttocks, furrows that went round his sides to meet across the belly. It was a horrifying sight.

Ogilvie said, 'Put your tunic on, Sergeant.' Makepeace did so. As he gave the old man a hand Ogilvie asked, 'What's the situation outside?'

'This fissure is under constant watch, sir. There are many men, with many rifles. You

141

cannot usefully engage them—they number upwards of three hundred. There are also enough heavy guns, but they will not be used. That is to say, if they are, they will blow up in the ruffians' faces!' Makepeace chuckled. 'That, I have this day arranged, sir. You see, sir, by this time they trust me, and I have been allowed a free hand inside the fort. I have never been allowed beyond the gates, except when ordered to lay the battery against you the other day, but inside I have not been watched. And the tribesmen know nothing of how to handle guns, sir, nor of how they should be maintained. They have not noticed my modifications!'

Barr said sourly, 'So you've been guilty twice of betrayal.'

'Only once, Colour-Sergeant, only once! Of my own country—to my great sorrow. Of the natives who made me do this—no! I regard this as no betrayal of any trust, Colour-Sergeant—'

'Nor I,' Ogilvie said quickly. 'As to the first betrayal, well, we'll see. There's a lot to be done before that can be considered—'

'Mr. Ogilvie,' Barr said. 'This old man killed five of the men and wounded others, I'll have you remember. One has since died from wounds received. Why, he's nothing but a common murderer who should hang as such in the greatest disgrace outside Nowshera civil jail, and—'

'As you'd have liked in the case of Corporal Nichol, no doubt? You'll please say no more, Colour-Sarn't. I want no unofficial Courts Martial here, and I mean to see there won't be any!' Ogilvie swung round on the others. 'That goes for everyone. Until it's decided differently, Sergeant Makepeace takes rank according to his seniority at the time of his capture. You'll all do well to remember that he *was* captured, and didn't desert.'

'So *he* says!' Barr snapped.

'I believe him, Colour-Sarn't. It would be a pointless lie in any case—it can be checked the moment we reach Peshawar. Now—more water for Sergeant Makepeace, and make it fast. Kinnear!'

'Sir!' Private Kinnear snapped to attention. 'Coming, sir.' He went towards where the water bottles were piled under guard, came forward with one, and held it out to Makepeace. 'Drink your fill, Sergeant,' he said. 'I'm one that agrees wi' every word the officer said . . . and it doesna worry me two hoots what Colour-Sergeant Barr has to say about it!'

Barr moved towards Kinnear, his face dark with fury. Ogilvie said, 'Colour-Sarn't! Leave it. If you touch Kinnear I shall ask for your Court Martial. Kinnear, you'll guard your tongue or you'll be on a charge for insolence as soon as we return to cantonments.' He looked at Makepeace, noted that the old man's eyes were filled with tears of gratitude at Kinnear's

143

words. He turned away in embarrassment and took up his watch duty again—after noting something else: Makepeace had taken only one small sip at the precious water.

Soon the old man's earlier words were borne out. When a second attempt was made to use artillery, the fresh guns blew up, as before, the moment they were fired, with devastating effect upon the attackers from the Black Fort. The old man said, 'You see, sir? I have destroyed the enemy artillery for you.'

His meaning was obvious and Ogilvie put a hand on his shoulder. 'It shall count in your favour, Sergeant,' he said. 'Meanwhile, is there anything more you can tell us about the fort?'

'Little enough that will help now, sir. The guns have gone, but the rifles are still there, and this place, this hole in the rock, will be well surrounded. They'll not want to let me get away, sir. But you'll understand that it was my duty to come, even though my presence may make things the worse for you and your men.'

'Don't worry about that,' Ogilvie said, glancing momentarily at Barr. 'Of course it was your duty to join us, Sergeant, and you've more than proved your worth already. You certainly haven't made things any worse!' He added, 'I understand the fort's in the hands of a man known as Masrullah Sahib, who has the reputation of being friendly towards us. How is that?'

Makepeace said, 'He is no longer in full

command of the fort, sir. He takes his orders now from a man called Shuja Khan, from Afghanistan, a young man, a *rat* of the line of Shah Shuja who once occupied the throne in Kabul. A rat of a Pathan who was personally responsible for many of my own more recent torments, sir, and who means, as I believe, to bring out the tribes against Her Majesty, all along the Frontier, as far as Chitral and beyond.'

Ogilvie nodded thoughtfully; Chitral, of course, had been in the air back in Peshawar. What Makepeace said linked with the situation as indicated by Andrew Black. Ogilvie questioned the sergeant further but Makepeace was unable to add more, except that he believed the rising of the tribes to be partly due to the actions of a sepoy regiment in the north, which had tortured some captives— the sepoys had been guilty of bayonetting the dying, also of heaping dry rubbish against the wounded and setting light to it. This was as far as Makepeace could go; his scanty knowledge had been gleaned from half-overheard, and in some cases only half-understood, snatches of conversation in the fort and in Kabul. Ogilvie turned his attention now to the problem, the worsening problem, of water and provisions. There were less men to feed than he had started out with, but their stocks would not last long beyond the date when the patrol had been expected to return to cantonments, unless

145

there was a tightening of the rationing. This, Ogilvie arranged with Barr. There were no further attacks from the fort and it became obvious that the tribesmen of Masrullah Sahib—or Shuja Khan—had finally decided to starve them out.

*   *   *

On the evening of the day Ogilvie's patrol should have marched in, an urgent despatch reached Peshawar with word that an attack had already been mounted by the tribes in the north upon Fort Gazai and that the garrison, with its women and children, was under strong pressure. A relieving force sent from nearby Chitral town, which was still garrisoned by British troops since the earlier trouble, had been cut to pieces and the commander in Chitral, himself under threat, could spare no more men. Lord Dornoch's face, when he returned after a summons to Division, was grey with anxiety. At once he called a conference of his officers, informing them that a strong force was to march north into Chitral province as soon as possible. The Royal Strathspeys were in fact ready in all respects, thanks to the Colonel's foresight. Dornoch gave them a summary of the situation so far as it was known. Standing before a large wall map of the North-West Frontier he said, 'You're all familiar enough with the nature of the terrain,

146

gentlemen, and the general lay-out—at least in theory. As for the actualities . . . it will be far from an easy march. As you know, Chitral state lies in the spurs of the Hindu Kush, and is inhabited by some of the most turbulent and savage hillmen along the whole Frontier. It is these hillmen that are rising and are currently besieging Fort Gazai, and it seems likely the fort may be over-run before we can reach it. History, gentlemen, is repeating itself—rather too closely upon its own heels than is comfortable. I refer to the march on Chitral in March last. On that occasion, you will recall, there were two columns of advance, one from here, and the other from Gilghit under Colonel Kelly. The same strategy will be employed this time. The Peshawar column, that is, the whole of our Division, will march at first light the day after tomorrow, while the column from Gilghit will march the following day. The Gilghit column will be under Brigadier-General Preston and will consist chiefly of Indian units—infantry, cavalry, artillery and supporting corps. Now, we have a little under two hundred miles to cover, the 2nd Brigade from Gilghit has a little over. We are ordered to rendezvous east of Fort Gazai as soon as possible—that's vague, I know. Last time, the march from Gilghit to the Chitral River took Colonel Kelly twenty-six days. The 1st Division from Nowshera took a few days longer than Kelly to reach the garrison in

Chitral city, after delays in action along the route. This time we shall both attempt to make the march faster. Twenty-six days is a long time to a garrison under siege. If we fail to arrive in less time, then it is feared we shall have to regard Fort Gazai as lost. The restoration of the *status quo* will then be a long and costly business. But even that is not the worst aspect, gentlemen. I have it very much in mind that there are women and children in Fort Gazai. If *they* are taken, we know what will happen. The children will be killed, and the women will be used by the tribesmen. I think I need say no more about that.' He paused scanning his officers' faces. 'Are there any questions, gentlemen?'

Black said, 'Yes, Colonel. What do you wish me to do about Ogilvie?'

'Ogilvie . . .' Dornoch ran a hand wearily along his chin. 'Overdue, isn't he, but only by a few hours.' He pulled out his watch. 'We'll give him until tomorrow morning, Andrew, then I'll review the position. Bring this to my notice again at 8 a.m., if you please. Oh, and while we're speaking of Ogilvie, Andrew—and the rest of you, gentlemen. I think you will all have met his cousin, Mr. Hector Ogilvie of the India Office.' Hector had arrived from Simla via Murree three days before, and all the officers had been more than a trifle wary of him; something of a blight had been cast over the Mess and its off-duty life, though in all

148

conscience the preparations put in hand by Lord Dornoch had left little time for anything but work. Dornoch went on abruptly, as though he didn't much care for what he had to say, 'Mr. Hector Ogilvie ... I have been personally informed to this effect by General Fettleworth ... Mr. Hector Ogilvie wishes to see as much of the Frontier as he is able before he returns to Whitehall. It has been decided that he shall accompany the march with the 114th.' He caught the adjutant's amazed eye. 'Yes, Andrew?'

'I call this monstrous!' Black said angrily. '*Monstrous*, Colonel! To be burdened upon the march—and then in action—with a—'

'Yes, yes, Andrew. I have to say I entirely agree, but my hands are tied. I have already pointed out the hazards and the inconvenience and I have been over-ruled. In view of Mr. Ogilvie's appointment—I think you will understand me—I thought it in the best interests of the regiment not to protest too far, or I would certainly have refused to take him, orders or no orders, in which case he would have been allocated to some other regiment. I want you all to bear in mind that he is Sir Iain Ogilvie's nephew, and to remember Sir Iain's own long service with the 114th Highlanders. That is all I have to say on the matter, gentlemen—except this.' Dornoch paused, frowning. 'While you must feel no constrictions upon your actions as a result of Mr. Ogilvie's presence, you will bear constantly in mind that he—er—that he—'

Major Hay saved his Colonel his embarrassment. 'We all understand very well, Colonel,' he said. 'The utmost care will be taken at all times.'

Dornoch smiled in grateful relief. 'Thank you, John,' he said.

*   *   *

Hector had in truth been far from pleased at the turn of events that seemed likely to project him into violent action; action was not in his nature. He was an observer, an administrator, a man of affairs most at home behind an expensive desk with a secretary to take care of the detail, the donkey work and the visitors. But the bland suggestion, albeit with tongue in cheek, had been put to him by his Uncle Iain in Murree, and conveyed to Major-General Francis Fettleworth in Peshawar. Fettleworth, though disliking Sir Iain heartily enough, was always willing to oblige any Army Commander under whom he happened to be serving, and, after half an hour spent in Mr. Hector Ogilvie's company, had become even more obliging. Mr. Ogilvie should most certainly see all that was going—and damn good luck to the clerkly little bugger! It was seldom that serving officers had the opportunity to watch a Civilian squirm under the harsh realities of forced

150

marches in adverse conditions—and such a one as this especially! Besides, Fettleworth was good at reading between the lines, and he knew Sir Iain pretty well. The Army Commander was anxious for his nephew to be given the best of all possible insights into the hard life of the Queen's military service.

He would be.

Hector sensed all this, and felt vindictive about it; but, short of appearing to be a coward, there was no way whatsoever of backing out. A faked-up illness would be seen through, and would rank with cowardice. It was thoroughly filthy luck that he should have come on to Peshawar at just the very time there was trouble in the air; but now that it had happened, it had to be put up with. His uncle was by no means incapable of dropping some adverse opinions into high Civilian ears, and Sir Iain, though merely a soldier, would be listened to with respect. But the following afternoon Hector fancied he smelt reprieve, at least to some extent. In the middle of the last-minute touches being put to the forthcoming march, the man who had been allocated to Hector as a servant came to his quarters and informed his temporary master that the adjutant would be much obliged if he would step towards his office.

'Very well,' Hector said ungraciously, and after delaying ten minutes, did as he had been bid. He found Andrew Black in an unpleasant mood.

'Ah—Mr. Ogilvie.' Black looked up at the clock on the opposite wall. 'Kind of you to come. Did your servant take all this time finding you, may I ask?'

'I imagine he did, yes,' Hector answered, adjusting his spectacles. 'He's just this moment come to my room.' In view of Black's expression, he had deemed the white lie, as he considered it, expedient. He preferred, when possible, not to fall out with people to their faces.

Black said, 'H'mph,' disbelievingly. 'Sit down, Mr. Ogilvie, if you please.' Hector sat, and Black continued. 'With regard to your accompanying the Division tomorrow. I regret to say, something else has cropped up. Or should I say, *may* crop up. You're aware, of course, that your cousin is away with a patrol towards Sikat, and has not yet returned.'

'Yes, indeed, Captain Black.'

'This means he is overdue.' Black tapped irritably on his blotter with a pencil. 'A confounded nuisance, at a time like this. It makes for a deal of complications—a deal! The Colonel has ordered that if no word is received of Lieutenant Ogilvie by dawn tomorrow, a half-company will detach from the column when the advance is past Abazai, and will proceed to search for the patrol. The Colonel has allotted me the responsibility of commanding this half-company.' Black's voice gave the appointment honour; in his heart, he was furious, sensing that Dornoch's action was a slight and that the Colonel preferred to have his company commanders with him on the march rather than detach one of *them*. To command a mere half-company was no part of an adjutant's duty. However, he went on, 'I am ordered to locate the patrol and, depending on the state they are in when found, either to bring them back to cantonments or lead them north to rejoin the column of advance towards Fort Gazai. Now, what I am coming to is this, Mr. Ogilvie: Lord Dornoch suggests you may prefer to come with me, rather than remain with the column. After all, your cousin . . . and you will see a very representative slice of the Frontier.' He stopped; he did not in the least want Hector Ogilvie with him. 'It is your choice entirely,' he added with a shrug.

Hector jumped at it. 'I would much like to accompany you, Captain Black. As you say— my cousin and—and all that. Yes. Thank you.'

'That's your decision, Mr. Ogilvie?'

'Oh yes, indeed it is—'

'Very well, then,' Black said, and added acidly, 'I shall look forward to the pleasure. And now, if you don't mind, I'm a very busy man just now.'

'Of course.' Hector got to his feet. As he made for the door Black's sharp voice reminded him that he must be up and ready to march at the crack of dawn.

By next morning Ogilvie's patrol had still not returned, but during the night a report had been received from Brigade concerning the observations of the Political Service, where information had filtered through from a source hitherto believed to be defunct, to the effect that an exchange of fire, and what appeared to be a siege, had been noted in a remote valley south-east of Sikat village. Lord Dornoch was at once roused from his bed; and to him it seemed too much of a coincidence to be neglected. Together with Andrew Black, he studied detailed maps of the area and brought a finger down on a valley running roughly parallel with that of the Panjkora River. 'That's where you'll find him,' he said with decision.

Black murmured, his head bent over the map, 'A bad business, Colonel, a very bad business. The boy—'

'Boy, nonsense. He's a grown man.'

'Yes, Colonel. Boy or man, he was under orders to avoid an engagement—'

'But not necessarily to run away if attacked. We can't make any judgments without the facts before us. So don't try to.' Dornoch tapped the map and looked keenly at his adjutant. 'The report is precise, so location shouldn't be hard—and I want that patrol brought in intact and without any accusations having been made. One thing more: your half-company will act as escort only. Ogilvie remains in command of the patrol. Is that clearly understood?

Black scowled. 'It is, Colonel.'

'Good. You'll inform Ogilvie accordingly, of course.'

'Yes, Colonel. When we detach from the column—'

'You won't do that now,' Dornoch cut in. 'You must leave at once, Andrew. Every moment counts now.' As Black lingered, he asked sharply, 'Well? Is there something else?'

'Yes, Colonel. Perhaps I should have asked you this earlier. Why are you sending me to escort Ogilvie back ... when you spoke only recently of possible spite on my part against him?'

For a moment Dornoch seemed taken aback; then he said, 'I'm sending you because you are an efficient, knowledgeable and thorough officer, Andrew. I know that if it is possible to reach Ogilvie's patrol and bring it back to the column, you will do so. You've never fallen down on a job yet and I don't ever expect you to. In my view you're the best choice this time and that's all that concerns me. I am trusting you not to allow personalities to interfere with action, and I don't believe you'll let me down. Do you understand?'

'Yes, Colonel.' Black turned away, mollified but only slightly. The Colonel was not giving him command of the patrol and he fancied he knew why: Dornoch didn't trust him far enough to be sure he would not haze young Ogilvie, whatever he might say.

Within the hour a half-company of the Royal Strathspeys was on its way, marching through the star-filled night, north and west for Sikat, with three pipers and three drummers, and Captain Andrew Black scowling with loss of sleep, and Mr. Hector Ogilvie only half awake on the horse that had alarmingly been provided for him on the Colonel's order. And back in cantonments soon after this, as the first streaks of dawn lit the distant hills beneath their snow mantles, the strident bugles, and the trumpets of the cavalry regiments, woke the Peshawar garrison from its slumbers, and the great force, drawn in from the whole area, began to assemble unit by unit on the regimental parade grounds, to march and link up into the column of advance outside the town. With the 114th Highlanders the column would include three entire infantry brigades of four battalions each, three regiments of cavalry, six batteries of Mountain Artillery, sappers, miners, and a vast number of pack animals and coolies to carry the rations and water that would be needed on the march—small rations they would be, and a minimum amount of water for each man per day. No wagons would be taken, for the terrain was totally impossible for any wheeled transport other than the elephant-drawn guns. To ensure swiftness of advance the column would travel as light as possible, without the usual heavy baggage train, and each officer was

156

allowed forty pounds weight of baggage only, and each other rank ten pounds; and there would be no tents taken.

The various units made contact as the sky lightened and, under a great cloud of dust, and amidst the shouts of the sergeants and the neighing of the horses, the rattle and clash of equipment and the rumble of the gun-limber wheels—all this overlaid at intervals along the column by the drums and fifes, and the pipes, and the brass until it returned to base—the Division began its march through almost unknown territory upon Fort Gazai and the impudent disturbers of the Pax Britannica; and there was not a man among them whose thoughts were not with the women and children in that distant beleaguered fort, or who would not willingly have torn out the guts of any native who molested them.

CHAPTER SIX

'Captain Black ... oh dear, oh dear. *Captain Black*!'

Black looked round. 'Yes, Mr. Ogilvie?'

There was an indistinct torrent of words. Black called, 'Catch up, if you please, Mr. Ogilvie! I cannot make out what you are saying at this distance.'

Hector sighed miserably, and urged his

horse ahead, suffering the most acute discomfort. His clothing was filthy, his white shirt and starched collar—no one had bothered to tell him what he should wear—was as limp as a rag and sticky and foul with sweat. It clung round his neck like a soft wet limpet; and his behind was quite raw, so were the insides of his thighs. Not expecting to have to ride horseback, he had not come prepared, and Black had ill-temperedly refused him the time to go back to his room and change; and, more-over, had angrily sent back the trunk he had packed for the journey. Reaching Black, Hector panted, 'Captain Black, how far is it now?'

Black's mouth opened, then shut again. Restraining himself icily he said, 'A long way, Mr. Ogilvie, a long way yet.'

'Yes, yes, but *how* long?'

'Oh, two days' march, I don't doubt.' Black stared hard at the man from Whitehall, looking down his nose from beneath the peak of his Wolseley helmet. He saw the way Hector was so gingerly seating himself in the saddle, as if the thing were biting, as in a sense no doubt it was. Black smiled inwardly.

*　　　*　　　*

'Did ye hear that, sir? Did ye hear that?'

The man's excitement was intense; he had been at his post at the fissure entry, and now

158

he turned, and ran up to Ogilvie. 'Sir—*it's the pipes!*'

'The pipes!' Ogilvie and Barr ran to the entry and listened. Sure enough, in the distance still, very thin but coming closer, they heard the wailing of the pipes and the beat of drums advancing along the valley from the south. 'It's the battalion,' Ogilvie said. 'It must be!' He felt a thrill of pride; this was how the defenders of besieged Lucknow must have felt, when they heard the pipes of Havelock coming to their relief.

'God be thanked for it, if it is,' Barr said. He was trembling with thankfulness, a smile spreading across his coarse red features. 'We've done it, after all! Those buggers out there—oh, they'll run the moment they see the bayonets, I'll be bound!'

'I wouldn't be too sure of that,' Ogilvie warned. 'Have the men ready, Colour-Sarn't, including Sergeant Makepeace. I'm going to make a sortie out into the open, when the battalion comes up—just to give them support.'

'Sir!' Barr turned about and began shouting out the orders. Men stood by their rifles, with bayonets fixed now, waiting for the word. Barr thrust a rifle into Sergeant Makepeace's willing hands. 'There y'are, Makepeace,' he said grudgingly. 'Be sure ye make good use of it—but remember, ye'll no' act the sergeant. Times have changed since you pissed off, my friend! An' mind this, too: *I'll be watchin' you.*'

Ogilvie, at the entry still, heard the injustice but said nothing. This was scarcely the time to raise any such issues. His heart swelled still as he heard the pipes come nearer, nearer ... they were sounding out loud and clear now, a stirring note over the beat of the drums, playing Pipe Major Ross's Farewell to Invermore, a tune the Pipe Major had composed shortly before they had entrained from the depot a year before. A while later, the music stopped; the relieving force was near enough now for Ogilvie to hear the jingle as bayonets were fixed, and, soon after, the working of bolts. He looked round. 'Stand by now,' he said. His revolver in his hand he edged forward, with Barr close beside him. The Colour-Sergeant's face was tight and eager, full of relish for the killing that was to come. There was a pause; nothing seemed to be happening, outside. Then Ogilvie heard a voice that he recognized as Andrew Black's, a voice calling an order, and a split-second later the rifles of the relief force crashed out.

Ogilvie waved his own men out, he and Barr running ahead; the remnants of the patrol came out raggedly but with spirit, along with Sergeant Makepeace. As they came clear of the scrubby growth, they stared down the valley into the surprised faces of Black and the fresh troops. There was no more firing; Ogilvie looked around, somewhat dazed by the totally unexpected lack of opposition. Black shouted, 'Well, Mr. Ogilvie? *Where's the enemy?*'

'I don't know,' Ogilvie called back. He felt remarkably foolish. 'Who were *you* firing at?'

'I caught a sight of what I took to be movement,' Black answered, 'although I, too, have failed to see any enemy since entering the valley.'

'It's a bloody ambush!' Barr said suddenly. He swung, and, almost without taking aim, fired at some bushes. There was a cry and a man fell out from cover, a man in dirty white robes and wearing a shaggy beard. A private ran over to him and covered him with his bayonet. Everywhere the soldiers stood to, swinging their rifles around cautiously, but there was no more firing. Barr said roughly, 'The buggers have all gone, Mr. Ogilvie. They left just the one, to report when we moved out. Man, you've been holding us in yon bloody hole on false pretences!' He began to laugh, and went on laughing till tears streamed down his face.

Ogilvie turned on his heel and walked towards Black. His cheeks were scarlet. He said, 'I'm glad to see you—thanks for the relief, Andrew.'

'My dear James, I think you scarcely needed it. Come with me, if you please.' He added as he turned away, 'Incidentally, your cousin is with us.'

'My—' Ogilvie stared; he didn't know how

161

he had come to do so—except perhaps that Hector's clothing was now khaki-coloured from the dust—but he had quite failed to notice his cousin; and now he was furious that the fellow should be witness to his discomfiture—which undoubtedly Black was going to make the most of. He growled, 'The last person I expected to see.' He advanced on the figure on horse-back. 'How are you, Hector? Sore?'

'Oh, damn you,' Hector said childishly—and unexpectedly. Ogilvie grinned and turned back to the adjutant. 'Where do you want me to go with you?' he asked.

'To have words with that tribesman your Colour-Sergeant removed so neatly from the bushes, James. What he has to say may be interesting, don't you think?'

He turned about and strode off along the valley. Ogilvie followed, with Barr and some of the men. Reaching the native, who was groaning in pain—Barr had got him through the groin—Black asked for a rifle. Barr snapped an order and a man came forward and handed over his weapon to the adjutant. Black laid the point of the bayonet against the tribesman's wound, which was bleeding profusely; the features twisted in fresh pain as sharp steel met mangled flesh. Black said, 'Now you will talk, blast you! You'll tell me what's been going on and where your friends are at this moment.' He had spoken in English;

162

there was no response beyond a rolling of the eyeballs. Black shrugged, and tried a hill dialect. He struck lucky; the man answered him.

'What does he say?' Ogilvie asked.

'He says he won't talk,' Black said, 'but I'm going to prove him wrong.' With a jerk of his wrist he drove the bayonet home a little way, and then gave the blade a twist. The man roared out in agony and threshed his body like a landed fish. Ogilvie's hands clenched at his sides. This was going too far.

'Steady, Andrew,' he murmured.

'Why so—Mr. Ogilvie?' Clearly, they were back to parade ground formality again.

'The man's in pain—sir.'

'Pain? Nonsense. He's a native, Mr. Ogilvie, a damn dirty native!' Again Black twisted the bayonet; even Barr looked a trifle white, and Hector, who had moved up on his horse by now, looked as though he was about to be sick; but the torture worked. The man began talking before Black could twist the blade again, and as he talked, Black nodded away to himself. When the man had finished Black said, 'Mr. Ogilvie, he tells me the tribesmen have returned to Sikat, all of them. They were withdrawn, leaving him alone, to join the general rising along the frontier. They were withdrawn *two days since*. How have you spent the last two days, Mr. Ogilvie?' His voice had risen now; Hector—all the men—were

163

listening. 'Playing dice?'

Ogilvie didn't answer; Black turned to Barr. 'What were you laughing at just now, Colour-Sarn't?'

Barr, to do him credit, looked confused. He said, 'Just a passing fancy, sir, nothing more.'

'Indeed?' Black's eyebrows went up. 'I think I know what you were laughing at, Colour-Sergeant, and I cannot blame you for it, in all conscience!' His eyes lit then on Sergeant Makepeace. 'Good God, Mr. Ogilvie. In the name of all that's wonderful, who's this?'

Makepeace himself stepped forward. Saluting he said, 'Sergeant Makepeace, Royal Regiment of Artillery, sir. If I may make so bold, sir . . . young Mr. Ogilvie's a fine officer and gentleman, and he kept our spirits up nobly, indeed he did—'

'I didn't ask for your opinion!' Black snapped rudely. 'In future, hold your tongue, or you'll be on a charge for insolence! No officer needs *your* defence.' He looked closer. 'Did you say . . . the Royal Regiment of Artillery?'

'I did, sir.'

'I fail to understand . . . where from, and how, in heaven's name, were *you* drafted, Sergeant? Do you belong to—to some kind of reserve, or what?'

Ogilvie said quickly, 'I can explain, sir.'

'Good. Then pray do so, Mr. Ogilvie.'

Ogilvie told Black the outline of the story.

164

Black listened intently but made no comment. When Ogilvie had finished he nodded and asked, 'How fit are your men, Mr. Ogilvie?'

'Fit enough. They've been on short rations, but no one's gone without. I have one man wounded—the other wounded have died, and must be buried before we move out. The wound is in the arm, and is not espccially serious.'

'Then I can take it you are able to join the column of advance?'

'The column of advance, sir?'

'Yes, Mr. Ogilvie. I have orders to rejoin the Division in its march upon Fort Gazai.'

'Fort Gazai—near Chitral? So it's begun, has it?'

'Yes, it has begun, but please answer my question. Are you all fit to fight? I wish your opinion.'

'Yes, we're fit. But aren't we going to mount an attack on the Black Fort? They—'

'No, we are not, Mr. Ogilvie. I have my orders as already stated, and they will be adhered to. Rest assured the Black Fort will fall once the general rising is crushed and broken—as it will be. Now—bury your dead, Mr. Ogilvie, if you please, and then we shall march. We shall be hard put to it to overtake the regiment now, so you will work fast. Every man will be needed at Fort Gazai. There are women and children besieged by the damn niggers.' He looked coldly and disdainfully at

165

Sergeant Makepeace, whose old eyes were shining at the thought of being on the march with British soldiers once again. This was his chance to take his revenge for his many years of slavery and torture and brief. But Black said, 'The traitor will march in handcuffs.'

*   *   *

By the time the dead had been buried in shallow, rock-marked graves after a brief reading of the burial service by Captain Black, the wounded tribesman had also died. His body was on Black's order left for the vultures to pick and the patrol, refreshed now with water from the bottles of Black's half-company, formed up for the march. Black had duly if grudgingly informed Ogilvie of Lord Dornoch's order that he, Ogilvie, should retain command of the patrol with Black's detachment forming the escort only; but had insisted that he, Black, was to give the orders concerning Sergeant Makepeace, who could not be considered any part of the actual patrol. Ogilvie grieved that he had lost control of Makepeace's destinies. The old fellow had been shockingly treated, in his opinion—and, he knew, in the opinion of all the others except Barr. There was nothing he could do about it, however; he had raised the issue with Black as Colour-Sergeant Barr had clapped the steel handcuffs on, but had been told to hold his tongue. The man, Black said, was a self-confessed traitor. And twenty-eight years' absence from his regiment could not be so easily written off the books, either; it was normal for a recovered deserter to travel back to his unit in handcuffs—even in chains.

'But he's not a deserter,' Ogilvie pointed out. 'He was captured in a raid.'

'So he says. In any case, I will not have such hair-splitting. Makepeace fired on British troops and that's an end of it, d'you hear?'

So the detachment moved off, heading away from the vicinity of Sikat village, across the hills to the east of the valley by way of a pass further up, expecting to cut across the main British column in the region of the Malakand Pass above Dargai. Makepeace hobbled along in the rear between an escort of two privates and a lance-corporal, who gave him a helping hand whenever Barr and Black were not nearby; in front rode Black, and behind him both the Ogilvies upon a single horse. Ogilvie the soldier sat ahead of Ogilvie the civilian and both hated their mode of progress. Hector groaned continually as the animal jogged him, and kept cannoning into his cousin's back. Ogilvie told him, sharply, to keep still.

'I can't possibly,' Hector whined. 'It's the horse, not me.'

'A bad rider always blames his mount.'

'Don't *nag*.'

'Why the devil did you come in the first

place?'

'Because Uncle Iain suggested it!' Hector snapped.

Unseen by his cousin, Ogilvie gave a wide, wide smile; the humour of this situation appealed, and made up for the less happy aspects of the day. He could so well imagine the glee that would have been on his father's face when he had thought this trip up for cousin Hector.

CHAPTER SEVEN

By this time the Division from Peshawar had reached the vicinity of Abazai and was on the fringe of virtually unknown tribal territory— territory, indeed, that had remained completely unknown and unexplored until the recent march on Chitral by the 1st Division under General Sir Robert Low. It was now known that the Mora, Shahkot and Malakand Passes gave access to the Swat valley, through which the regiments must pass to reach Chitral and Fort Gazai. These passes were high and treacherous, with no more than rough tracks running through. General Fettleworth knew that Sir Robert Low had had comparatively little difficulty in moving his troops through the Malakand Pass, however, and thus decided to follow in his more illustrious predecessor's footsteps. But, unlike Sir Robert, who had made feints against the Mora and Shahkot Passes whilst concentrating his main thrust on the Malakand, General Fettleworth decided to throw his total weight against the one pass which he intended to force. Proceeding beyond Abazai with a fair degree of ease and speed considering the rough nature of the country, the Division headed on for the entry to the Malakand Pass. There was no opposition, although the sweat-soaked scouts expected to find the enemy rifles lurking behind every bend of the treacherous track, behind every boulder that they passed along the way as they marched and climbed and cursed, feeling their feet swell painfully in their boots.

They were now well ahead of Ogilvie's reinforced patrol.

*   *   *

Black, as usual, nagged continually. It was not in his nature to overlook the smallest detail, even under the exigencies of a forced march through hostile and difficult country, and he was constantly urging on Ogilvie the importance of smartening up the men. Ogilvie's reasoned protests only worsened Black's temper, and in the men's own interests Ogilvie was forced to concede to the adjutant and chivvy them along. The men understood, though they grumbled enough as they set one

169

weary, aching foot down after another; Black was detested throughout the regiment for his unfair treatment of the rank and file, his unnecessary harrying of the subalterns, and his murderous ill-will the morning after a drinking bout—not an uncommon occurrence under normal conditions.

Ogilvie was convinced that, in point of fact, he was drinking now. During the halts when the men fell out for a rest Black would call for his servant, ferret in the pack which the man brought, bring out something wrapped in a towel and retire behind a rock. Unlike Barr, who was still smelling from time to time of his illegally-bottled rum, the adjutant's breath held no evidence of drink, but his general demeanour did. His face was flushed and heavy and the good temper that followed upon each wayside halt evaporated quickly as the day's ferocious heat drew out the liquor in sweat and left the uncomfortable dregs behind to plague the man.

As they marched or rode along, with the pipes and drums mostly silent now, with scouts posted ahead as they went on through the narrow, sun-dried defiles towards Abazai, Ogilvie had time to talk to his cousin. Hector was in a thoroughly depressed and nervy mood; he saw danger in every small sound, and danger again in the very silence of the halts. Ogilvie did his best to take his cousin's mind off his bleak surroundings; and because he was intensely concerned about the answer, he probed for some information as to how things had been in Simla in regard to Mary Archdale. He asked as casually as he could, 'Do you know if mother's met Mrs. Archdale?'

'I believe so,' Hector answered. 'I—er—I understand she went round to the Archdales' bungalow soon after your recall came through.'

'And?'

Hector shrugged behind Ogilvie's back. 'If you want to know what she thought of the lady, you must ask someone else, for *I* don't know.'

Ogilvie ran a finger around the inside of his sweat-damp collar. 'No ideas on the subject at all?'

'You know as well as I do, Aunt Fiona has never worn her heart on her sleeve. Besides, dear boy, if I may remind you, you told me quite plainly it was no business of mine.'

'True, but—'

'So it doesn't become you to question me now.' Hector sounded smug. A moment later, however, he clutched tightly at his cousin and said in a high, scared voice, 'What's that—ahead at the side of the track?'

Ogilvie looked. 'A body.' He had noticed the busy vultures some way back, rising hastily because the pipes and drums, starting up just then, had frightened them away from their meal. The corpse, a native one, was now half eaten.

Hector said, 'Oh, my God.'

171

'You'll get used to that.' They rode by. What was left of the corpse was filled with a seething mass of wriggling white maggots, smooth and cheesy-looking, and there was a foul stench; Hector gave a sound of retching.

'Hold it,' Ogilvie said, thinking of his uniform.

Hector was shaking. He said with loathing in his voice, 'I suppose they'd do that to us as well.'

'Who?'

'The vultures.'

'I suppose they would,' Ogilvie said irritably. 'I doubt if they realize the essential difference between the local banditry and the rulers of British India. They might baulk at a Civilian, though. I wouldn't worry too much, Hector. You can always send them a Note, or whatever it is you do in Whitehall.'

'Don't be such an ass,' Hector snapped back. Ogilvie's thoughts returned to Mary; he realized now that he had hardly had her in his mind at all since the day he and his patrol had marched away from Peshawar. He didn't know what this might mean, whether it indicated that deep down he was looking upon her as no more than a bird of passage, or whether it meant simply that he had his priorities in order. He had to be a soldier first—that had always been instilled into him, and he didn't dispute what he knew to be a fact. In a sense he had been a Royal Strathspey from birth and even now, even in this terrible dry dust that seemed to creep insidiously into every part of his body, he could still feel the surge of pride run through his veins as the pipes and drums beat along the track, could still feel the deep emotions aroused by race and regiment. And in a situation such as they had been in, such indeed as they were still in and would continue to be in until stability had been restored, temporarily at any rate, along the Frontier, he had no business to allow his mind to be distracted from his military responsibilities. But, now that Hector had turned up, having been so recently in Simla and thus within Mary's ambit, he found his mind once again divided. His thoughts roamed towards the husband Mary didn't love, that elderly major who was riding somewhere in the main column of the grand advance ahead, fussing around Major-General Francis Fettleworth and very probably getting his field lavatory all tangled up with the commissariat . . .

That night, when they halted for a few brief hours' sleep, well guarded on the perimeter of the makeshift bivouacs by watchful sentries, Ogilvie was taking his turn as officer of the guard when he was approached by Andrew Black, whom he heard come stumbling out from the eerie shadows cast by the high peaks against the moon.

'A word in your ear, Mr. Ogilvie,' the adjutant said with much formality.

'As you wish, sir.' Ogilvie sniffed; this time Black's breath did smell—of whisky, and very strong. The man's movements were a trifle stiff too, though his speech seemed unaffected, and he was wearing khaki drill though the night air and a chill wind had been enough to make Ogilvie put on a blue patrol jacket; the whisky was keeping Andrew Black warm, perhaps. 'What can I do for you?'

'That damn deserter—Makepeace. Sergeant he calls himself, you say. Well, I've been thinking. I've reached certain conclusions.'

'Oh?'

'You may well say "oh", Mr. Ogilvie. You're responsible for his presence.'

'On the contrary. Sergeant Makepeace is responsible for his own presence.' Ogilvie shivered slightly in that cold wind coming down from the distant peaks of the Hindu Kush. 'His action in joining us—in rejoining the service—was entirely voluntary. And I would point out, with respect, sir, that he is no deserter.'

'So you've said before.' Black's voice was heavy with anger now. 'I'm tired of hearing you try to vindicate him. In my opinion it's a thoroughly bad example to the men.'

'Keeping him in handcuffs is, yes.'

'Don't be impertinent, Mr. Ogilvie. You know well that I was referring to no such thing. My action in regard to the handcuffing was and is perfectly proper and I do not intend to have

174

it called into question, or even commented upon, by a subaltern—which you still are, Mr. Ogilvie, I'll have you remember!' Black breathed heavily and more whisky came across to Ogilvie. 'I say that man's a damn disgrace and—'

'Would you,' Ogilvie interrupted coolly, 'see your wife and children tortured, and yourself flogged repeatedly, and still be of the same opinion?'

'Whatever the provocation, there is no excuse for firing upon your own comrades in arms, Mr. Ogilvie. I am highly astonished that any officer should hold any different view from that. One who does, Mr. Ogilvie, is not worthy to hold the Queen's Commission—or to be a Royal Strathspey. I trust you will keep that well in mind.'

Ogilvie stood silent; Black, of course, was only too right within the letter and the spirit of Queen's Regulations and the Army Act. It couldn't be denied—except on the grounds of humanity. Yet even on those grounds, once the principle itself was breached, there was no knowing how far things might drift. The logical conclusions might well be that whole regiments would refuse their orders, that men might stream from the enemy. The discipline *had* to be iron hard, the men *had* to be treated as mere receptacles for orders, machines that fought and died on an officer's or N.C.O.'s word of command. It was unpleasant but it was

175

true. In current conditions you couldn't have an army under any other terms. It came down to the well-established fact that the men must be a damn sight more scared of their own colonel than of the enemy, for then there would be no question of disobedience or of cowardice in action. And captives like old Makepeace must stand and watch the horrible things that were done to their defenceless families, and turn the other cheek to their own tortures, and watch the British regiments march by. They must never aid the enemy. When Sergeant Makepeace returned in handcuffs to Peshawar, he would very likely receive the death penalty. After all, Corporal Nichol's crime had been far less heinous in a sense. The hanging came back vividly to Ogilvie and he felt shivers run up and down his spine, this time not from the wind off the distant northern snow.

Meanwhile Black was speaking. '. . . so the man must be made an example of, Mr. Ogilvie. It is not good for the men to see him being treated almost as one of themselves, given the same food, the same water, wearing a sergeant's stripes—'

'You can't remove them,' Ogilvie said. 'Only the Colonel can do that, Captain Black, and then only—'

'On the contrary, on detached service *I* am in the room of the Colonel, Mr. Ogilvie. I can do precisely as I wish. Precisely—d'you hear—

as I wish!' He rasped a hand across his moustache, as if to brush away the fumes of drink. 'And now I shall tell you what I wish, Mr. Ogilvie.'

'Well?'

'As I have said . . . the man must be made an example of, and in public—before the men, who will be left in no uncertainty as to what happens to deserters.' Black took a deep breath. 'My decision is that before the march is resumed, Makepeace will be flogged. He will receive one hundred and fifty lashes, Mr. Ogilvie, and Colour-Sergeant Barr will administer them.'

Ogilvie, utterly amazed, laughed in the adjutant's face. 'You must be mad,' he snorted. 'Why, flogging's been abolished in the army, Andrew, you can't—'

'Kindly do not teach me the regulations, Mr. Ogilvie. Flogging may have been abolished; what has *not* been abolished, to my certain knowledge, is the absolute prerogative of an officer in command of troops to discipline his men in the way he thinks fit. I shall be well able to justify my action to the Colonel, Mr. Ogilvie, and to anybody else too, on the ground that in current circumstances, the circumstances of war, I considered it the right and proper thing to do in order to keep the men up to the mark. You will kindly see that the preparations for the flogging are made.'

Black started to turn away; Ogilvie reached

out, took his shoulder and swung him round. In the moonlight Black's face was devilish. 'What does this mean?' he asked sharply.

'It means I'm refusing the order, Andrew.' Ogilvie's voice was almost pleading. 'Don't you see? It's an illegal order and whatever you say you can't justify it. You'll wreck your career. I refuse to be implicated!'

'Except by way of mutiny, Mr. Ogilvie? You realize the penalties for mutiny, of course?'

'This is not mutiny, Andrew, it is sanity. If you think for a little longer, you'll see it that way too. If you have that flogging carried out, you'll be cashiered.' His voice hardened now, passionately. 'Not that that would bother me in the very least. What does worry me is Makepeace. He is not going to be flogged. Why, damn it to hell, man, if you stop to think you'll realize there isn't even a cat-o'-nine-tails outside a museum to carry it out with!'

Black seemed to be on the verge of a fit; his breath was coming in jerks and he was shaking all over. The moon's light showed the deep, bitter lines cutting into his bleak face. Thickly he said, 'Mr. Ogilvie. You will consider yourself under arrest.'

Ogilvie shook his head. 'Oh no, I won't,' he said. 'The boot's only too likely to fit the other foot far better! There will be no flogging as far as I'm concerned. If you persist in your attitude I shall order your own Colour-Sarn't to place *you* in arrest, and I shall take over the

178

command of the detachment on the grounds that in my opinion you are drunk—drunk on active service—embittered by sheer temper, and in no fit state mentally to command even your own servant. And you know as well as I do that with the exception possibly of Colour-Sarn't Barr, I shall have every man on my side.'

'You—you—' The adjutant struggled, gasping, for words. Ogilvie said, quietly now, 'If I were you I wouldn't say any more, Andrew. Don't make it any worse. You know I'm right, and would be acting within my rights. I mean every word I've said. But if you go to sleep now and forget all this—well, I'll forget it too. Nothing will be said in Peshawar. It's your choice, Andrew.'

Black stood for a moment, his arms waving stupidly; then, without another word, he turned and went off. When the adjutant had gone, Ogilvie turned away also and some dozen paces in rear found MacInnes, Colour-Sergeant of Black's half-company. Abruptly he asked, 'Did you hear all that?'

'Aye, sir, every word. I couldna help it, first off. Then I remained, in case you wanted a witness later. It's always advisable to have that, sir.'

'Thank you, Colour-Sarn't. But now I'll be obliged if you'll forget it.'

'I'll do that, sir. And see to it as well that the men do, any that happened to hear.'

'Thank you again.' Ogilvie hesitated. 'I'd

179

appreciate it if you'd tell me ... whether you think I was right, or not?'

He saw the gleam of MacInnes's teeth in the moonlight. The N.C.O. said, 'Dead *right*, sir, without any doubt at all.'

Ogilvie nodded and continued on his rounds of the perimeter; after three hours, the sergeant of the guard and the sentries were relieved; no relief came for Ogilvie. Black was sleeping it off, or was simply in a savage mood. When the march was resumed, Ogilvie had had no sleep at all. Black kept well clear of him; but there was no more talk of a flogging.

There was, however, an aftermath that greatly saddened Ogilvie. At the first brief halt that day, he walked along the line of men, having a word here and there, keeping their spirits up as they penetrated farther into the unknown tribal lands north of Abazai; and as he reached the end Sergeant Makepeace, still handcuffed, tried to scramble to his feet, assisted by his escort.

Ogilvie said, 'Sit down, Sergeant. This is a rest period.'

'Yes, sir. Permission to speak, sir?'

'Of course. And there's no need to stand up for it,' Ogilvie said, smiling down at the old warrior. 'Look, I'll sit beside you.' He squatted on the dust of the track, and signalled the escort to withdraw. He saw tears once again in Makepeace's watery eyes. Encouragingly he asked, 'What is it, Sarn't?'

'You're very kind, sir. A real gentleman, the finest I ever met, sir. They tell me your father is Lieutenant-General Sir Iain Ogilvie, sir. I served under him when he was a young Staff Captain attached to the 1st Infantry Brigade, outside Kandahar. A true gentleman, sir, and admired by all the men. A gentleman with a temper, sir, but always fair and just. It's in the blood, I dare say. But it is not of your father I wish to speak, sir. It is of myself, and you.'

'Me, Sarn't?'

'Yes, sir. You see, sir, I was told, I shall not say by whom, of what took place last night. I thank you, sir, from the bottom of my heart. But I do not wish you to suffer on my account sir. I am an old man and have few years left to me, and besides, my family is long since gone. I have no wish to live on, sir, without them. Now you, sir, are a young officer with his full career before him. You must not incur the displeasure of your senior officers, sir. This can be fatal, as you must see.'

'You mustn't worry, Sarn't, I can look after myself! I'm damned if I'm going to stand by and see injustice done.'

'It does you great credit, sir. But foolhardiness does not. I ask you to have a care for the future.' He paused moving his body uncomfortably on the hard, barren ground. 'I ask something else of you, sir, a favour.'

'Well?'

'All I have left, sir, is the hope of undoing

181

some part of what I have done.'

'You mean—'

'I mean, sir, that I wish to fight the enemy when we reach Fort Gazai. I have scores to settle, sir, above all with the young rat Shuja Khan of whom I have already spoken. And I can still lay a gun, sir. I am still an artilleryman, and I guarantee I have not lost my skill. But I cannot fight with my hands held as they are now, sir.'

'I'll do what I can for you, Sarn't.'

'God bless you, sir. There's one thing I must add, since I do not wish to deceive you. Once the handcuffs are off my wrists . . . Sir, I shall fight before Fort Gazai and fight as well as may be for the women and children, but I shall not wish to return to Peshawar. If God is kind, He will allow me to kill many of the enemy, and then He will allow the enemy to kill me. If He is not so kind . . .' He shrugged his thin shoulders, on which his tunic hung like a rag. 'I have no doubt you understand me, sir.'

Gently Ogilvie said, 'I think I do, Sarn't.' There was a lump in his throat as he pressed the old soldier's arm and got to his feet, and marched away up the line towards Black and his cousin.

*   *   *

'Where's Archdale?' General Fettleworth demanded. He was standing in his stirrups, a thick, portly figure looking out through field-glasses over the entry to the Malakand Pass, staring at that hostile place with worry nagging at his mind and that nervous, horse-like grin baring his teeth. All was oddly—*most* oddly—peaceful, yet the pass looked the most appalling place for any body of men to force—if force it they had to, which most assuredly they would, for the peaceful state could not possibly last. When General Low had gone through, the trouble had been chiefly in Chitral city itself; not right along the Frontier. Expecting trouble, Fettleworth was worried chiefly because it had not so far manifested itself.

An *aide-de-camp* answered his question: 'I haven't seen Major Archdale, sir.'

'Use your eyes, then, and go and get him.'

'Yes, sir.' The A.D.C. turned his horse and rode off. Ten minutes later he returned with Major Archdale. Fettleworth stared with his protuberant blue eyes and said, 'Ah, Archdale. I'm bothered.'

'Really, sir?'

'Yes. Can't for the life of me understand why we've had no damn opposition so far. Not *like* the tribes, you know. I'm told you have some knowledge of this district. What d'you think—hey?'

Archdale considered the point, pulling at his thick moustache. After a moment he suggested, 'They may be heading us into a trap, sir.'

'Ha—that's what I think, damn it! Crafty so-and-so's, y'know, Major—crafty so-and-so's. Artful as a cartload of monkeys.' Up went the glasses again. 'Can't *see* anything, though.'

Archdale coughed. 'They would keep concealed, sir.'

'Yes.' The General blew through his moustache. 'Don't like fighting in this sort of country. No good for forming square, that's the long and short of it, Archdale. Can't have a square up a damn hill! Not a steep one, I mean. If only there was a plain, I'd bring the enemy to battle—Damned if I wouldn't!'

'The Swat valley has flat ground, sir.'

'Ah, so had Waterloo,' Major-General Fettleworth said sagely. 'But like Waterloo, Swat is inaccessible from here! That's to say, it's on the *other side* of the pass. I don't mean to say we won't *reach* it.' Baulked of his pitched battle for the time being, Fettleworth frowned and puffed out his cheeks. 'D'you know, Archdale, my dear fellow—there are people who say the British square has had its day?'

'Really, sir?' Archdale gnawed anxiously at his upper lip; of course he knew. He fully agreed, privately, but had never dared to say so to Major-General Fettleworth. In Fettleworth's view the British square was sacrosanct, was still even in the mid-nineties the basis of all his military thinking, strategy and tactics. In this he was not entirely alone, as it happened. The square had proved itself time and time again throughout its long and honourable history as the British Empire's most publicised secret weapon. Archdale said diplomatically, 'One wonders what the devil they'd propose to put in its place . . .'

'Artillery, shouldn't wonder,' Fettleworth grumbled. He walked his horse around in a circle, followed punctiliously by his Staff Officers until the latter realised their lord and master was not going anywhere in particular. 'Well, well!' Fettleworth cried. 'This will never do. We must get on, gentlemen, on to Fort Gazai.' He took a deep breath. 'We must remember the women and helpless children threatened by the heathen. We must remember them—and Her Majesty.'

He nodded at his Chief of Staff, who nodded down the line of command until the last nod reached the A.D.C. The A.D.C. sent his right hand swinging against his helmet in a salute, wheeled his horse and called for a bugler; and within the next few minutes the Division was once again on the move, its bands playing stirring tunes, its colours and standards and guidons flying bravely and its poor despised guns trundling over the horrible ground behind the elephant-drawn limbers. It was an inspiring sight, a great colossus moving for Armageddon, a monstrous sprawl of arms geared to the whim of Major-General Francis

Fettleworth, marching into the jaws of hell to form square on the fertile plains of Swat, with Major Archdale's field lavatory, the mobile commode that had been so offensive to Sir Iain Ogilvie, trundling incongruously on a gun-limber behind a glittering and purely fortuitous escort of the Bengal Lancers.

*   *   *

'I only hope to very God,' Lord Dornoch said fretfully, 'that he does know what the devil he's doing! That's all.' Dornoch had temporarily handed his horse over to a groom and it was being led by the bridle while the Colonel and Major Hay picked their way, stumbling over the thickly-strewn boulders, half sliding down the hillside into the deep canyon that lay to the left of the track taken by the column of advance. The 114th had been ordered to the head of the Division to act as vanguard and to provide the advanced scouting parties. Lord Dornoch's uniform was torn and dirty and he was covered, as they all were, by thickly clinging dust that body-sweat had turned rapidly into a sticky film of yellow mud that soiled tunics and accoutrements. They were tired and footsore and hungry—their rations were meagre and unappetising, and were very rigidly measured out by the quartermasters as they were brought up on the backs of the native bearers from the supply train for

186

distribution. They had had to bring all the basic essentials with them; here in this desolate, sun-dried land under brazen skies, there was little hope of being able to live off the country, though the wild berries, scavenged on the march by ravenous men, brought a small bonus to the daily issue. The thirst was far worse than the hunger, and the water-containers were guarded every minute of the days and nights. Behind Lord Dornoch came the main body of the regiment, followed in a long straggled line by the remainder of the troops, interspersed at intervals by the ponies and mules and camels labouring with the commissariat and ammunition, all the impedimenta of even a lightly-provisioned column on the march. The entry to the pass seemed alive with those pack animals and their native tenders, stumbling, in constant danger of slithering over sheer drops into seemingly bottomless gorges, bleating, breaking legs and having to be shot ... the regimental veterineraries were having a field day. So were the farrier-sergeants, and the quartermasters who had to supervise the transfer of valuable stores to other, already overburdened, animals. The air was filled with hoarse shouts, orders, curses, argument. 'For want of a nail ...' Dornoch quoted, shading his eyes to stare back along the moving line of khaki enlivened by the kilts of the Highlandmen, and then ahead again along the pass. 'I don't like this,' he remarked to Hay. 'For one thing, we're far too spread out, in my opinion. The tail of the column isn't even in sight yet. That's no way to go through a hostile pass, John. God help us all, if the enemy decide to mount a full-scale attack now!' He added, flinging sweat from his forehead with the back of his hand, 'I could have wished Black and Ogilvie to have rejoined before we reached the Malakand. If they miss us, and try to come through on their own . . .' He left the sentence unfinished.

'I'd not worry, Colonel. I doubt if they would do that. My guess is, they'll have returned to cantonments, maybe on account of wounded men, or—'

'Possibly—assuming Black did find the patrol, and he may not have done, John. But I don't believe I really agree with you in any case.' He smiled momentarily, and put an affectionate hand on the shoulder of his second-in-command. John Hay was a quiet, shy man, undemonstrative, not perhaps a man of great personality, but there was no one Lord Dornoch would rather see take over the battalion when his own time was done. Hay was a good man, and kindly, and a methodical, efficient soldier. Dornoch said, 'You've too much faith in human nature, John. Too inclined to think everyone has your own view of life!'

Hay looked across at him, half smiling, as they stumbled past the strewn boulders. 'I

188

don't follow, Colonel.'

'You don't? Well—never mind, John, never mind.' Dornoch moved on. He was more worried than he had shown, as to the fate of the patrol. Things could have gone badly wrong with Ogilvie, and so they could with Black and his half-company. But Dornoch certainly didn't see Black missing any action by, for instance, taking his wounded back to Peshawar; ambitious officers did not miss action, and Black was a very ambitious officer indeed. There was almost no promotion without a war, and it was always better to have taken part in the action personally, when the names came up for captaincies and majorities and so on in the room of the men who had fallen. No one wished anybody else dead, of course, but it was said to be a subaltern's and a captain's prayer that God should send them a nice, bloody war! It was natural enough; in Dornoch's view the old men clung on too long to high command, long after they should have retired to make way for younger, more able, more resilient-minded, more physically fit men. The old fellows—why, look at Fettleworth, Dornoch thought. A fine case in point! Lion-hearted—dashingly brave as a young officer by all accounts—he had epitomised the old army, the days when war was more of a gentleman's game than it was becoming now. In his day Fettleworth had won many battles, for then his mind had been in

189

tune with his times. But now that mind was about as resilient as a piece of cast iron—and you could scarcely blame Fettleworth for that, it was part and parcel of his weighty years. And take the poor old Duke of Cambridge: seventy-six years of age—and only now had it been decided he should finally be prised loose from the Horse Guards and his office of Commander-in-Chief of the British Army in favour of Lord Wolseley.

Dornoch scrambled on ahead of the 114th. Looking round soon after, he caught the eye of the Regimental Sergeant Major, heaving his vast chest and tattered, muddy tunic out from behind a boulder. Dornoch wriggled his fingers in front of his lips, miming the fingering of the pipes. Cunningham understood. He called out to Pipe-Major Ross, who was coming into view behind him. Ross gave a thumbs-up to his fellow Warrant Officer and a few moments later the pipes blared out, stirring the hearts of the Highlanders. Arms swung more proudly, shoulders, bent by sheer weariness and hunger, straightened; the battalion came on as though swinging down through the Pass of Drumochter on a long route march for the depot at Invermore. They were an Army yet, Dornoch thought with swelling pride in his men. Nothing would ever beat the British soldier, in the long run.

It was little over an hour later that Captain MacKinlay, in the lead of his company, saw, just for a moment, the shape of a man on one of the peaks far ahead to the right of the column. Just for an instant, and then it was gone as though it had never been there at all. The great jags of rock seemed totally empty beneath that brassy sky, and there was no movement visible anywhere. MacKinlay put on such speed as he could, making towards the Colonel.

He saluted, breathlessly.

'Hullo there, Rob. How goes it?' Dornoch shaded his eyes with a hand.

'Colonel, I saw a man ahead, a tribesman.' MacKinlay reported in detail.

Dornoch asked, 'What d'you make of it, Rob?' Then, before the other could answer, he said, 'No, don't bother. It's clearly an ambush—if you're sure of what you saw.'

'I'm positive, Colonel.'

'Very well. In that case, I'm afraid they'll have got our scouts. There's been nothing from the heliograph. No shooting either.'

'*Thuggee?*' Hay suggested.

'I wouldn't be surprised. It lingers still.'

'Will you inform the General?'

Dornoch gave a short, hard laugh. 'I will—but first gentlemen, I shall halt the column. The General won't like it, but I'm afraid he'll have to lump it.' He held up a hand, shouted along the pass for the R.S.M. 'Bugles to sound the halt,' he called. 'I want a subaltern to act as runner back to Division.'

In the still air, the 114th's bugles sounded out loud and clear and melancholy, echoing stridently across the desolate hills of Malakand, beating back from the tall jags of rock.

The column came slowly to a halt.

In the centre, Fettleworth looked astonished, even shocked. He clicked his tongue in annoyance. 'What the devil!' he said. Breath hissed through his teeth as he dismounted from his horse to stretch his legs while he awaited some word of explanation. This came when a young subaltern of the Royal Strathspeys dashed up, red in the face and steaming like a kettle.

Identifying his General, seated by this time on a tartan rug and surrounded by the deferential and dismounted Staff, the subaltern saluted. 'Sir, I am—'

'Regiment, young man?'

The subaltern stared; his kilt, he fancied, should have spoken for him. He answered breathlessly, 'The Queen's Own 114th Highlanders, sir. I—'

'Name?'

'Urquhart, sir—'

'Very well, Mr. Urquhart, now that we are decently introduced, you may proceed. Tell me—what has happened in the van?'

'Sir, my Colonel—'

'Who is he, pray?'

'The Earl of Dornoch, sir—'

'Ah, yes, yes.' The argumentative man, Fettleworth remembered. 'Go on.'

'My Colonel has sighted a tribesman on a peak—'

'Indeed. Really, my dear young man, I find this not so very surprising. Surely not of enough importance to halt my Division without reference to me? This is tribal territory, is is not?'

'Yes, sir! But my Colonel believes the man may be a hostile sentry, a lookout, and that we may be heading into a trap, sir.'

'An ambush?'

'Yes, sir.'

'Very possibly.' An obstinate look spread across Fettleworth's face. 'Very possibly, indeed. However, I happen to be under orders to advance into Chitral, and really I cannot allow the whole Division to be brought to a standstill every time a man is seen upon some peak or other! We are here to fight, not to run away—and fight we shall, whenever necessary. What, pray, do the scouts report?'

'There has been no report from the scouts, sir.'

'Well! That speaks for itself.' Fettleworth pursed his lips and brought out a handkerchief with which he mopped at his cheeks. 'No, no. My compliments to your Colonel, Mr.—er. I am much obliged for his intelligence and have taken due note of this. But the Division will advance nonetheless. Archdale.'

'Sir!' Major Archdale stepped forward and seized hold of Fettleworth's right arm. Grunting, the Divisional Commander was hoisted to his feet. Leaning, until he got his full balance, for the ground was uneven, upon Major Archdale, he said, 'Thank you, thank you. Yes. Now then, Chief of Staff, kindly sound the Advance. Young man, go back to your Colonel quickly.'

Once again the bugles sounded, sending out their contradiction, once again the regiments got on the move as the calls were repeated down the line.

*   *   *

Some seven miles in rear of Major-General Fettleworth's physical presence, Ogilvie and Black caught the faint echoes of those bugle calls. 'British troops,' Black said. 'It will be the column, God willing!'

Ogilvie had given an involuntary sigh of sheer relief; glad to be about to rejoin his regiment, he would be doubly glad to be relieved of the current situation. Hector didn't seem quite so joyful; to him, joining up with Division meant only closer proximity to war, with the last chance gone of being able to make for safety in Peshawar. But he uttered no protests; he was too far gone in weariness by this time. Black snapped his orders to the escorting half-company; Ogilvie followed suit

194

with his patrol. The pace of the small force quickened. Men threw off their tiredness now; heartened by the prospect of rejoining their comrades and perhaps getting a little more food and water as a result, they found the soreness of their tortured feet vanishing miraculously, found they could march on beneath the cruel rays of the sun and no longer notice them so much. It was not long before they heard the distant sounds of a large troop concentration on the move, and soon after that they saw the native-led pack animals and the native troops, the rear of the column toiling up into the Malakand Pass far behind the vanguard, and then, later, as they began to overtake, they saw the khaki-drill tunics of the British regiments.

It was a happy moment. Even though home was on the move in hostile country, this was, indeed, home.

CHAPTER EIGHT

Brushing stinging insects from his face Major Hay reported, 'Colonel, Captain Black is rejoining with the patrol. Word has come through from the rear of the column, via Division.'

Dornoch was greatly relieved to hear this. 'That's good news, at all events. Any casualties?'

Hay said, 'I'm afraid so, Colonel. Eleven men killed or died of wounds, and one man wounded, though not seriously. Corporal Phillips is among the dead.' He added, sounding puzzled, 'We have actually been reinforced, I gather, by one man recovered from the enemy—a sergeant, a gunner sergeant named Makepeace.'

'Oh?' Dornoch raised his eyebrows. 'Sounds odd.'

'Yes, Colonel. I haven't the full details yet.'

'Very well, John. Send word down the column will you, to Black and Ogilvie—I want them to try to reach us as soon as they can move up to overtake. And inform the General accordingly, please, John.'

'Very good, Colonel.'

The second-in-command turned away. He despatched a runner to the rear and then rejoined his Colonel. The regiment proceeded towards a bend in the pass, closing the region where the man had been so distantly glimpsed on the peak. There was no attempt being made to conceal their approach; this would have been an impossibility in any case. So all along the column the bands were playing and the 114th were moving on behind their pipes and drums. There was as yet no sign of the enemy in all the surrounding wildness of the hills; as they approached the bend, and rounded it, the pass seemed clear ahead. Dornoch wondered

196

if the alarm had been a false one after all, though on the face of things it could be considered highly unlikely that the tribes would allow a strong force to pass through without hindrance. When that hindrance came, the defence of the long column was going to be extremely difficult, especially since there was not physically room for the whole force to fight and manoeuvre between the great jagged peaks that hemmed them in. Dornoch's mind dwelt on the new rifle that had recently been issued to the 114th for trial under action conditions—the Long Lee Enfield. Great things had been said of it, and it would very likely replace the Snider and the Martini-Henry as issued to the other regiments. Soon now it might prove its worth—or not. Meanwhile, Dornoch strongly mistrusted the silence, the brooding quiet and the total lack of activity ahead of the column pressing on into the pass. He was right to do so. The van of the advance had just spotted the bodies of the scouts, lying with bloated faces and thin cords drawn tightly about their necks, when that peculiar silence was broken, shatteringly. The hillsides ahead seemed to come alive within a second as hordes of armed tribesmen materialized with a terrifying suddenness from behind the boulders and the scrub and came yelling and screaming into the open. A murderous rifle fire swept down upon the British column, volley after volley coming from the ragged but well-disciplined hillmen.

There was a moment of utter confusion.

All around Dornoch men and animals fell screaming. The column swayed and broke. Neither Dornoch nor his officers could make themselves heard. Then a somewhat astonishing thing happened. A bugle sounded stridently and Dornoch saw Major-General Fettleworth charging down the line for the van, alone, scattering men to right and left, shouting something out, his face red, his sword lifted high, the blood-lust in his eyes.

He charged straight for the enemy, who were forming now in the middle of the pass ahead of the column. His sword flashing, he cut right into their centre. The hillmen reeled back from the General's horse, leaving their dead to be trampled into the ground. The effect upon the British infantry was immediate and almost magical. Training and discipline reasserted themselves and the men steadied, and then surged forward towards their Divisional Commander, giving a kind of baying cheer as they did so. But even as he went forward with his Highlanders, Dornoch knew in his heart that it was a useless endeavour, a purposeless and potentially dangerous display of courage on Fettleworth's part that was going to lead to immense and wasteful killing. A quick reconnaissance told him that the Staff were nowhere to be seen. He caught Hay's eye and beckoned him on, then he pressed through towards Fettleworth, who was still laying into the tribesmen, and had still not himself been so much as lightly wounded, by some miracle; but who was visibly tiring. Dornoch came up beside him, with Major Hay on the other flank. 'You must fight back to the column, sir!' Dornoch said. 'We're standing by you. We must not lose the Divisional Commander whatever happens!'

Fettleworth appeared not to hear. Shoulder to shoulder with him, Dornoch and Hay, sweating blood, fought off the tribesmen and, almost without his knowing it, Fettleworth was urged back towards the protection of the infantry as the men surged, milling and cheering, around his horse. There was still no apparent sign of the Staff. Dornoch yelled at his men. They were in hand now, the company officers and N.C.O.s taking charge. Dornoch ordered them to scramble behind what cover they could. They did so, and began to return the rifle fire of the hillmen. The leading machine-guns, the Maxims, were also in action now. From the rear the following regiments, with no orders to hold back, pressed on until lack of space alone forced them to a standstill, and the Division became, in effect, wedged in solid upon itself. It was a grotesque situation. Dornoch, widely separated from Fettleworth by now, was firing point-blank with his revolver into a press of advancing tribesmen who were still keeping up their rate of fire in face of the bullets from the head of the column. Whilst metaphorically with his back to the wall he saw the Staff trying to press through the ranks to reach Fettleworth, who seemed unperturbed at what was going on around him. The native casualties were in fact immense from the rifles and the Maxims; the hillmen were taking no cover now, were coming blindly on, but their numbers seemed not to grow any less. There was evidently an endless reserve somewhere behind the crests. Meanwhile the British casualties were mounting fast. Dornoch was in a furious temper as he saw his Highlanders fall around him; the enemy seemed in a fair way to destroying the whole Division, and if that should happen, then Fort Gazai with its women and children was lost. Fettleworth had refused to heed the advance warning and here was the result of his folly. Fettleworth's recent plunge down the line into the battle had been one of extreme personal bravery and Dornoch was the first to admit it, and, for what it was worth, admire it too. But it had not helped the action. It had committed the infantry too soon, when in fact Fettleworth should have stayed where he was in the centre, halted the column way back when MacKinlay had spotted the lookout man, and sent the guns ahead, followed up by the cavalry. Had that been done, there would have been a very different story told.

Dornoch made contact again with Hay.

Hoarsely he shouted in the Major's ear, 'John, I want you to take over. I'm going to try to reach the General.'

Hay nodded, his revolver pumping out bullets. Dornoch turned away, took over his horse from his servant, and rode through the massed ranks of men towards Fettleworth, scattering infantrymen as he went. Here, where the main body was not yet in action, the confusion was still evident, was if anything worse than the initial confusion that had hit the van. Officers and sergeants were shouting contradictory orders, horses were rearing up in fright, the commissariat and ammunition packs were being scattered from the backs of the milling mules and ponies. The native muleteers were jabbering away nineteen to the dozen and in the distance, to the south, Dornoch could see a swarm of coolies beating it fast for safety and taking their laden ponies with them. It was a disastrous and disheartening sight and when Dornoch reached the General his temper was worse than ever.

He rode straight up to Fettleworth, pushing his horse unceremoniously through the surrounding Staff. Hotly he said, 'Sir, you have seen for yourself what conditions are like in the van. In the rear your coolies are deserting and your mules stampeding—'

'The devil they are! Cornforth-Jarvis.'

'Sir.' A dandified young Captain wearing

201

white cotton gloves moved forward and saluted.

'The rear, Cornforth-Jarvis. Go and take charge.'

'Yes, sir.' Looking down a long nose, the Staff Captain rode away. Dornoch addressed the General once again. He said, 'The situation is worsening in the van, sir.' He could scarcely make himself heard at all above the continual volleys of fire from the rifles and machine-guns, and the screams of men and horses.

Fettleworth shrugged. 'You should expect no less, Lord Dornoch, no less at all. As it is, I have given orders that the regiments behind you are to press on with all despatch—'

'They'll do no good!' Dornoch snapped. 'There's literally no room to fight. The tribes on the hills have it all their own way, General. To send in more men . . . is only to increase the target for the attackers!'

'It is all I can do,' Fettleworth said calmly, almost, Dornoch thought, smugly. 'Casualties must be expected in war, Colonel, you know that—'

'I am not throwing away my Highlanders uselessly, sir. I realise you have no personal fear for yourself—neither have my men. But with respect, sir, I suggest you use your imagination and accept that this is a situation for tactics rather than physical bravery alone. I beg you, sir, to order me and the other forward battalion commanders to withdraw and reform to the rear.'

'Fiddlesticks! I shall do no such thing!' Fettleworth's obstinate face had reddened dangerously. 'By your own admission there is no room, so how can you proceed to the rear without—'

'I did not mean to—'

'Kindly listen to me, Colonel. The van is to fight it out—this must be so. It will be supported by all means in my power.'

'*All* means, General?' Dornoch took up his words with vehemence. 'Sir, in my opinion the infantry should be withdrawn *in toto* and re-formed in rear of the guns. The guns should then be sent forward ahead of the cavalry, and should put down a curtain of shrapnel as heavily as possible and then—'

'Hoity-toity! So we have a brilliant tactician . . . an infantry Colonel, instructing his Divisional Commander in the art of war!' Fettleworth puffed out his cheeks. '*Artillery*, Colonel? Damme, I shall *not* use the artillery! The artillery is there merely to blow down walls and pierce forts. It is not to be used in open action, in column . . . God bless my soul!' Fettleworth seemed to bounce on his horse. 'What the devil next?' He glared round at the Staff.

Dornoch, hanging on to his temper, said, 'It's the only hope, General, the only way to get the column through, do you not see? Every

203

minute, every second, is counting at this moment and we must not delay. So far only one thing has saved us at all—and that is, a tactical error on the part of the tribes. If they had deployed themselves along the pass, and waited for the whole column to move into the trap, we'd have been cut to pieces by now.'

Distantly Fettleworth said, 'I'll not use the artillery. Battles are won by infantry and cavalry alone. Besides, the ground is really scarcely suitable for the deployment of artillery—'

'That can be quickly remedied. If you will order the sappers to lay tracks, we can move the guns quite fast enough.'

'I do not agree. No, Dornoch, no. No artillery.'

Dornoch, in desperation, swung round on the Staff. 'Is there not one of you, gentlemen, who'll support me?' He addressed the Chief of Staff. 'Sir, I beg of you to reason with the General before he loses the whole Division!'

The Chief of Staff shrugged. Stiffly he said, 'Colonel, you forget yourself. You will be good enough to rejoin your regiment at once.'

'But—'

'That is an order, Lord Dornoch. Disobey it at your peril. Remember you have left your post in action.'

'By God, so he has!' said Fettleworth.

Dornoch started in sheer surprise, his face darkening with fury at the slur. He was about to open his mouth when he saw the fractional closing of the Chief of Staff's left eye and read the message plain on his face. He said no more, but gave a stiff salute and turned away, riding back towards the hard-pressed vanguard. After he had gone the General said pettishly, 'Really! I always distrusted the Scots. *Terrible* lot—no damn discipline. Mere killers the lot of them. Clans ... little to choose between them and the damn tribes, what?'

The Chief of Staff said, 'A disrespectful officer, sir. But he has made a valid point nevertheless. You will recall, sir, that I advised precisely the same thing?'

'Yes!' Fettleworth said surlily. 'No, Forrestier.'

'I am aware of your dislike of using guns, sir. If you cannot overcome this dislike, I suggest that in place of the guns you send forward four squadrons of the cavalry to clear the ground, in the meantime withdrawing the foot. The foot to advance again in the wake of the cavalry.'

'But the ground is totally unsuitable for cavalry! Too damn rocky! They cannot fight to advantage.'

'I disagree, sir. The pass is quite open enough for that. If they can move at all, they can fight.'

'Oh, dear ...'

Forrestier, his hands shaking with frustration, persisted. 'The action is going remarkably badly. I know you do not wish to fail to reach Fort Gazai, sir.'

'H'm. You think we may?'

'It is not a question of thinking, General Fettleworth.' The Chief of Staff suffered something like a rush of blood to the head. 'For God's sake, sir, do *something* before it's too late!'

Fettleworth pretended he had not heard that. He was thinking furiously. Calcutta would be most upset at failure; Whitehall would be more so. And there was the Press— so damn scurrilous! Half-pay was a nasty prospect; Fettleworth thought anxiously of Bath and Cheltenham, and all the other retired warriors who would know precisely why he was joining them. 'Oh, very well, very well,' he snapped. 'Have it your own way, do.'

As Dornoch rejoined his men he was vastly relieved to hear the bugles sounding the Retire for the infantry. As quickly as possible the 114th were withdrawn, running and sliding away from the terrible advance, leaving too many dead behind them, dead that were overrun within minutes by the triumphant tribesmen from the hills. Then, as the infantry regiments pulled back off the track to the rear, a trumpet sounded the Cavalry Charge. There was a wonderfully heartening rattle of equipment and a jingle of harness and, as a band somewhere broke into 'Bonnie Dundee', two squadrons of the Guides swept thunderously past, supported by two squadrons

206

of the Bengal Lancers, their guidons fluttering out along the pass and their sabres glinting in the sunlight.

A tremendous cheer broke out, all along the ranks of infantry, as the horsemen charged into the tribal mass. The hillmen, taken by surprise now, scattered to right and left, running, climbing the steep sides of the pass, fleeing from the hooves and from the sabres that slashed and tore. When the charge had passed through, the cavalry turned to deal with such of the natives as were left on the track, supported now by another squadron coming up from the rear. Now the slaughter was the other way round; as the cavalry charge ended, Fettleworth ordered the infantry in. The bugles sounded the Advance; and they advanced, with sheerly murderous intentions. Rank upon rank of men climbed the hillsides, fast behind the enemy, led once again by the Royal Strathspeys wielding broadswords and bayonets savagely and without mercy or quarter, and using their rifles with devastating effect on the turned backs of the tribesmen. After that it was all over quickly; the native horde, leaving their many dead behind them, fled over the crests and away and the column began to sort itself out again.

The wounded were tended and handed over to the doolie-wallahs, the stretcher-bearers, where necessary. The water-bottles were opened. Fettleworth, disinclined to linger now, gave orders that the dead were to be left unburied. Ogilvie and Black, though they had made all possible speed with their men to come up the column and over take the 114th, had missed the action; but the considerable delay while the column was re-formed and the pack animals recovered gave them the time to join up again and Black at once made his report to Lord Dornoch.

'The patrol brought safely back, Colonel, less the casualties which occurred before my arrival. I think Mr. Ogilvie will have some observations to make on that.'

'Thank you, Andrew. You will resume your normal duties, please. We shall be marching again at any moment.'

'Very good, Colonel.' Black hesitated. 'There is nothing further you wish of me just now?'

'No, Andrew, thank you. Not unless you have anything else to report?'

Black's cold face darkened. 'There is the man Makepeace, Colonel. I—'

'Quite so. What's his story, Andrew?'

Briefly, Black passed the details. When he had finished Dornoch said, 'A most remarkable thing. Did you make the . . . shall I call it, the reception of this man?'

'No, Colonel. Mr. Ogilvie bears the full responsibility for the patrol, and the man was apprehended before my own arrival.'

'Apprehended?' The Colonel gave him a

shrewd look.

'The exact word will be a matter for an enquiry, I fancy, Colonel.'

Dornoch's face was expressionless as he said, 'I see. Very well, Andrew, then that's all for now.' As Black went off with his long stride, calling for his servant, Dornoch turned to Ogilvie. 'Very quickly, please, James—how did you get on?'

Ogilvie made a full and honest report, leaving out nothing except the personal behaviour of Colour-Sergeant Barr. Dornoch said, 'You might perhaps have investigated a little more closely from the fissure and found the enemy had left their positions.'

'I'm sorry, Colonel.'

Dornoch smiled kindly. 'Oh, don't worry too much about it. You did very well indeed in the circumstances. I'm only sorry the patrol turned out to be unnecessary in the end, James. However—that can't be helped now,' he went on briskly. 'Tell me—what d'you make of this Sergeant of Artillery?'

'I'm impressed by him, Colonel.'

'You believe his story?'

'Absolutely.' Ogilvie added with a touch of diffidence, 'Colonel ... the fact he's handcuffed leaves him defenceless if we're in more action.'

'Which undoubtedly we shall be! I'll have a word with the adjutant about that,' the Colonel promised. 'All right, James. Off you go and rejoin your company. I'm glad to have you back.'

'Thank you, Colonel.' Ogilvie saluted and turned about. Before he had taken a couple of paces Dornoch called him back. 'One moment, James. How did Colour-Sarn't Barr behave?'

Ogilvie knew quite well what the Colonel meant. The eyes of the two men met and after the briefest hesitation Ogilvie said formally, 'He gave every satisfaction, Colonel.'

'No complaints?'

'None, sir.'

'I'm delighted to hear it. All right, James, thank you.' As Ogilvie saluted once more and went towards B Company, Dornoch thought: He's damn loyal to his men, even when they're not over-loyal to him. Stupid in a way, but a very excellent quality in a young officer all the same. But Barr would have to be watched . . . Dornoch sent once more for Black, and with asperity ordered Sergeant Makepeace to be freed of the handcuffs. The most he would permit, he told Black, was an escort. Before the column moved off along the pass Dornoch went himself to talk to Sergeant Makepeace. He questioned the old man about the Pathan, Shuja Khan, but quickly realized that Makepeace had no information to offer that would be of help to Division. Nevertheless he sent back a report to the General in case Fettleworth should wish Makepeace brought before him. The march was then resumed through the shadow of the peaks and crags towards the greater freedom of movement offered by the Swat valley and that evening the Division poured out from the Malakand Pass and made camp in the open beneath the stars, with the mountains rearing skyward behind them. A cold wind was blowing, refreshingly after the day's heat, but becoming hard to bear after a while. Word came down the column to the 114th that General Fettleworth wished words with the man Makepeace. Lord Dornoch waited himself upon the General, along with Black and Ogilvie and Makepeace's armed escort of kilted Highlanders. Fettleworth questioned the old man closely and competently in their presence, and came to the same conclusion as had Dornoch regarding Makepeace's scanty information about the rising. But when he had finished his probing he said gruffly, 'I remember the raid you spoke of, Makepeace. A bad business—a bad business indeed. I also remember that a sergeant of the gunners was missing afterwards, with his family, and was deemed to have been captured. I am most sorry—*most* sorry—for your really dreadful misfortunes, Sergeant.'

'Thank you, sir, thank you indeed.' Tears came to the old man's eyes, poured down his weathered cheeks. When he was able to speak again he asked, 'May I take it, sir, that you believe what I have told you?'

'I have no reason to disbelieve it,' Fettleworth said.

'Thank you, sir, thank you from the bottom of my heart, and may God bless you, sir, for your kindness.'

Fettleworth tweaked at his moustache, seeming embarrassed. 'Very well, Makepeace. That's all. You understand there will have to be a full enquiry—of course?'

'Indeed, sir, yes.'

'I shall speak for you, you may be sure. This is a terrible business. You must not worry unduly, Sergeant.'

Again tears sprang to the old fellow's eyes as the escort led him away. Black's face, Dornoch noted, was stiff with disapproval, with fury that there should be any suggestion that Makepeace should get away with it. Leaving the General's presence, Dornoch felt almost humble. He would never have believed Fettleworth could show such humanity and understanding. He thought again of the Divisional Commander's undoubted heroism during the attack in the Malakand Pass. Brave, with a demonstrable capacity for compassion ... it was a pity his mind was so closed and unadaptable to present-day methods of making war, a great pity, for he was in basis a good and honourable man. Such attributes went a long way; but, in action, not far enough unfortunately.

The column remained bivouacked for a

good portion of the dark hours, the cold dark hours when the wind increased and whistled about ears muffled into balaclavas. Before first light next day, the Division was on the march again. Here in the Swat valley the going was much easier. The men moved through coarse scrubby grass, past tall and stately deodars, making good speed now. On two occasions they saw the tribes gathering with obviously hostile intent, but each time the natives were dispersed by cavalry charges. There were no losses to the British other than some pack animals that had to be shot after being hit by bullets; the stores were redistributed and the column moved on again.

At the first halt for rest that day, a surprising announcement came down the line from the General: Fettleworth intended holding a religious service, to be conducted there and then by the Divisional Chaplain. There was a good deal of disrespectful comment from the ranks, and ribaldry about church parades in the desert, and Private Burns, self-appointed barrack-room lawyer, was heard to say something to the effect that Bloody Francis would go on parade wearing a crown of thorns, a halo, and crossed shepherd's crooks on his shoulders instead of his normal insignia of rank. 'Christ's Major-General upon Earth,' Burns scoffed. 'The fat-arsed wee birkie!' But most of the men were pleased; their dead had been left without burial and this was a fitting time to pray for their souls, which was no doubt what the General had in mind. Besides, plenty of the 114th had witnessed Fettleworth's heroic dash into the enemy ranks earlier and they admired him for this, and were less inclined to criticize now. And in the event the service was an impressive occasion. The whole Division, with their officers out in front of the regimental lines, stood with bared heads while the Chaplain read a simple but moving service in a strong, clear voice, praying to God for victory and salvation for their kith and kin in Fort Gazai. It was all over within thirty minutes and it ended with every man singing a resounding hymn:

> 'Forward! be our watchword,
> Steps and voices joined;
> Seek the things before us,
> Not a look behind;
> Burns the fiery pillar
> At our army's head;
> Who shall dream of shrinking,
> By our Captain led?
> Forward through the desert,
> Through the toil and fight;
> Jordan flows before us,
> Sion beams with light.'

The words, in those strong voices, beat out across the valley, seeming to reach right into the surrounding hills. It was, Ogilvie felt, a moment to treasure, a jewel for a store-house of memories. The hymn rose and fell over the lines of war-accoutred soldiers, over the horses and the lances and the grim grey guns of the batteries; and when the last echoes had died away into the stillness the sergeants began shouting their orders and, once again, the Division formed column for the march.

*   *   *

Next afternoon the column began to close the Swat River; this they would need to cross before they could proceed through Kohistan, unless they were prepared to make a wide detour to come up south of the Shandur Pass and then drop down to the west upon Fort Gazai. This would mean an unacceptable delay. Word was passed down from the Staff that the Swat River was to be reconnoitred by the Royal Strathspeys ahead of the main force. Dornoch sent for Ogilvie.

'James, I want you to take a detachment, a covering party only, to have a look at the river.' He pointed across the plain, ringed in by the distant ranges brought to pinnacles of gold by the sun. The air was very clear. 'We need to find a ford, and also we must have an estimate of the strength of the current. Bear in mind that heavy stores and ammunition, to say nothing of the guns, have to go across—so we may need a bridge to assist the pack animals

215

and the batteries. Of course, the Sappers will have to take a look later, but a lot is going to depend on your preliminary report, James, so let's have a painstaking one. All right?'

'Yes, Colonel. Do you wish me to leave now?'

Dornoch nodded. 'Yes, at once, as soon as you've detailed your party. I'll leave its composition entirely to you.'

Ogilvie saluted and turned away. Shortly after this he rode ahead with his detachment of thirty men, plus a sergeant and two corporals. This time Barr was not with him. In the interests of speed all the men were mounted, and a curious sight they made. Ogilvie himself was wearing trews, but the men were still in their kilts, which were rucked up over their thighs and trailing down behind over the horses' rumps. There was laughter and a good deal of cat-calling and other chaff as they rode out; and Ogilvie knew that by the time they rejoined the column his men would be pretty sore. It took Ogilvie some little time to reach the southern bank of the Swat and on arrival he found a force of around five hundred tribesmen waiting on the other side. Some shots were exchanged but there were no casualties and the native levies retired to a safe distance under the concentrated fire of the Scots and remained there to watch events. Undeterred by their brooding presence, Ogilvie and his sergeant carried out a quick but thorough survey of the river, riding some ten miles in each direction to make their observations. The river, they discovered, was in fact fordable in a number of places but the current could prove too strong for the heavily-laden pack animals and too deep for the guns in most places; a bridge, it seemed, would be necessary as Lord Dornoch had predicted. His survey completed, Ogilvie rode back with his men to the column and made his report, which was duly conveyed to General Fettleworth. The column moved on and that night made camp on the river bank in full view of the tribesmen. There was no attack; at dawn a brigade with two cavalry squadrons in support was ordered to cross by one of the fords noted and mapped by Ogilvie. Under fire now, this brigade forced the crossing and at once engaged the enemy, who beat a rapid retreat in face of a charge from the 11th Bengal Lancers, thundering across the plain beneath their streaming pennons and backed by the infantry. With the ford safe, the Sappers threw a makeshift pontoon bridge across the river and as soon as this was completed the supply and ammunition train, and the guns, were moved across while at the same time the rest of the infantry and cavalry and support corps crossed by the ford. It was a tricky business; the men had half to wade, half to swim across; but they made it in safety, all of them, and began to form up on the other side, still watched from a distance by the warring tribesmen, while their General, almost the last to make the crossing, was tended through the current by the Staff, whose horses acted as makeshift, mobile waterbreaks for the delicate operation.

As once again column was formed for the march, sporadic attacks came but were beaten off easily enough; such a force as Fettleworth's was in fact virtually impregnable to all but picking-off tactics when in the open; the tribes preferred on the whole to mount their assaults from cover and to avoid pitched battles, concentrating their strength mainly in the forts. From now until the link was made with the column from Gilghit, when they would be close to journey's end, the Division anticipated little real trouble, except possibly when they came to the next river crossing, which would be the Panjkora. As the column pressed forward there was singing from the men, not hymns this time but army songs of the barrack-room kind. Ogilvie, who was currently marching with Hector—whose horse had been commandeered to help replace casualties— noticed the pained look on his cousin's face as the bawdy words floated about his ears. He laughed and said, 'You're certainly having your mind broadened, old man.'

'I'm trying not to listen!' Hector snapped, brushing the swarming insect life from his face. He walked on in silence for a while then said, 'You know, James, I've been doing a great deal of *thinking* the last few days. I admit I had no idea the Frontier was like this. Oh, I knew it all in theory, but—'

'Seeing it, that's different?'

'Yes.' Hector blew out his cheeks, which were now dark with the sun and the fresh air of the days and nights. 'Those natives who attacked—they were skin and bone, you know. Under-nourished. It's dreadful to think of. Contrast *that* with Simla!' He shook his head. 'One day, India will have to be democratised if we're to go on holding it at all.'

'Sooner you than me,' Ogilvie said with a laugh. 'Try democratising a Maharajah and see what happens to you!'

'It will have to come,' Hector persisted. 'They must succumb to the pressures from below sooner or later. So will your people have to, James—the military.' He shambled along in silence for another spell, then asked suddenly, 'What do you think of General Fettleworth, dear boy?'

Ogilvie glanced sideways; his cousin's owlish face was innocent, the eyes blinking behind the spectacles with a total lack of guile, but you never could tell with Cousin Hector. He answered briefly, 'I think he's a General. And that's all.'

'Um?'

'And my Divisional Commander to boot.'

'I'm afraid I don't quite—'

'And I'm a subaltern—'

'Yes, but I—'

'—with ambitions.'

'Come, dear boy—'

'And I don't want to end my career as a dead-end Major in charge of command transport or something like that, back at base. Follow, Hector?'

'Oh . . . well, yes, I think perhaps I do.'

Ogilvie was suddenly and uncomfortably aware that he might well have put his foot in it. As clearly as if he'd said the words outright, he had given his frank opinion of Bloody Francis. Men like Hector often needed only the sense, the feeling. They could fill in the rest with winks and nods or with delicately worded reports. Ogilvie sighed as he trudged along through the dust; he should cultivate the double tongue, the diplomatic lie, become the fulsome flatterer. That way, an officer could survive for much longer in the twice-dangerous life of the Frontier.

*　　　*　　　*

They approached the Panjkora River; this time there was no fording operation. The Panjkora could not be forded at the place where Fettleworth fetched them up, the sides were far too steep and sheer, and it was seen to be necessary to build a full-scale bridge across the gorge. The Sappers informed General Fettleworth that it might well take forty-eight

220

hours to construct and position a suspension bridge, but this delay had to be accepted. 'We shall make camp,' Fettleworth briskly informed the Staff. So the Division settled itself down, and because they were in any case well visible from the ridges fires were lit and a decent meal prepared by the field kitchens. Men relaxed, under the watchful sentries of the guard. The perimeter was constantly patrolled. A few isolated shots came across the gorge but served only to keep the sentries even more vigilant. But the general relaxation was in part denied the 114th Highlanders, to whom came a string of unnecessary and irritating orders from their adjutant. Uniforms were to be smartened up, cleaning of boots and equipment was ordered within the capabilities of the reduced kits. Spit and polish became the order of the day once again, just like at the depot at Invermore in Scotland or the Peshawar cantonments; there would be an inspection the next morning and woe betide any man who had the misfortune to incur Captain Black's displeasure.

Ogilvie heard some of the comments during his spell as one of the officers of the guard.

'Did you ever hear the like?' one old soldier said, spitting into the ground as he sucked away at a foul-smelling pipe. 'Yon bastard'll get his due one o' these days, however. I hope it comes before my time expires, that's all.' The man added, 'Black's twisted ... twisted up inside like a rotten snake, and as vicious too. D'ye mind the way he treated poor old Makepeace, eh? Now, if I was Makepeace, d'ye know what I'd do?'

'Go on, Ben.'

The old private sniffed, then chuckled and spat again. 'I'd say to meself, I would, that I'm going to be shot or hanged whatever happens, so before they shot me I'd put a bullet where it'd do the most good—right up Captain Black, so help me!'

Ogilvie walked away discreetly, unseen. It would never do to be noticed listening to such a conversation unless he intended putting the man concerned on a charge.

CHAPTER NINE

In Simla the news from the Frontier, such as it was, had been studied avidly; most of the English inhabitants had a relative or friend who was fighting either with Fettleworth's Division or with the column marching through the country's hazards from Gilghit under Brigadier-General Preston; and the fate of the garrison in Fort Gazai was everyone's concern. Fort Gazai must not be allowed to fall; but the whole might of Empire would be on the march to avenge the dead in the name of the Queen Empress if it did.

But despite all this there was little interruption in the social programme, though now there were not so many officers available to take part in it and to lend their colourful uniforms as plumage to grace the parties given by the Simla ladies; and when Sir Iain Ogilvie visited Simla, snatching a few days' respite from his cares at Murree, he took his wife to an afternoon's racing at Annandale, riding his horse through the narrow Simla streets while the native population cringed back obsequiously so as not to restrict the passage of the General Sahib and his ladies, riding in the rickshaws behind. The Ogilvies were accompanied that afternoon by their younger daughter, Anne Farquharson, whose husband John had now started on safari in Africa. Anne was very close to her father, though she had more of her mother's gentle yet sometimes artful ways with her; and Sir Iain idolized her. She was dark like her mother, and pretty, and vivacious. And after the third race, looking around at the elegantly dressed gathering, she caught the eye of a young woman escorted by a good-looking Indian; the woman seemed to be studying the Ogilvies, but looked away when she saw she had been observed.

Anne nudged her father. 'Somebody,' she whispered, 'seems to know us, papa. Who is she?'

Sir Iain lifted an eyebrow at his daughter, then looked around, 'She? Who? Where?'

'She's going away now ... with an Indian who looks as though he's somebody very special, judging from the turban and the jewels.'

'Oh. Yes. Yes, indeed. That's young Shandapur. Capital feller, capital. Maharajah. Very friendly.'

'But who is it with him, papa?'

Sir Iain refocused. 'It's a Mr. Archdale. Damn stupid husband on Fettleworth's staff. Pretty woman, damned attractive in fact...' At that moment the Indian, turning, happened to catch Sir Iain's eye. He smiled with genuine pleasure, took his companion's arm, and moved towards the Ogilvies. He was a tall man, of graceful movements, and very richly dressed, with a light blue turban whose peacock feather was held by a brilliant ruby, the biggest Anne had ever even imagined, let alone seen. Mary Archdale, though nicely and appropriately dressed in white silk with a large and decorative hat, seemed completely overshadowed by her escort's grandeur. Sir Iain muttered into his moustache. 'Damn! This is going to be awkward, Anne. Your mother isn't anxious to meet the Archdale girl.' He reached out and put his hand over his wife's— she had been concentrating on a gush of conversation from a Civilian wife transferred with the Government from Calcutta—and Lady Ogilvie turned, thankful enough for the interruption, not yet knowing the cause of it, as the Maharajah of Shandapur came up. She gave a small start as she recognized Mary Archdale and for an instant her face went stiff; but she recovered her poise well and displayed her innate good manners. Sir Iain said, 'You remember young Shandapur, of course.'

The young Indian bowed. 'It is such a pleasure to see you, Lady Ogilvie. May I present Mrs. Archdale?'

Lady Ogilvie inclined her head, kept her hands clasped in front of her. 'We have met.'

Sensing an atmosphere, the Maharajah glanced quickly at Mary and then turned to the General. 'I understand the columns have not yet reached Fort Gazai, Sir Iain,' he said. 'Is there recent news of their progress?'

Sir Iain shrugged. 'Little enough, little enough—but I gather there's been good speed made, considering the immense difficulties of the march. Yours is an inhospitable land, Your Highness, in its remoter parts.' Shandapur smiled. A stir in the well-dressed crowd indicated that another race had started; as the thunder of hooves reached him, Sir Iain put up his glasses for a moment before continuing, 'I understand the Peshawar column has reached the Panjkora. The trouble should soon be over, in my opinion.'

'I'm glad to hear that,' the young prince said, smiling again. Educated at Eton and Christ Church, Oxford, he was one of the most British of Indian princes and a whole-hearted admirer of the way in which British India was run. He had no wish to see unruly elements succeed in upsetting the *status quo*. 'I was talking with Lord Elgin only the other day. I told His Excellency I should be only too pleased to send any of my own troops he might need—but he assured me the Commander-in-Chief had all the men he needed. I imagine you would concur in this view, Sir Iain?'

'Oh yes, assuredly. Very good of you, though. Very good. We're most appreciative.' Sir Iain, always interested in a good-looking young woman, found his attention was straying to Mary Archdale, who was talking to his daughter. Unceremoniously he butted in. 'I have word from our agencies that your husband is about to cross the Panjkora River, Mrs. Archdale.'

'Indeed? Your son also, Sir Iain.'

'Yes.' The General went no farther in that direction; his wife's face had a tight, tense look and he knew very well why. James was being a young fool, but he could scarcely blame the boy; Mary Archdale was damned attractive, he thought, and didn't look her age, which he had discovered was twenty-eight. She had a fine figure, well-breasted, but not too much so, and James—thank God—was a very normal young man ... hastily, Sir Iain shifted his gaze and coughed. 'Yes. I see you've met my daughter.'

'I would have known her anywhere,' Mary said brightly, seeming quite unaware of the chill from Lady Ogilvie. 'She's so like your son—and you.'

'Really, really. Have you had any luck with the horses, Mrs. Archdale?'

She shook her head, her eyes merry. 'I'm afraid I haven't, Sir Iain. But then I haven't lost much either.'

'Glad to hear it. I'm sorry to say I have. Confounded brutes!' Sir Iain tugged at his moustache; it was time the conversation was ended—more was the pity—or he would have to endure a monologue from his wife afterwards. Always in full command of the situation when dealing with men, the General was frequently at a loss with young women when it came to sending them on their way—chiefly because he never wanted to. This time, however, Mary Archdale herself put him at his ease. She said, 'I know you'll excuse me, Sir Iain, but I really must go. I have an aunt arriving from Calcutta shortly, and—'

'Oh, really, really, that'll be pleasant for you. Goodbye, Mrs. Archdale.' He stood puffing through his moustache as Mary and young Shandapur took their leave. He watched them go, with regret. 'Capital young feller,' he said to his wife. 'Nice woman, too. Damn pity about this business.'

'Not in front of Anne, please,' Lady Ogilvie whispered sharply in his ear.

'Oh, rubbish, she's a married woman—'

'That makes no difference. There's no

reason why she should ever know.' Imperturbably Lady Ogilvie checked once again through her race card and turned her glasses on the next race. But that night, after Anne had gone off early to bed with a headache, she brought the subject up of her own accord. She said, 'Iain, we've never had a proper talk about James and that woman.'

'I thought we had.'

'Not what I call a proper settling talk. It must be settled once and for all.'

The General rustled irritably in his chair. 'Leave it, leave it. Let sleeping dogs lie.'

'This dog is sleeping only because James is in action and she's here in Simla. Let them be together again in Peshawar, and it'll all start again where it left off. It won't do, Iain.'

'He's old enough to see that for himself.'

'Old enough, yes—but *will* he? You know what young men are like, Iain. Headstrong, stupid. He *must* be made to think of the family and his own career. The best thing would be to interest him in someone more suitable.'

Smiling, Sir Iain said, 'That's your province, my dear. You can't expect me to go round digging up suitable females—for another man!'

'Oh, dear,' she said. 'Please don't joke, Iain.' She sighed, and stared out into the purple darkness that hung over the hills. She looked immensely sad as she sat there in the shadows. 'It's his whole career, after all. You should know that—both as a father and as a soldier.'

'I do know it, Fiona. Of course I know it. But it's damn hard to interfere. Oh, I agree it wouldn't do—but it's a pity. She seems a nice young woman.'

'What *do* you mean—a pity? Iain, she's *married*!'

'Yes, yes—that's bad—I wouldn't condone anything that could lead to a divorce, naturally, if that's what you're driving at, but I'm damn sure it'll never go as far as that. I repeat, she seems a nice young woman.'

'I'm quite sure she is. She was perfectly pleasant when I . . . spoke to her, but—'

'What exactly did you say?' Sir Iain asked curiously.

'It was what I *didn't* say, really. But I know I left her in no doubt that I considered it far better the friendship should be broken off, and that she was the one to do it. As I say, she was perfectly pleasant—quite charming, in fact. But she has a tough streak, Iain, and she's full of determination. I could see that *quite* clearly.'

With a sly expression Sir Iain asked, 'So it was a case of what *she* didn't say, too?'

Lady Ogilvie nodded. 'I suppose it was. That's why I'm so worried. For another thing, I don't believe she cares for her husband—'

'I'm not surprised—'

'—and that's a terribly dangerous situation, Iain. It simply isn't good enough just to—to shrug it off. We can't possibly have a—a—'

'Oh, say it!' her husband snapped. 'I've said it already myself—divorce!'

'Please don't speak so loud, Iain! It's such a horrid word.'

'I don't believe there's the slightest danger of that. James has far too much sense, anyway. You're making a mountain out of a molehill and running much too far ahead of the facts. Damn it, the boy's never so much as mentioned the woman's name to me!'

Again Fiona Ogilvie sighed. 'Iain, you're very dense sometimes. Young men never mention these things to their fathers, not until they've talked to their mothers, anyway—and mothers always know a long time before they talk about it. I tell you, there is a very real danger of James doing something very, very stupid. It's up to you to put a stop to it, and you know quite well you can.'

'How?'

'Why, firstly by having a very strong talk to him. A lecture, Iain. Tell him exactly what effect all this could have on his life, and point out that he's not behaving as a gentleman in even *seeing* a brother officer's wife while her husband is absent. If that doesn't work—arrange for him to be posted elsewhere. Or Major Archdale to be sent home. He'd be bound to take his wife. I think I should prefer that. I dislike the idea of James leaving the regiment, and I suppose that is what it would mean if he were to be posted, wouldn't it?'

Sir Iain was glaring at her stonily, his colour having risen throughout. 'Fiona, my dear, I'm devoted to you as you know. But I've never held any opinion of an officer who allowed his wife to dictate to him how he should run a regiment—let alone a damn Army! I'll tell you straight, I'm having no interference of that sort!'

Lady Ogilvie nodded submissively enough, but she was smiling inwardly. Iain had always reacted strongly to what he considered interference; but time would work wonders and he would see, it having once been said, that she was perfectly right; and in due course he would himself come up with the same suggestion, trumpeting it loudly from the rooftops as his very own idea. She adroitly turned the conversation onto the Maharajah of Shandapur after that and let her husband have his head on one of his pet subjects, which was the great wisdom of the British administration in allowing the Indian princes to retain in full their time-honoured powers and huge wealth, and in bolstering their position and treating them as equals. They made magnificent buffers, wonderful defences against the other half of India. A very sound policy, Sir Iain considered—and in any case they were mostly capital fellows, gentlemen in fact. Much more so in truth than some of the officers the army was getting these days . . .

The morning after the arrival on the south
bank of the Panjkora River, two companies of
the 88th Foot, The Connaught Rangers, were
sent across a rope bridge during the night and
took up their positions on the north bank to
cover the work of the Engineers as the main
bridge was extended over the river. The 114th
were ordered to stand to on the south bank, to
give additional fire should this become
necessary. From some distance in rear, on
rising ground, Major-General Fettleworth
watched from horseback, through fieldglasses.
He watched until the field kitchens had
prepared his breakfast and that of the Staff,
and then he dismounted. With his senior
officers he walked towards the trestle table
that had been laid with a starched damask
cloth, silver plate, and knives on which much
knife powder had been expended. Breakfast
was porridge, fried eggs, dry bread and
marmalade and steaming hot Camp coffee.
With the coffee Fettleworth lit the first cigar of
the day, a fat cheroot, and then announced
that he would walk down to the lip of the gorge
for a personal word with the bridge-building
sappers. At once a procession formed up,
headed by the Chief of Staff; and the senior
officers moved towards the river. The water
gave off a most offensive smell which a change
of wind brought hurrying across towards the

encamped troops. 'Pah!' Fettleworth said, wrinkling his nose in disgust. 'Damn good thing we finished breakfast before the wind shifted, what?' He brought out a handkerchief of coloured silk and held it to his nostrils; the Staff did likewise.

'Carry on with the work,' Fettleworth said, sounding muffled through the silk-clenched nose as the Major of Engineers dropped everything and hurried to greet him. 'I don't want to cause too much trouble.'

'Sir!' The Major saluted and turned about, and marched back to his duties. Amiably, Fettleworth moved to the gorge and surveyed the scene, sending an occasional word of advice by Captain Cornforth-Jarvis of the white gloves. After a while, however, the smell grew much too strong; for a little longer Fettleworth watched carcasses and other debris floating down on the swift current, then he turned away. 'Too smelly,' he said. 'Thank God I'm not a sapper! And I hope the wind changes again before luncheon, gentlemen.'

Thankfully, the Staff retired. Ogilvie, standing by with his company, watched them leave for the rear, one anxious Staff Major sniffing the air ahead and moving his nose from side to side as though carrying out a nasal probe for patches of clean air fit for his General. Joining Ogilvie, MacKinlay observed, 'It's a trifle too thick for the gilded Staff, James. But I dare say we'll be the same if ever

233

we reach those dizzy heights! There's not really much point in hanging around where you can't do any good, I suppose.'

'The men might appreciate the gesture, mightn't they?'

'Some would, others wouldn't—and give the old boy his due, James, he's *done* that, even if he did beat a retreat pretty soon!'

Late the following evening, a little ahead of the Sappers' estimate, the bridge was in position across the Panjkora River and the column was formed for the crossing after the structure had been tested for strength. A squadron of the Guides moved across first, and then the infantry, followed by the rest of the cavalry, then the guns, the support corps and the pack animals. They all crossed in safety; the bridge had been well and truly built and General Fettleworth was sufficiently impressed with what appeared to be its lasting qualities to name it Fettleworth Bridge, an act of egoism that brought many groans from the ranks. Joining up with the 88th on the other side, the troops bivouacked once again; General Fettleworth disliked being on the move during the hours of darkness, and with some justification in so difficult and treacherous a terrain. Once again a peaceful night was passed, though they could see the distant flickers from the watchful enemy's camp fires. At dawn the march was resumed, with the pipes and drums of the Royal Strathspeys still in the van of the advance behind the scouts. They had some fifty miles left to cover now. As they pressed on to the accompaniment of their martial music, they saw the wild tribesmen from time to time; it seemed they were being shadowed, and shadowed only, for no attacks developed.

The impression grew and spread that they were once again advancing into a trap.

*   *   *

In the name of Captain Black, Colour-Sergeant Barr was harrying the men. Ogilvie watched the process with misgiving but hesitated to bring it to the particular attention of his company commander. MacKinlay, naturally, was aware of Fettleworth's personal order some weeks before that he, Ogilvie, was to continue with Barr as his Colour-Sergeant, and, friendly as Rob MacKinlay always was, there was still the possibility that he might see personal feelings emerging in any adverse comment upon Barr's methods. If MacKinlay had seen nothing wrong himself, this impression would be strengthened. That was inevitable. Nevertheless, it would be a subaltern's duty to bring to his company commander's notice any facts that might prove prejudicial to the company's welfare and fighting efficiency—so long as they *were* facts. It would be almost impossible to accuse Barr of inefficiency; and discipline-wise he always kept just within the letter of Queen's Regulations. As the slow miles wore away and MacKinlay still appeared to notice nothing amiss with Barr's raucous, bullying voice, Ogilvie began to wonder if after all he was the one at fault. Possibly Barr's way of driving weary soldiers on to battle really was the only way; but he doubted it all the same.

In the end he decided to take a risk and sound out the old brigade discreetly and indirectly. He dropped down the column to the rear of his company and pulled in alongside Makepeace just as the order came to halt for a rest. He gestured to the escort. 'I want a word with the Sergeant. Fall out for the time being.'

'Sir!' The lance-corporal and two privates of the escort moved away and Ogilvie sat and yarned with the old man, asking him about the territory and the fighting he had seen in his younger days. Old Makepeace grew reminiscent about his service as a young gunner. Casually, choosing his moment, Ogilvie asked, 'How did you find the discipline in general terms, Sergeant?'

'Hard, sir, very hard. The men have it easy now, compared to them days, sir. Why, sir, I've seen men flogged for being sloppily dressed on parade, sir. Going back to before my time, a man could be awarded two thousand lashes for desertion, but they changed that back in '48 I think it was. Fifty became the limit then, and

236

that was bad enough. I doubt if any man ever survived the two thousand, sir.'

'So do I, Sergeant! Tell me—what were the N.C.O.s like? How would they compare with today's?'

Makepeace scratched his chin, his fingers rasping over the many days' growth that was fast becoming a straggly, snow-white beard. 'Hard to say, sir. Some were always bastards, so were some of the officers, sir, begging your pardon. But there's not been a great change really, sir, taking it all round. I reckon my lads used to think I was a bit of a bastard myself, sir, from time to time, though such was never my intention. You see, sir, you had to be hard if you was to enforce all the petty regulations, the sort of regulations that can break a man's spirit and make him feel less than a man, if you follow me, sir. I don't see a great deal of change today in that respect, sir. A soft N.C.O. is no use, sir, indeed he's worse than useless, though there's ways and ways, of course.' He paused, panting. This march was becoming far too much for him. 'You're young, sir, if I may say so. I have seen in your face that you can feel with the men, sir. That is an admirable thing in an officer, but not one that helps the officer who has it. To win battles, sir, an officer needs to have a total disregard for anything but the act of winning, in my opinion. I myself—though merely a Sergeant, sir—was not hard enough to do that, when it came to the point, as you know. That is why I shall be punished.'

'Don't jump to conclusions too quickly,' Ogilvie told him.

'Ah, sir, you may say that, but it must be. You know that is true.'

There was little Ogilvie could say to that, but he was trying to think up a consoling response when suddenly the old sergeant took his arm in a hard grip, an almost fierce grip, and said in a harsh whisper, 'Sir, I am worried about the outcome of this march. I am greatly worried as to the chances of success.'

'Why's that, Sergeant?'

'I have heard stories about the General, Mr. Ogilvie. I know him to be a brave man, with no thought of his personal safety, and an honourable one too. But I am told . . .'

'Told what.'

Makepeace gave a sigh and scrabbled about with a thin brown finger in the dust of the track. 'Perhaps I should hold my tongue, Mr. Ogilvie. It is scarcely my concern, though I can still lay a gun with the best of them.'

'Go on,' Ogilvie said.

The old gunner drew a deep breath and then, after a long pause, said heavily, 'Sir, I am told the General does not like the guns, that he will not make use of them in open battle, but only to do such things as destroy the walls of a fort. Tell me, Mr. Ogilvie: Do you know if this is true?'

'I believe it is,' Ogilvie said cautiously. 'The guns weren't used when we were attacked in the Malakand, certainly.'

'It is not wisdom, Mr. Ogilvie. It is not good sense. The natives fear the bayonet, I agree, but they also fear the guns. I have a feeling that if the guns were used before Fort Gazai, the General would destroy Shuja Khan's force much more quickly.'

'But the General is the only one who can order them into action, Sergeant.'

'Aye, sir—and he will not, by all accounts. Not to do so is waste of good men and good material. Mr. Ogilvie . . . I am no strategist and I am no tactician. But I am a Sergeant of Artillery . . . and I know the natives have few capable gunlayers. If the guns went through— if they reached the vicinity of Fort Gazai in advance of the main column—we would be in a fair way to the total destruction of Shuja Khan!' The old man's voice was trembling with some strange and deep emotion, some inner conviction, as it seemed to Ogilvie, that he alone had the key to a victory in arms. His grip tightened on Ogilvie's wrist and he said in his ear, 'Sir, I know a way the guns could—'

'Ssh!' Ogilvie hissed the warning; he had seen the approach of Captain Black through the dusty scrub, Black on the lookout for trouble. Makepeace's whisper died away and Ogilvie scrambled to his feet as Black came up. The adjutant didn't say a word, but his eyebrows went up sharply and his lip curled in disdain. Looking Ogilvie up and down as he sauntered on, Black went past. Flushing, Ogilvie gave Makepeace a curt nod, called out for the escort and went back towards the other officers of his company. He felt he had really learned little from the old man except perhaps that the men expected to be chivvied and bullied. Yet that too could well be wrong; Makepeace would be too old and too set in his ways, in his former service, to understand the changing times. Not only Makepeace. That very afternoon, the trouble Ogilvie had been expecting blew up in his face, if only in a mild way. Colour-Sergeant Barr gave an order that was disobeyed. Ogilvie guessed something had happened when Barr marched stiffly up the column with a face like thunder, a private soldier ahead of him. By-passing Ogilvie, who happened to be with his company commander, Barr marched straight up to MacKinlay.

'Sir!' he reported in a carrying voice. 'Private Yelf, sir. Refused to obey my order, sir.'

MacKinlay stifled a sigh, rather obviously. 'What was the order, Colour-Sarn't?'

'This man, sir, was acting as escort to the prisoner Makepeace. I ordered him to stop assisting the prisoner. Sir.'

'Stop assisting him, Colour-Sarn't?'

'Sir, Private Yelf was supporting the prisoner, who was malingering. He is fit to

240

march unaided, and to assist him was to place extra strain upon a man needed to be fit for action.' Barr blew through his moustache. 'When ordered to desist, Private Yelf refused to do so. Sir!'

'Very well, Colour-Sarn't. You do not dispute the facts, Yelf.'

'No, sir, I do not.' The young private spoke with a firm, hot honesty, looking MacKinlay right in the eye.

'Then you will be placed in arrest and will appear before the adjutant in due course. Carry on, please, Colour-Sarn't. I'd like a word with you when you've seen to Yelf.'

'Sir!' Barr turned away and marched Yelf back down the column, shouting out the step loudly. MacKinlay said, 'Oh, hell and damnation, James! You'd think the bloody man'd have more common sense.'

'You mean Barr?'

'Of course I mean Barr. He'd better watch his step, or he's going to have to be taken down a peg or two.' MacKinlay paused, then looked sideways at Ogilvie. 'You've never said so, James, but I've a feeling you didn't get along too well with him on this last patrol. Am I right? I'd like you to tell me, you know.'

After some hesitation, Ogilvie said, 'Yes, you are right, Rob. The man's impossible, really, but you know what the situation is— thanks to Fettleworth's order. I didn't feel inclined to say too much to the Colonel when

241

he asked me.'

MacKinlay nodded. 'I can understand that, but you may be sure the Colonel knows the score, James. Tell me all about it.'

Ogilvie did so, and when he had finished MacKinlay said, 'Well, don't worry too much, old boy. Give Barr just a little more rope and he'll hang himself in the end, you mark my words. That sort always slips up sooner or later, even if he seems to take a long time doing it.' He paused. 'Regarding this current business . . . *is* your old warrior malingering?'

'No! He'd never do that.' Ogilvie hitched at the straps of his equipment. 'I've seen for myself that he's feeling the strain. I think he's been treated damned unfairly all the way along, frankly.'

'Well, don't be too frank, or at least, not too loud when you are! Forget his age, James. Just remember he *has* done just about the worst thing in the book, whatever the reasons.'

Ogilvie felt inclined to argue that, but bit down on his retort. He thought once again of the conversation he had had with Makepeace at the last halt, wondered what the old man had been going to say, what his particular piece of knowledge was all about, and just then Barr came back with his kilt swinging, his face dark beneath the khaki brim of his pith helmet. 'Sir! You wished to see me again.'

'Yes, Colour-Sarn't. I'd be obliged,' MacKinlay said sourly, 'if you'd keep

242

defaulters to a minimum whilst on the march. We have scarcely the facilities for dealing with them, except for important offences.'

'The man disobeyed a *direct order*, sir!'

'Oh, I'm not disputing that—or the gravity of his doing so. But the offence was given rise to by something—well, by something minimal, Colour-Sarn't. Very minimal. Sergeant Makepeace is an old man. A blind eye would have been the better way, don't you think?'

'Sir!' Barr's face was livid, but he wasn't saying a word out of place.

'We don't want him to die on the march.'

'That we *don't*, sir!' There was relish in Barr's tone; the hangman must not be cheated of his due victim—and perhaps another ceremony on the parade at Peshawar.

'Then, that being agreed, Colour-Sarn't, I want Sarn't Makepeace to be carried by his escort from now on.'

'*Carried?*' Barr's face was a picture this time.

'Yes, Colour-Sarn't. In a *doolie*. See to that, if you please, and quickly.'

Barr's mouth opened and he gasped, audibly. 'This will be a burden on the men detailed, sir.'

'Oh, no, I think not, Colour-Sarn't. You'll give them easy spells, of course. Let's say, half an hour each. We have enough men and it can be kept as a company affair.'

'But sir—but sir—in the Black Watch we would never—'

'Please do as I say, Colour-Sarn't Barr.'

'I would prefer—'

MacKinlay, smiling icily, said, 'I am not asking for your preferences, Colour-Sarn't, I am giving you an order. I take it you are not proposing to disobey?'

'*Sir!*' This time the word was an explosion of sheer wrathful disbelief and astonishment rather than the customary acknowledgement of an officer's command. Barr glared, but turned away smartly. The affair, however, had not yet run its course. At that moment Black rode up and happened to see Barr's face. He asked, 'What's the matter, Barr?'

'Matter!' All Barr's fury came out in a rush. 'Matter, Captain Black, sir! I am ordered by Captain MacKinlay, sir, to *carry* that deserter of Mr. Ogilvie's! In a *doolie*, sir!'

Black smiled thinly. 'Personally, Colour-Sarn't?'

'Er . . . not *personally*, sir, no.'

'But even if you were, Colour-Sarn't, you would, as I do sincerely trust, carry out the order?'

'Why, I—I . . .' Barr was stuttering with rage now. 'Yes, I suppose I would, sir. Yes. I would have to—wouldn't I?'

'Truly put, Colour-Sarn't, well and truly put. That is all.'

'But—'

'I said that is all.'

'Sir!' His thick wrestler's body quivering,

indignation and horror in every pleat of his kilt as it swirled about his thighs, Barr marched away. Black looked at MacKinlay. As usual, he made no attempt to keep his voice down. 'It would appear you have surpassed yourself, Captain MacKinlay. You have gravely upset Colour-Sarn't Barr, and no wonder—and all in the interest of a damn deserter.' Black looked coldly at Ogilvie, the officer primarily responsible. 'Captain MacKinlay, you will observe that I have supported you, as was my duty. You will now undo the harm you have done.'

'How?'

'How, you ask? Think, man, think! You will at once countermand your order, Captain MacKinlay—yourself. Thus due dignity will be preserved. No deserter is going to travel in a *doolie* while I am adjutant of the 114th. Be very sure of that. One other thing: I have noticed signs of much slackness in your company, Captain MacKinlay. Idleness, slovenliness, talking in the ranks, never made a soldier yet. From now on, all of B Company will march at attention, Captain MacKinlay, yourself and Mr. Ogilvie included of course, and half an hour after the column halts for the night there will be another dress inspection of B Company, which I shall once again carry out myself.'

Without waiting for MacKinlay's reaction Black spurred his horse on towards Lord Dornoch. At once, loud talking broke out in the ranks behind. As Ogilvie turned to put a stop to it, he saw the same men as had been discussing Black in the bivouacs earlier. Their faces were ugly and menacing. But from then on Black's order was rigidly obeyed—and MacKinlay's duly countermanded. Sergeant Makepeace struggled on behind a silent company, men carrying their rifles at the slope, keeping their dressing by the right and marching in step along the treacherous, rocky ground. And all the time Barr was busy, yelling out the step, taking names, straightening rifle-butts roughly, criticising the set of helmets and of kilts; and Black was riding up and down the company column, smiling with devilish sarcasm at the men's discomfort, which increased progressively as the day wore along. When the column halted that night, the men of B Company were given no respite before they had to begin smartening up their uniforms, polishing buttons and boots as best they could, shaking off dust, washing mud-stained stockings in such evil-smelling water as they could find in the gullies, and putting them on again, wet, for Black's inspection, rigorously carried out. That night Ogilvie felt the men were on the point of mutiny and he reported as much to MacKinlay. MacKinlay pooh-poohed his fears, however. He said, 'I shouldn't worry too much, old boy. Blacks come and Blacks go—the men have mostly met them before and will meet them again. They ride the storms, you know.'

'I'm not so certain.' Ogilvie was worried. 'Don't forget it's the first time in India for most of the men—agreed we've been out here a year, but Black's the only one of his kind they've encountered yet.'

'The old hands'll keep the hotheads in check, James. And don't *you* forget we have some first-class N.C.O.s. If there's any real trouble brewing, they'll be the first to spot it.'

'Barr isn't much help.'

'He would be, in a situation of that sort. You can rely on that. He's a so-and-so with the men, but he's a very loyal N.C.O., even if you don't always hit it off with him. I know he talks too much about the Black Watch, but he's very jealous of the Royal Strathspeys' reputation too.' MacKinlay clapped Ogilvie on the shoulder. 'Just keep an eye open now and again, but don't let it get on your mind. Soldiers always grouse—it's much more dangerous when they don't. All the same, you were quite right to tell me, and I'll be keeping an eye on things as well, you may be sure.'

'I was wondering if it mightn't be a good thing if you were to have a word with Black.'

MacKinlay unfolded a camp chair and sat himself down on it. 'That would only make things worse,' he said, lighting his pipe. 'Black's not the sort to appreciate comment!'

'The company's still your responsibility, Rob.'

MacKinlay looked up sharply at that. 'I don't need you to remind me of my responsibilities,' he said in a cool voice.

Ogilvie flushed. 'I'm sorry. I didn't mean it quite like that.'

'Damned if I know how you *did* mean it, then. Do stop fussing around like an old hen, James! If I thought there was anything seriously wrong, I'd go for Black like a dose of salts, don't you worry. But this isn't the moment. I don't want to worsen his mood when things are nowhere near danger point. If I saw that point really coming up, James, I'd go over Black's head and straight to Hay or the Colonel. Now—just leave it at that.' He broke off. 'I see cousin Hector looming up, James. We don't want our domestic troubles to be brought too closely to Whitehall's attention!'

Hector came up, looking disconsolate. Ogilvie asked, 'Found yourself a good billet, Hector?'

'Not very. It's going to be frightfully uncomfortable, and I didn't get much sleep last night either.'

'That's active service for you,' MacKinlay said. He looked quizzically at Hector. 'Didn't they warn you before we started?'

'Yes, but—'

'You thought soldiers always exaggerated?'

'It was rather my impression.'

MacKinlay laughed. 'I think this march has opened your eyes a little, old boy! Well, that's

248

all to the good; and if you don't mind my saying so, I think you've shown a remarkable amount of guts in coming with us. I really mean that.'

Hector looked pleased. 'I think you fellows have more guts than anyone I've ever met,' he said. Then he coloured, and, seeming confused, muttered some excuse and went off. Ogilvie said, 'That's the first time I've heard Hector use a vulgar word like guts. This experience *is* doing him good!'

'And us, I rather believe. Cousin Hector has the look of a man who's going a long way, James. It never does the army any harm to have the top Civilians sympathetic towards them.'

Ogilvie nodded, and soon after that moved away, back to the men's bivouacs, trying to get the feel of the situation. The murmurs, now that the cleaning operation and the inspection were over, had died away. The rations had been brought up the line by the bearers and the men were talking together quietly. When the wretched fare had been eaten there was even some singing that swelled then gradually tailed away, and soon they began to settle down for the night in the hollows and behind the rocks, in the *nullahs* or in shallow trenches that they had excavated for themselves. A moon came up, lighting the hills, lighting the country they had yet to march through before they could join up with the column from

Gilghit and cover the last miles to Fort Gazai. After a while Ogilvie went back to his own bivouac and slept; tonight, as it happened, he had no guard duties and he looked forward to a long rest until the dawn bugles blew. But this was not to be, and, oddly enough, when the trouble came, it was Hector who was the first to spot the signs. Ogilvie had been asleep for no more than a couple of hours when he felt a hand shaking him awake and he heard his cousin's urgent voice in his ear.

He sat up. 'What is it, Hector?'

'I don't know. I couldn't sleep—I've just been lying awake, you know. I saw some sort of movement on the hillside, ahead and to the left. Over there.' He pointed.

Ogilvie, looking hard, saw nothing. The moon had gone behind low cloud. He asked, 'Just what did you see?'

'I can't be sure, really. It looked like a man, visible on the summit. I only saw it for a moment, a fraction of a second. I could be wrong. I thought I'd come and tell you, though.'

'Quite right. But we do know we're being watched along the way, of course.' Ogilvie took another long, intent look through his field-glasses—and then he saw a movement on the hillside as the moon came out from behind the cloud. It was no more than a sudden brief glint, a shining of the moon on moving metal, but it was enough. The movement was down the

250

hillside. Ogilvie scrambled to his feet and ran for the Officer of the Guard, a subaltern of the 88th. He said breathlessly, 'There's movement on the hills, O'Rourke. If I were you, I'd sound the alarm.'

'The devil you would!' The Irishman brought up his glasses and searched the hillside. 'I see nothing.'

'I'm not surprised. They're a slippery lot ... I've been caught like this before. We can't take a chance, believe me.'

In the moonlight Ogilvie saw the officer's hard stare, summing him up. Then the subaltern nodded and turned to his bugler. 'Alarm to arms,' he said curtly.

The bugle sounded out over the sleeping men, was taken up by others along the spread-out bivouacs. Everywhere soldiers scrambled to their feet, reaching out for their rifles. The machine-guns swung to cover the perimeter on all possible arcs of fire. Action had been taken just in time; as Ogilvie ran towards his half-company a mass of bodies was seen scrambling back for the summit, natives beating it fast for safety now that the column was ready for them. There was a burst of fire from the machine-guns, and a number of rifle shots; there was some return fire from the tribesmen as they fled, and that was all. There were no casualties in the British lines—except for one flesh wound; and the wounded man was Captain Black, who had been hit in the left arm just

251

below the shoulder. It was far from being a serious wound, though Black was making a good deal of it. Surgeon Major Corton attended the adjutant together with two orderlies and decided to extract the bullet, which had embedded close to the bone, immediately.

'Hold still, Andrew,' he said. 'It'll not hurt. I'll give you a local anaesthetic.' He prepared his hypodermic with cocaine, sent a squirt into the air by the light of a storm lantern, then slid the point of the needle into the fleshy part of Black's upper arm. When the cocaine had taken its effect he began to probe. Black's eyes rolled and his face glistened with sweat; his teeth were held fast together and he wore a martyred look. Corton hummed a tune to himself as he worked; the job didn't take him long. After a few minutes he sat back on his haunches and said, 'Well, Andrew, there she is, all out in one piece, and you'll be none the worse.' He gestured to an orderly, who swabbed at the wound. 'I'll put a couple of stitches in and you'll be fine. D'you want to keep the bullet as a souvenir, Andrew, for posterity?'

Black made a grimace, then asked, 'Where is it, Doctor?'

'Here,' Corton said, and passed it over. Black took it in his right hand and studied it in the lantern's light. Then he gave a start, seemed about to speak, but thought better of

252

it; his face, as Corton deftly inserted the stitches and then bandaged his arm, was white and stiff and he didn't seem to be aware of what was going on around him. When he was lifted to his feet and assisted back to his bivouac, he was shaking all over; and when he had been made comfortable he sent for Colour-Sergeant Barr. Then he sent for MacKinlay. Next morning MacKinlay told Ogilvie the story in confidence. The bullet that had entered Black's arm had been fired from a Long Lee Enfield rifle. The hill tribes along the Frontier were known to be in possession of British arms, some of them actually supplied by British firms whose purses were of more importance to them than their consciences, but it was most unlikely that any of the new rifles would have reached them. The Long Lee Enfield had been produced only that very year at the Royal Small Arms Factory at Enfield and was not yet in service except with the 114th as guinea-pigs. So far as Ogilvie knew, no other British regiment had them, and would not have them, probably, for many months to come.

MacKinlay said, 'Well, old boy, you were quite right, and I apologize most humbly. This could have been so damn serious it doesn't bear thinking about.'

'What's going to happen now?'

'Nothing, except Andrew's going to take off the pressure.'

'He's not taking any action at all?'

'No. There will be no report to the Colonel. He swore Barr and me to secrecy, and I'm doing the same with you, James. This is to go no further and I don't want to hear it discussed again. You can take that as an order. It's over.' He grinned suddenly. 'But our adjutant's had a God Almighty shock! I had a talk with him after Barr left us. He knows there isn't a hope in hell of ever finding out who fired that bullet, and he feels the least said the better, in case he gets another with a better aim to it. For my part, I remembered what you'd told me and I laid it on very, very thick, I can tell you! I don't believe we'll have any more trouble from Black on this march, James.'

Soon after this the troops breakfasted and then the column of advance re-formed. Black kept well out of the way of B Company and there was no repetition of the order to march at attention. Before the men had moved off, Hector had been sent for by Lord Dornoch and taken to the Divisional Commander, who was drinking coffee at his trestle table. Fettleworth had congratulated Hector on his voluntary vigilance. 'Damn good effort, Mr. Ogilvie,' the General said. 'You saved a great many lives, let me tell you—a great many lives—and much valuable ammunition. Well done! We'll make a soldier out of you yet—what?'

James was glad enough that his cousin's act,

which he himself had reported to Lord Dornoch, had received its due recognition; but he couldn't help smiling to himself as he saw the suddenly acquired military straightness in Hector's back and shoulders as he joined that day's march.

*   *   *

Three days later the scouts picked up a wild-looking man whom they had believed to be a surrendering Pathan, a ragged man smelling to high heaven who turned out to be one Captain Hopkiss of the Political Service. Hopkiss, sent at once to the General, reported that he had left Fort Gazai four days earlier and had slipped in his disguise through the enemy lines. The garrison of the fort, he said, was in a sorry state, being much reduced in numbers by continual sorties from the enemy; the food and ammunition were running out, and the daily ration reduced to below subsistence level even for the women and children. There was hysteria among the latter each time rations were issued; and there was a strong likelihood of an epidemic breaking out if the fort was not soon relieved and fed. Meanwhile more and more of the Frontier tribes were coming out and were joining up with the 60,000-strong army encamped before the town and fort. Shuja Khan had arrived, and was in personal command of this army in the name of his

255

father in Afghanistan. By now there was full expectancy that the final assault would be mounted at any moment and the garrison over-run. Major-General Fettleworth called a conference of Commanding Officers, together with all Staff Officers from Division and the various Brigade Headquarters. He addressed them at some length, and fulsomely, about the serious consequences throughout the British Raj if Fort Gazai should fall and its occupants be murdered, as they would be. He talked much, and quite unnecessarily, about the urgent need to reach especially the women and children in time; every man in the column was already well enough aware of what would happen to them. Fettleworth added that Captain Hopkiss had information from his department that the column from Gilghit under Brigadier-General Preston would by now have most likely reached Laspur and would be across the Panjkora River. 'If this is the case,' Fettleworth said, 'I would expect that column to be marching down the west bank of the Panjkora for Fort Gazai. In which case, gentleman, I shall expect to rendezvous late tomorrow evening. That can be considered good news. There is, however, less pleasant news. I am informed by Captain Hopkiss that General Preston's column has been badly mauled whilst marching through the Shandur Pass, and its fighting strength reduced to one half. It will be up to us, gentlemen, to redress the balance.'

*　　　*　　　*

In Murree Sir Iain Ogilvie pushed his maps aside, rubbed wearily at his eyes, and irritably dismissed his Chief of Staff. All that could be done, had been done. The rest was in the hands of the Almighty—whose representative in Murree, by virtue of his office under Her Majesty in Windsor, Sir Iain in a sense was. He was in fact tremendously aware of his responsibilities for the lives of a vast number of men; he was not a general who cared to have high casualty lists. There were such; to some high-ranking officers, a large casualty list was a measure of their own effort in victory, of their own struggle in defeat. Not that anyone wished men to die; it was simply that they were not impressed with the tragedy, with its consequences to the bereaved families. Of course, you couldn't fight a campaign if you were afraid of losses, but there were ways of minimizing them all the same. Some generals took pains to minimize them, others did not— that was all. Bloody Francis was in the latter category, and currently held in his inept hands the life of Sir Iain's son. Sir Iain's nephew too, blast it to hell ... Sir Iain champed angrily, gnawing at the ends of his drooping moustache. Brother Rufus would never forgive him if the feller should be lost. Couldn't blame

him, either. But James . . . he was really very
fond of the boy. Didn't show it much, but . . .
Sir Iain thought momentarily of Archdale's
wife. A damn good-looking filly, that! The
General's blue eyes, so like Fettleworth's,
gleamed. Why, he wouldn't mind bedding her
himself, he was still capable—still all right to
look at, too, if a trifle paunchy and grey.
White, his wife said, but he disagreed. He
could see no traces of white. She said it only to
destroy his confidence *vis-a-vis* young women,
he felt sure. If so, it hadn't worked . . .
Moodily, he crossed the room and brought out
a whisky bottle and poured himself a *chota peg*,
which he downed fast. He took a pinch of
snuff, then looked at the bottle again, but
regretfully put it back in the cupboard. He
needed to be mentally alert now of all times;
no one could tell what the next news from Fort
Gazai might be; already he had asked for
Peshawar to be strengthened by troops from
Southern Command at Ootacamund, and he
might yet have to fling them across that
treacherous country towards Chitral . . . if only,
he thought suddenly, men had wings! There
had been some talk of flying machines, but that
was a lot of hot air, they would never get off
the ground, and if they did, they would only
carry the driver or whatever he would be
called. But what a miracle it would be . . .

Sir Iain blew out his moustache. Mary
Archdale . . . damn! Possibly Fiona was right;

besides, he'd always wanted to rid his command of that fool Archdale, hadn't he? It might cause some ill feeling, but he could always go over Fettleworth's head and have the man sent home. Reasons could always be trumped up—medical if no other. Have the man invalided—he'd probably drunk quite enough whisky in his time to have the makings of cirrhosis of the liver and if he hadn't, why, he could always be adjudged too thin or too fat for the climate. In Archdale's case, too fat. Or—with that damn mobile commode of his— too turgid in his bowel movements. Sir Iain thought once again, lustfully, of the wife. How she could bear that great, gross, constipated body . . . he shook himself; this was getting him nowhere at all. He had to do what he could to protect his son's career. Yes—damn it—Fiona *was* right, it simply would not do at all to have a scandal and James had been infernally indiscreet if all Fiona said was true, which it would be; she didn't embroider as much as most women, never had. Sir Iain banged a bell on his desk and a messenger doubled in and crashed to attention.

'Sir!'

'My compliments to the Director of Personnel Services, and I'd like the particulars of the career of Major Thomas Archdale, 178th Mahrattas. At once.'

'Sir!' Boots crashed again and the messenger turned away. There was no time

259

like the present, Sir Iain reflected, even if within the next few days he had no son to consider.

*   *   *

As forecast by General Fettleworth, the rendezvous was made the following evening with Preston's force. Marching north in the purple Indian twilight, along the western river bank, the scouts saw the dust-cloud ahead and word was sent quickly back to Bloody Francis. Soon the battalions in the van of the advance heard the heartening sound of the fifes and drums beating out into the still air, and then they too saw the dust-cloud and, emerging from under it, the weary but still proudly marching troops of Brigadier-General Preston, battle-scarred and with bloodstained uniforms and bandages, and burdened with what seemed to be a colossal number of wounded being borne along in the *doolies*.

There was a resounding cheer from the Peshawar column as the men from Gilghit marched to join them, but the cheers fell away raggedly as they saw the extent of the force's mauling in the Shandur Pass. It had been reduced to little more than a skeleton and there seemed to be more wounded than fit men if the count included the walking wounded. General Fettleworth rode through the column preceded by a mounted escort and accompanied by his Chief of Staff, to greet Preston. Fettleworth knew of Preston, who was one of the younger brigadiers and a man of what he considered advanced ideas; thus Fettleworth was inclined to caution.

'Delighted to join you,' he said, returning the junior general's salute. Preston, he noted, looked sick and drawn. 'You appear to have had a bad passage.'

'God, that's an understatement if ever I heard one,' Preston answered. He was a small man, slim and spare, with a sharp, intelligent face and bright eyes—too bright, Fettleworth fancied as he studied him; and he hadn't much cared for the tone. 'I'm sorry to have to report that I've lost two thousand men killed, and I'm carrying another three thousand wounded. It was bloody murder.'

Even Fettleworth was startled at the figures. 'Good gracious me! Shocking—shocking! I'm very sorry. And your supply train?'

'Gone,' Preston answered briefly and bitterly. He passed a hand across his eyes. 'My Indian commissariat and camp followers bunked. We were ambushed, you see—in an especially difficult defile. We couldn't fight back with any effect. We were sitting targets almost—for an ambush of twenty thousand tribesmen at a guess. They were deployed along the crests and firing down right into us and there was no cover.' He added, 'I have also to report . . .' he was swaying in the saddle

261

from sheer weariness '... I've lost almost all my guns.'

'Poof!' Fettleworth said. He bared his teeth in his horsey grimace; he looked remarkably like a Japanese general.

Preston said, 'I beg your pardon, sir?'

'Oh, nothing ... but guns are of little account to me. I dare say you know my views on the use of guns.'

'As a matter of fact, yes. Allow me to predict, however, you'll never win a battle without 'em.'

'Nonsense. I think I may say I've been successful enough in winning battles, Brigadier-General Preston, with my artillery held in reserve throughout.'

'Well, let us not argue the point now,' Preston said coolly. 'I—'

'By Jingo, sir, I think you must be tired!'

'By God I am.' Preston's tone was cooler than ever. 'I'm ready to drop, and so, I might add, are my men. I couldn't have moved 'em a step farther.' He gave a nod of his head to the westward. 'I hear things are not too bright in Fort Gazai, sir.'

'They're not,' Fettleworth agreed disagreeably; he had not liked having the subject changed for him. 'However, the arrival of our joint force will alter the balance—'

'If we're in time.'

'What?' Fettleworth's eyebrows shot up.

'I said, if we're in time.'

'Damn it, of course we'll . . .' Fettleworth suddenly changed what he had been going to say; even he could scarcely forecast when Fort Gazai might fall. 'We'll use our best endeavours,' he said stiffly, instead. 'We shall not fail.'

'May I remind you, I have three thousand wounded, give or take a few. Of those, something in the region of fifteen hundred should really be stretcher cases. They're going to hold us up and we must face the facts of that, sir.'

Fettleworth clicked his tongue; the fellow was only too right. 'We shall have to discuss the matter in detail,' he snapped.

'Yes, of course. There's just one thing I'd like to make clear before any discussions take place, however.' Preston looked round at his depleted, forlorn column, at the wounded, at the men still on their feet, their bodies swaying from the effort of the march and from lack of food. Then he turned back to Fettleworth and said, 'I shall not leave a single one of my men behind, General, and I must state that quite clearly.'

Bloody Francis blew his moustache up angrily. 'Well, General Preston, we shall see, we shall see.'

'No. We shall *not* see, General Fettleworth. I am adamant.'

They glared at one another.

'I have heard,' Hector said, 'that he's an excellent general.'

'So've I.' Ogilvie looked round the bivouacs; both the columns had intermingled now, and some of the strain was going from the eyes of Preston's troops, who now had a meal under their belts and were falling asleep already. Ogilvie, understanding the dialect, had overheard some comment on the recent march from the sepoys, and every one testified to the bravery of their General and to his regard for his men, who clearly loved him. Physically Preston was somewhat like Lord Roberts, and it seemed he inspired his men in much the same way as Bobs Bahadur, as Roberts was known to his troops, inspired his. Ogilvie wished Preston had been given their own Division; he was, frankly, fearful of the outcome once they reached Fort Gazai. After that terrible display back in the Malakand Pass, it seemed clear enough that Fettleworth knew little of how to deploy men in battle in anything approaching modern conditions; and if the rot set in outside Fort Gazai, there might well be considerable trouble with the men, who were never slow to realize when they were being badly led in action; the comment after Malakand had been ripe enough. It was sheer luck that had pulled Fettleworth through that time; he would scarcely be lucky twice in a row! Ogilvie could foresee that, if he and his brother officers were to abide by their orders and their loyalty to their commander, it could become necessary to drive the men uselessly to their deaths. With men like Fettleworth in command, an officer's loyalties were constantly torn in two, which was, to say the least, hard on the nerves.

At dawn next day the Divisional Commander called a massive conference of all officers down to and including company level. The officers sat in a ring around the General, who produced a large map of Fort Gazai and its surroundings and had this map carried around his audience by two Staff Sergeants, so that all could have a brief look at it. When the map had been paraded it was fixed to a blackboard on an easel in rear of Bloody Francis, who then outlined his tactics, which were simple enough to be followed by the meanest intelligence.

'Gentlemen, we march, as you know, in one hour from now. I expect to be in position before Fort Gazai by noon tomorrow. This schedule will be kept to even if we have to march throughout the night. As you also know, the reports from Fort Gazai via Captain Hopkiss are not encouraging. Now, Captain Hopkiss tells me the enemy forces, up to the time he left the fort, were encamped *here*.' Fettleworth picked up a long pointer and laid its end on a spot to the east of the fort. 'The estimate of numbers is 60,000 but it is believed that this figure may have been quite considerably added to. We must, I believe, base our expectations upon having to face an army of between, say, seventy and eighty thousand men. We can muster little over twenty-four thousand fit men all told. In these circumstances, gentlemen, I do not propose to attack immediately upon our arrival unless the enemy shows signs of mounting an attack of his own. If this does not happen, the Division will dig itself into trenches at a suitable distance from the enemy—about *there.*' He tapped with his pointer. 'Yes, Captain Hopkiss, what is it?'

'That will not do, sir. The—'

'Won't do, won't do? What the devil d'you mean, won't do?'

'The ground where you are indicating is solid rock, sir.'

'Oh. Oh. Oh, damn! Are you sure, Captain Hopkiss?'

'Yes, sir. Any trenching will have to be a little farther to the south of east.'

'Oh. Come and show me, Hopkiss.' Hopkiss did so. The General went on, 'Well, *there*, then. Now, as I was saying . . . the Division will dig in at a suitable distance from the enemy, such distance to be decided upon arrival according to the conditions as we find them. From these trenches, gentlemen, I shall hope to reduce the enemy by sorties, which will be made as frequently as possible. Also by rifle and machine-gun fire, naturally. Thus, by a process of attrition as it were, we shall reduce the enemy to more equitable proportions before the main attack is mounted—which will be done as soon as the enemy is seen to be making clear preparations to move in on the garrison in Fort Gazai. Is that clear so far?'

There were murmurs of assent, accompanied by many looks of total incredulity. Brigadier-General Preston, occupying the centre beside the thick figure of the Divisional Commander, had his eyes closed as if in mental agony; and was saying nothing whatever. Dornoch guessed he had already said plenty and had been sat on, hard. Fettleworth went on, 'Good. Oh, I almost forgot, gentlemen. The trench-digging operation will be covered by the cavalry and the machine-guns, also by the rifles of the 1st Brigade. Understood? Very well. Now—if we should be attacked ourselves upon arrival, or if an attack appears likely after we have taken up our position in the trenches, we shall at once form square by battalions—'

Preston opened his eyes and said, 'By God we won't.'

'By God we *will*! How dare you, sir! Never in all my service . . .' Fettleworth bounced on the balls of his feet; his obstinate face was as tight as a drum. '*I* am in command here, Brigadier-General Preston—not you.'

'I don't dispute that, sir. But to form

267

square—'

'Silence, sir!'

'I will not—'

'Hold your tongue, sir! I will not have this! I shall place you in arrest if you won't be quiet.'

The briefing proceeded in an angry atmosphere. As MacKinlay remarked later to Ogilvie, Bloody Francis was still chained to the Iron Duke. He said, 'Really, everyone was thoroughly embarrassed but no one except Preston had the guts to tell him what a bloody ass he was. It's obvious enough what he ought to do—forget his trenches and his infernal squares and smash the tribesmen up with an artillery barrage first of all, then send in the cavalry with the infantry in support. But he's too thick-headed to see that.'

*　　　*　　　*

Before the word was passed to march Lord Dornoch walked along the battalion's bivouacs with the Regimental Sergeant-Major, talking to the men as they waited to move out. He spoke with his usual cheery confidence and managed to impart some of it to the men, but his face was heavy and sombre and anxious as he walked away afterwards with Mr. Cunningham alongside him. The Warrant Officer, too, was looking immensely preoccupied.

'A penny for your thoughts, Sarn't-Major,'

268

Dornoch said with a smile as he eased the chinstrap of his helmet.

'Sir! I was just thinking ... I never did like the hours before action. There's many men we're not going to be seeing again, sir.'

'That's usual.' Dornoch's voice was sad. 'I regret it as much as you, Sarn't-Major—but it's usual.'

'Yes, sir. But this time more than usual.'

'I wouldn't say that, Cunningham.'

'I would, sir. Begging your pardon, sir.' Bosom Cunningham heaved his big chest and squared his shoulders. 'It's going to be the worst action we'll ever have fought, sir. They do say the General will not be using the guns except as a last resort.'

Dornoch gave a quiet laugh. 'Is that what they're saying, Sarn't-Major?'

'It is, sir. And I'm not keen to see the regiment carved up by ... well, I have to say it, sir ... by an act of folly. We're a good regiment, sir, the best, with a fine tradition, and a happy one too, thanks to you, sir.'

'It's good of you to say that.' There was emotion in the Colonel's voice now. 'Not only me, though. It's the R.S.M. who sets the tone. Remember that. And remember that part about the tradition, Cunningham. It's going to be important tomorrow. I think you know what I mean.'

'Aye, sir, I do that. We must carry out our orders, no matter how daft they are. Well, I'll be doing that, of course, sir.'

'Of course, Sarn't-Major.'

'If you're not requiring me any more, sir, I'll be about my duty.'

Dornoch smiled warmly. 'Off you go, Sarn't-Major. And good luck to you. Of all the faces in the regiment, yours, my dear Bosom, is the one I'll most want to see again.' He held out his hand, and Bosom Cunningham took it in a warm, fierce grip and then turned about smartly, marching off with his pace-stick under his arm as though back on the wind-swept parade at the depot in Invermore. His eyes were a trifle moist. He and the Colonel ... they had been good friends for many a long year, had almost grown up together with the Royal Strathspey. Cunningham had followed his own father into the regiment at much the same time as Lord Dornoch had followed young Mr. Ogilvie's father as a company commander. Years ago now ... and all those years good ones, serving Her Majesty the Queen in the Empire's cause along with fine comrades. The regiment was a family. The army was a very rewarding life when you had the good fortune to serve under good officers, and the 114th had mostly had good ones because their Colonels, which had included Sir Iain Ogilvie in his turn, and Sir Iain's father before *him*, had always chosen well from the Gentlemen Cadets at Sandhurst.

*　　　*　　　*

The regiments moved out in one column. The pipes and drums of the Royal Strathspeys led the Division still, behind a vanguard provided by the Bengal Lancers in their colourful uniforms and turbans and with the magnificent shabraques of their horses, and the pennons fluttering boldly from the lances. Bawdy song came from the Highland ranks when the pipes stopped, snatches of vulgarity to sear Hector's soul, though he had passed almost beyond caring now.

'We're the heroes o' the night,
For we'd sooner bed than fight—
We're the heroes o' the Nightgown Fusiliers.
Eyes right!
Kilts up tight!
Weapons to the fore!
We're the boys the deil deploys
Whene'er he sights a whore . . .'

But the singing didn't last long; the men were dog tired even after a night's rest. They were shadowed along the way by distant tribesmen, visible as stark silhouettes out of rifle range against the skyline, men who sent the word ahead that the British soldiers were now approaching Fort Gazai. They were forced-marching now, with few halts, and those of the

271

briefest duration only, and keeping up as smart a pace as the sergeants could induce. Overhead the loathsome vultures, the watchful birds of prey, hovered in their customary grisly fashion. The early part of the march was easy enough, in the day's initial freshness; but when the sun was up the discomfort set in again and in spite of the lesser heat up here in the northern hills the men were soon soaked through with sweat that ran down into the Highland kilts so that they sagged damply against sunburned knees. From time to time the bands started up again, temporarily lifting men's spirits; the sergeants and corporals were busy all that day, moving up and down the column, shouting, cajoling, harassing or encouraging according to their several natures; and all of them forcing the pace to the limit of endurance. Colour-Sergeant Barr snarled and barked at his Scots like an officious, surly-tempered sheepdog. Black was still being circumspect, and he kept away from B Company as much as possible, for which Ogilvie and MacKinlay were heartily thankful. Black, Ogilvie thought, must have some worries that he might be despatched by one of B Company in the forthcoming battle. After a brief halt, chiefly to rest the animals, Ogilvie, keeping a watchful eye on his men, found that Sergeant Makepeace had once again been handcuffed. He found Colour-Sergeant Barr and drew him aside.

He asked, 'Who gave orders for Makepeace to be handcuffed, Colour-Sarn't?'

'I took that upon myself, Mr. Ogilvie.'

'Then rescind the order at once, if you please.'

'Sir.' It was not a response of obedience, but one of intent to argue. 'With respect, Mr. Ogilvie. That man could be dangerous. We do not know where his loyalties lie for certain, but we know he is to face a Court Martial—if he remains with us.'

'Are you refusing to obey an order, Colour-Sergeant Barr?'

Barr snapped back, 'No, I'm not. I'm doing no such thing, Mr Ogilvie. I am merely pointing out the situation as I see it. It would be bloody daft to go into action with a possible enemy free to attack us from the rear as it were.'

Ogilvie gave a snort. 'An old man like Makepeace? What rubbish!'

'Rubbish it may be. It's my duty to put my point of view, Mr. Ogilvie. I do not wish to accept the responsibility of setting free a deserter who has already fired upon British troops and killed them.' Barr's face bristled with anger.

'All right,' Ogilvie said evenly. 'I shall take the full responsibility. Release the prisoner, Colour-Sarn't. That is an order.'

Barr stood his ground still. 'Sir. I wish to have that order repeated before a witness.'

'Then you shall!' Ogilvie snapped, getting hot under the collar now. He looked around, caught the eye of Bosom Cunningham. 'A moment, if you please, Sarn't-Major.'

'Sir!' Cunningham marched up and saluted, a cold eye running over Barr.

'Mr. Cunningham, I'd like you to witness that I am ordering Colour-Sarn't Barr to remove the handcuffs from Sergeant Makepeace.'

Cunningham's eyebrows lifted a little way and he gave Barr another sharp look. Then he said, 'I understand, sir. Begging your pardon, sir, but had I known the handcuffs were back on, I'd have taken the liberty of asking myself that they be taken off.'

Barr snapped, 'That's all very well, Sarn't-Major, but—'

'Hold your tongue, Colour-Sarn't. You have received an order from an officer. There are no buts. Obey that order at once, d'ye hear me, or so help me God, I'll have you in the room of Sergeant Makepeace. Jump to it, man!'

Barr started, paled, saluted, and turned about. He marched to the rear of B Company and began shouting at Makepeace's escort. Ogilvie said, 'Thank you, Sarn't-Major.'

'A pleasure, Mr. Ogilvie, sir. I never heard of such a thing. That poor old man could not hurt a fly, nor would he want to. It's a terrible story, a terrible story indeed.'

'What d'you think will happen to him?'

Cunningham hesitated. 'The worst, sir, I'm sorry to say. Discipline's discipline.'

'No points stretched?'

'No points stretched, Mr. Ogilvie.'

There was a pause. 'When you said "the worst", Sarn't-Major, did you mean death?'

'I couldn't say, sir. In view of his age, it might be life imprisonment. I've a strong feeling he'd prefer to die.'

'I have the feeling too, Sarn't-Major.'

'Aye, sir.' Cunningham's voice was sad and heavy. 'He can't be blamed for that. But if I may say so, sir—neither can the army.'

No, neither could the army. That was true. Makepeace had to be sacrificed on the traditional altar of 'pour encourager les autres'.

The march continued. Preston's men were in a bad way, and though their wounded had now been spread out among the troops from Peshawar they tended to slow down the advance; and Fettleworth's column was itself feeling the effects of the forced-marching after so many days on the move already. Men were falling out to be attended by the medical orderlies and either relegated to the pack animals for a spell or put unceremoniously back into the line of march. The column's advance was the only thing that mattered now. Fort Gazai must not be allowed to fall whilst the British relief force was less than a day's march away, and Fettleworth kept up the pace unrelentingly. That night there was just one brief halt, during which men fell exhausted to the bare ground, some of them finding instant sleep and others too tired even to find rest at all. The horses and mules were in a similar state, their eyes pathetic as they rolled on the earth with legs oustretched, tongues flicking out to lick at dust-dry lips and muzzles. They were given just one hour and then the bugles once again sounded the Advance as the order to move out came down the line from General Fettleworth. Sleeping men were roughly roused out and sent staggering with half-open eyes and rattling empty stomachs into the line to form column of route. Uniforms were awry and filthy, covered with layer upon layer of dust; the Wolseley helmets lay at all angles, the leather chinstraps held, in some cases, between clenched teeth. Boots pinched and hurt the grossly swollen feet. They marched, half asleep, into what was now, in this high ground, a bitter wind; and it was when bodies and spirits were at their lowest ebb of endurance that Shuja Khan mounted his attack in strength.

CHAPTER TEN

There was no warning, or very little: Ogilvie heard a curious high call, and then the native hordes came like devils out of the night, dropping down from the ridges, throwing themselves bodily on the British troops, attacking at the same time from ahead and in the rear. The column was a shambles of milling men and animals, of officers trying to sort out their companies and platoons and to form them into some semblance of fighting order. There was no lack of individual bravery. Ogilvie saw, close to him, a bearded pioneer-sergeant bring his great axe down to cleave a tribesman in two, although mortally wounded himself from several knife thrusts, before succumbing to an attack from behind that broke his spine like a rotten stick. Ogilvie, feeling the blood-lust rising in him like a tide, fired point-blank into the Pathan who had killed the pioneer-sergeant, watched the man curl and die with a tremendous satisfaction. Then he found himself overtaken by a company of the 88th and, ahead, heard the skirl of the pipes from the 114th as Lord Dornoch rallied his Scots. In the darkness lit only by the flashes of fire from the rifles, it was almost impossible to tell friend from foe until one was at arm's reach. The air was heavy with the stench of burnt powder and the ground slippery with blood. A squadron of cavalry, its trumpets sounding the charge, came riding fast through the lines of fighting men, the hooves of the horses impartial of race as they pounded the dead and dying into the ground. James

Ogilvie's last memory, as something took him hard on the back of the head, was of the screams as the cavalry rode by.

*   *   *

He had not, he fancied, been unconscious for very long, but when he woke the main fighting seemed to have drawn ahead of him. Cautiously, as life and feeling and awareness returned, he lifted his head. He was surrounded with dead men—Scots, Irish, cavalrymen, Pathans. From somewhere in the distance he could still hear the pipes coming shrill and defiant through the sounds of the rifles.

He struggled to a sitting position. Men and animals were still milling about around him, the rear of the column being pressed ahead by the attack from behind, evidently. Getting unsteadily to his feet, and then groping around for his revolver, he heard a voice calling out to him.

'Mr. Ogilvie, sir!'

It was Sergeant Makepeace. He moved towards the sound of the voice and found the old man sitting on the ground next to one of the men, now dead, who had formed part of his escort. The others were nowhere to be seen. 'Are you all right, Sergeant?' Ogilvie asked, bending—and feeling as he did so the pain shooting through his head. 'Are you hit?'

'No, Mr. Ogilvie, by some miracle I am completely unhurt. I have been looking for a weapon. Any sort of weapon that I can use against these filthy scum, sir.' A deep cough racked him. 'If only I could get to the guns, sir. If only I could get to the guns!'

'They wouldn't be much use at the moment, Sergeant.' Ogilvie stood up again and looked around in the enclosing dark. He had to rejoin his regiment, that was the thought uppermost in his mind, but he was reluctant to leave old Makepeace defenceless. He was about to tell the old soldier to lie down and sham dead for the time being when he saw a kilted officer loom up and, in the light of some rifle fire from close by, he recognized Urquhart, a brother subaltern of the Royal Strathspeys.

He called out to him. 'Alec!'

'Is that you, James?'

'Yes. I got laid out for a while. How are things going with the regiment?'

'Don't ask me. I got stopped as well, James.' There was pain in the voice, pain that couldn't be entirely overlaid by an obvious determination not to show it. 'I'm going to try to reach the front. Come along with me—we'll be needed pretty badly, I think.'

Ogilvie nodded, and bent down to speak to Makepeace again, but just at that moment a horseman came down the line at the gallop. As a shaft of moonlight came suddenly down from the edge of heavy cloud, Ogilvie recognized that the rider was an officer from the General's Staff. In the moment that he saw this, there was a flash of fire from the ridge on the flank and the officer slumped in his saddle and fell to the ground. For a moment his foot caught in the stirrup and he was dragged on by his horse for some yards before he fell free.

Ogilvie ran over to him with Urquhart. The officer was Major Tom Archdale and Ogilvie could see that he was badly wounded, with blood welling from his chest. Ogilvie supported his head; the face was grey, and he was gasping for breath. Blood was bubbling from his mouth as he tried to speak. Ogilvie could just catch the words. 'Orders . . . from the General. You . . . you must pass them now. The guns . . . are to be left—'

The voice stopped there, very suddenly. Archdale's body fell slack in Ogilvie's arms. That order would never be completed. Ogilvie felt urgently for the Staff Major's heart beats, but could feel no life. He might still be alive, but currently there was nothing to be done for him except to send back a medical orderly if one could be found. Ogilvie looked up and saw Urquhart and Makepeace standing by. Urquhart asked, 'What did he say, James?'

'He had orders—orders to be passed to the guns. I don't know what they were. He didn't finish.'

'How much did he say?'

Ogilvie repeated Archdale's few words. He

added, 'God knows what he meant, what was in the General's mind. I suppose we'll have to reach Division and find out.'

'I would not do that, sir,' Makepeace said. There was a curious quality in his voice, a firmness and a kind of elation.

Ogilvie asked, 'What do you mean, Sergeant?'

'What I say, sir! With respect. Listen to me, sir, I beg you!' He was speaking with great urgency and emotion. 'The guns are going to save Fort Gazai. That is the task of the column—the General's objective, sir. To save Fort Gazai, sir, and the women and children. And I do not believe the General meant, by his order, to use the guns at this moment to fight off this present attack. *The guns are to be left* was what you said, sir, is that not so?'

'Yes, but—'

'Sir, my interpretation of that would be, that the General intends to use the gunners as support infantry, that he intends to make use of them without their guns! Gunners without their guns—without their colours! Sir, it's a dreadful thought . . . when it is the guns that can relieve Fort Gazai if properly handled!'

Ogilvie looked hard at the old man, then caught Urquhart's eye. Urquhart was looking angry and impatient, and seemed about to speak his mind. Ogilvie laid a hand on his arm. 'Wait,' he said softly. 'Let's hear him out. Sergeant, I believe you have something else to

281

say. Out with it—we're all needed at the head of the column now and we haven't much time.'

Makepeace said, 'Once, I knew this country, sir. I remember now that I have been brought here in the past by the men who held me prisoner for so many years. Seeing it again has brought it back to my memory. There is another track to Fort Gazai, sir, away to the west and a little in rear of where we are now. The guns will not be far from the entry to that track. It is a difficult route, and one that would not normally be taken—but it is there, and with God's help we can make the passage—with the guns. Then we can reach Fort Gazai, and we shall not be expected. We can attack—with total surprise as an element in our favour. Do you see now, Mr. Ogilvie?'

'You mean the orders from the General—'

'Can be misunderstood, sir, and passed on by yourself. I stake my life the orders would not be questioned . . . if those orders were for the guns to detach and march to Fort Gazai! And there you have it, sir. It is in your hands, Mr. Ogilvie. As for me, I would be a happy man if my last act in Her Majesty's Service could be to guide the guns onto Shuja Khan.'

He said no more. Ogilvie took a deep breath, then felt Urquhart's hand on his arm. Urquhart said, 'It's madness, James. We'd all be Court Martialled and—and cashiered, if not worse! In a sense we'd be running away from action! You're not taking this seriously, are you, for God's sake?'

'Give me just a moment,' Ogilvie said quietly. He moved away a little, seeing for the first time that Makepeace had now got himself a rifle with bayonet fixed, from a man who had fallen. It was just as well he had, for at that moment their temporary oasis blew up around them as the fighting surged in from the flank. Ogilvie fired his revolver at a big Pathan; the man went down screaming and holding his stomach, and Ogilvie swung round to deal with another. From the corner of his eye he saw Makepeace drive his bayonet home into a tribesman's groin. As he fought, Ogilvie's mind was working hard, digesting and construing Makepeace's words of wisdom—or of folly. If he, Ogilvie, was prepared to take an enormous risk with his career, it could work out. He was willing to admit the truth of Makepeace's reasoning: a surprise attack by the British artillery could well send Shuja Khan's levies fleeing in rout; the tribes were poorly equipped with artillery, and, as the old man had said earlier, they had few expert gunlayers in their ranks. And, bearing in mind Fettleworth's almost insane mistrust of artillery, any deprivation of the guns could hardly have any adverse effect on the fortunes of the column at this stage. All he would be doing would be to deprive Fettleworth of some manpower— manpower which, it seemed, if Makepeace were right, the General meant to use as mere cannon-fodder in any case. If, as a result of his action in withdrawing the guns along another route, victory should be won, Fettleworth might well be content to take the credit without asking too many questions, a credit which in the circumstances Ogilvie would never seek for himself in any case. If they were to lose, it wouldn't matter, for it would end in massacre; the British would naturally fight to the last man . . .

And no one but themselves would know— he, Makepeace, Urquhart. Urquhart wouldn't be much help, but at least he might keep his mouth shut. He could do that without compromising his own fortunes. As for Major Archdale, he was almost certainly dead. Ogilvie's mind gave a sudden lurch as he thought of the terrible enormity of a subaltern swinging the tactics of a battle, even the strategy of a campaign really: the very idea was appalling. Yet—it could be done, it could bring victory. The overriding consideration now must be the women and children in that beleaguered fort, the people who would be torn asunder, raped, set on spikes upon the very battlements if Shuja Khan's hordes should sweep in and overcome them.

Ogilvie waited no longer. As there came a lull in the fighting once again in their vicinity, he pulled Makepeace and Urquhart to the ground where they lay shamming dead for a while. Ogilvie said, 'All right, Sergeant, I'm
284

with you. I—'

'Count me out, then,' Urquhart broke in.

'That's up to you, Alec. I can't order you to join us and if you're not willing we don't want you. All I ask is this: don't say a word to anyone about what we're going to do. Can I trust you to keep quiet, Alec? There's no one else to know you were here with us, and I give you my word I'll never let it out afterwards. All right?'

After a pause Urquhart nodded. 'All right,' he said. He added, 'Good luck to you both, then. You've always got away with too much for a mere wart, James. This time it isn't going to be so easy.' He moved away, to be swallowed up in the darkness and the mob of fighting, cursing men. Ogilvie put a hand on old Makepeace's shoulder. 'We'll make for the guns,' he said. 'Fast as you can, Sergeant.'

Scrambling up from the ground and half supporting the old man over the fallen bodies, he made his way towards the rear of the column, fighting off the Pathans, sustaining flesh wounds from the knives. He felt the blood running warm down his right sleeve though he had scarcely noticed the slash of the blade as it struck. The fitful moon's light had vanished again and they could see little as they plunged on through the ranks, past another cavalry squadron wielding bloody sabres, past infantry and sappers and support corps, past some of the commissariat animals and their native tenders. Ogilvie had no idea how long it took him to reach the batteries, the silent batteries whose gunners were standing-to and guarding their guns, fighting off the bloody attack from the long ridge above them. With Makepeace struggling along behind him, Ogilvie approached the Major of Artillery commanding the leading battery.

He saluted. 'Sir! Lieutenant Ogilvie, 114th Highlanders. I have orders from Division, from the General personally.' He felt the increased beat of his heart as he committed himself finally. 'All batteries are to withdraw to the west, sir—'

'Withdraw!' The Major, a tall, cadaverous man, stared at Ogilvie with red-rimmed, angry eyes. 'Withdraw! What the devil for?' he demanded. 'I've been waiting for orders to deploy here and now—though I'm dashed if I ever *expected* Fettleworth to show blasted sense enough to make use of us!'

Ogilvie spoke with total confidence, knowing he had to convince more than at any time in his life until now. 'The orders are that the guns should go on to Fort Gazai by a different route, sir, and attack the force *in situ* immediately upon arrival, using the element of surprise. I have been sent with Sergeant Makepeace to guide you through. Sergeant Makepeace knows the track.'

'Ah—I see. That's more like it!' There was clearly no doubt in the gunner major's mind,

286

no doubt at all that he was receiving the expressed wishes of the Divisional Commander. 'Sounds strangely sensible, I must say. Where is this track—hey?'

Makepeace stepped forward and gave a swinging salute. 'Sir! Approximately one mile to the rear, sir, and leading off westerly through the hills. I believe I shall have no difficulty in recognizing it again when we reach it, sir.'

'Right.' The Major stared at Makepeace, bending his tall, angular body as he did so. 'You're an old man, Makepeace. Do you think you can stand the march?'

'I shall do my best, sir, for Her Majesty and the women and children in the fort. I shall not fail, sir, if you will trust me.'

'Trust you?' The Major cleared his throat. 'I've heard the rumours about you—about your rejoining. I had scarcely entered Woolwich when you and your family were captured, yet I had heard about that by the time I joined my first battery. Yes, I shall trust you, Sergeant.'

'I am deeply grateful, sir, and—'

'Then we must channel your gratitude into action, Sergeant. Mr. Ogilvie, there is no time to lose now. Kindly go to the rear with the sergeant. Contact all battery commanders en route and pass the General's order. F Battery in the rear of the line will lead out. Carry on, if you please.'

The deception was complete, the die cast.

Ogilvie knew that the very fact the Major had not the smallest doubt about the authenticity of the order was in part a tribute to Makepeace's tactical sense: the order, however false, was a sound one. As Ogilvie saluted and turned away down the line with Makepeace, he heard the artillery commander calling for his Battery Sergeant-Major and soon after this the guns began to swing round behind their limbers and head to the rear. Making his way down the line Ogilvie found that of the five other battery commanders, four were dead or seriously wounded, as also were a number of captains and subalterns and gunners. The sooner they withdrew from the column now the better, or the guns would be silent before Fort Gazai. As he saw the carnage all around him, Ogilvie remembered Major Archdale, and remembered with a pang that he had taken no steps to send along a medical orderly. Perhaps Urquhart would think of it; but then, Archdale was merely one of very many that would be needing medical attention if by some miracle he still lived. The fact that he was Mary's husband made no difference to the Gods of war.

CHAPTER ELEVEN

As dawn came palely up over the eastern mountain ranges, casting a silvery green light

288

across the snow-capped peaks and bringing with it a chillier wind from those same snows, Fettleworth's column fought off the last of the night attack and then began to lick its wounds—and count its dead. The casualties were heavy, though not, surprisingly, as high as might have been expected considering the size of the Pathan force. There was no time for burial of the dead or even for a full count, but the estimates reaching Division totalled something over eight hundred dead with another nine hundred wounded in varying degrees of severity. The 114th Highlanders had lost eighty-odd N.C.O.s and men, two subalterns and a captain—Smith-Mackay of E Company. And totally unaccounted for was Lieutenant James Ogilvie; and also Sergeant Makepeace.

Barr was triumphant, gloatingly so. 'What did I tell you, Sarn't-Major,' he said to Cunningham. 'The old rogue's joined up again with his own friends—and yon Ogilvie's taken the opportunity of making himself scarce!'

Bosom Cunningham's face darkened dangerously and he put the end of his pace-stick against Barr's chest. 'You'll hold your tongue, Barr,' he said, 'or I'll have you in irons. That's a promise. You will not say another such word about an officer or about Makepeace either, do you understand me?'

Barr sneered openly. 'Aye, I'll hold my

tongue, but you can't stop my thoughts, Mr. Cunningham.'

The R.S.M. swung away angrily, and marched stiffly down the regimental lines. He was more disturbed than he had shown, and the Colonel was equally worried when the reports of the missing men reached him. He ordered another and more thorough check through the regiment's dead and wounded before the order came to move out, and when there was still no sign of Ogilvie or Makepeace he could only assume, as he said to Major Hay, that the two had been captured by the Pathans. But, when word came down the line from Division that all the artillery batteries had mysteriously vanished during the night, he was left with a fresh and perhaps illogical anxiety as to what might have become of James Ogilvie.

'He's an impetuous young man at times,' he said to Hay, 'and he's been very much influenced by old Makepeace. I wonder . . .'

'What's in your mind, Colonel?'

Dornoch shook his head. 'Damned if I know really, John. As I said, he's impetuous . . . and sometimes steers a pretty narrow line between obedience and—well, not quite insubordination. He's inclined to use his own interpretation of orders, I've noticed.' He rubbed at his eyes. 'I think we'll say no more about it for now, in the absence of any facts. There's just one thing, John: I'd like you to keep an ear open for anything Black may say about this. I think you'll understand what I mean?'

Hay nodded, pursing his lips. He had a shrewd enough notion in his head of what capital Andrew Black might make out of any suggestion that the disappearances of Ogilvie and Makepeace might be linked. He looked around the inhospitable terrain, at the high peaks, the scrubby track running below the ridge of the foothills, at the carrion birds hovering, waiting till the regiments moved out so that they could begin their horrible meal upon the dead. Anxiously he said, 'I wonder what the explanation is, Colonel. As to the guns, I mean.'

Dornoch gave a hard, mirthless laugh. 'My dear John, that's precisely my worry! Ogilvie, and Makepeace, and the guns . . . damn it all, I don't know! The batteries could simply have been captured, I suppose, and if that's happened, well, we'll not have a hope of getting them back, not in this sort of country—even supposing Fettleworth would delay long enough for a search, which I doubt he will! God's teeth, John, it's a damned disgrace to lose the guns! You'd think even Fettleworth—' He broke off sharply. Such behind-the-back recriminations didn't help at all. 'Let's hope they're not to be used against us outside Fort Gazai,' he said, 'that's all! There's a strong likelihood.'

At that moment the adjutant approached and saluted. As he returned the salute Dornoch noted the curious look in Black's eye, a look, he suspected, of restrained triumph. The man was mentally driving a very large nail deep into James Ogilvie's coffin, but was too astute to put anything into words, or even insinuations, at that moment. He had come merely to report the battalion ready to move out, and this he did punctiliously enough; after which the Colonel dismissed him with a nod and waited for the order to come down the column from Division—where, as it happened, General Fettleworth was having thoughts similar to his own as regards the eventual destination of the mysteriously vanished guns and was discussing the occurrence with the officers of the Staff. Although naturally angry at what he took to be the impertinence of the enemy, he was not unduly alarmed at the possible consequences of the loss itself. And despite the fact that Major Tom Archdale had been reported killed, there was no reason whatsoever to doubt that his, Fettleworth's, order had in fact been received by the battery commanders. Fettleworth's assumption, reasonably enough in the circumstances, was that his orders had been obeyed and the gunners had detached themselves from the guns and had joined the defensive action as infantry; and that some woodenhead, now, alas, beyond his retribution, had failed to leave any effective guard behind and the native force had made off with the guns.

'A pity, and the heathen will be made to pay in due course,' he said imperturbably, 'but I doubt if I would have found any employment for the batteries myself, gentlemen. I think you all know my views well enough by now. Of course, there is the fear that they may be used against us—but I still doubt the real effectiveness of artillery against well-deployed infantry and cavalry. Infantry, gentlemen, *infantry* is the acknowledged queen of battles!' He brought up his field-glasses and carried out a reconnaissance of the whole area. When he had finished he said, 'All quiet, gentlemen. Apart from the blasted guns, I fancy we taught the heathen a lesson he'll not forget in a hurry.' Indeed, the slaughter amongst the Pathans had been very heavy; a rough count of bodies had produced a figure in the region of three thousand. It was to be an excellent day for the vultures. 'Now we must not delay any further. Pass the word for the Division to move out, if you please—and I want a reconnaissance ahead. I think the Guides, what, Forrestier?'

'As you say, sir,' the Chief of Staff answered.

'Yes, quite. A message to the Colonel of the Guides. Two squadrons are to advance ahead of the column, and reconnoitre as far as the final ridge of hills—so they can see the enemy's camp. They are not to engage unless attacked, but are merely to observe and return as soon as possible.'

Brigadier-General Forrestier cleared his throat. 'The Bengal Lancers are already leading the column, sir. I would suggest you send them rather than bring the Guides through.'

'You didn't say that when I decided upon the Guides!' Fettleworth snapped. His tone was edgy; even the Staff were feeling the strain and were tending towards disrespect and argument; Forrestier had been unpleasantly forebearing during the night touching the use, or non-use, of the artillery—before it had vanished.

Now, Forrestier said, 'Then I apologize, sir. My fault entirely.' He gave an exaggerated bow over his horse's neck, an action that annoyed Fettleworth intensely.

'Damn silly suggestion anyway,' he retorted cuttingly. 'Think I want to leave the van unprotected, do you, just when I'm approaching the enemy?'

Forrestier gave a shrug of something close to weary indifference. The order was duly sent by runner, and the horses of the Guides ploughed solemnly and infuriatingly through the ranks of the infantry, a manoeuvre that perforce took far longer than a simple detaching of the lead squadron would have done. Reaching the head of the column, the Guides went forward at a canter and were soon obscured by their own dust-cloud, which itself vanished shortly after over some rising ground. The main column once again got on the move—like the walking dead by this time, numb in mind and body, stumbling onward by automatic reflex, the column dotted with the bloodstained white bandages applied by the medical orderlies to as many of the wounded as possible. The bands were not playing now; there was no wind to spare for that. Nor were the men singing any more; they simply hadn't the strength or the will. They scarcely cared even that the guns had gone. Leg lurched after leg and that was all; instinct and training and the fear of consequences kept the heavy rifles in their hands. The throngs of pack animals, the mules and the ponies and the camels, came on behind, driven by cries and sticks and abuse, carrying their burdens more or less uncomplainingly.

Four hours later an approaching dust-cloud gave warning of horsemen, and in the van the 114th stood to on orders from their Colonel, as a precaution. But soon the dust-cloud revealed the Guides, riding in with their report. The squadrons rode down the parting files of infantry and their Major reported in person to the Divisional Commander, who, shortly after, sounded the halt and then immediately called another conference, this time of Brigadiers and Commanding Officers only. When these officers were gathered together Fettleworth said, 'Gentlemen, the news is heartening up to a point. The British flag still flies above Fort Gazai.' He paused, as if awaiting the cheers; but the officers were too weary to raise more than a murmur of gladness. Fettleworth continued, 'The report from the scouting cavalry indicates that the enemy is present in force as I have already told you. The estimate is close to my own—some seventy thousand men including a large force of cavalry. Scarcely any artillery,' he added, with a glare at his Chief of Staff. 'This force is spread over a wide area of the plain, or plateau I should say, east of the fort—which they are in an excellent position to cut us off from until we can fight through their lines. I am told they are, or were at the time our cavalry withdrew, still encamped. Thus I can give no forecast, gentlemen, as to what their fighting disposition is likely to be upon our arrival. The tribesmen are, however, intelligently led, it seems, by this young man Shuja Khan, and I therefore expect them to follow broadly British battle tactics— which is to say I expect them to form square with their infantry to withstand any cavalry attack from us, and keep their own cavalry on the flanks for an attack upon our lines. After that—well, we shall see, gentlemen, we shall see. When we leave the trenches we may need to form square ourselves against the native cavalry, as I said earlier I believe.'

For some minutes Fettleworth carried on in

similar vein; Lord Dornoch returned to his regiment as filled with misgiving as before. Quite apart from the lack of tactical sense being displayed, there had been rumours that the Staff was falling out—and now Lord Dornoch had seen for himself that there was a most decided atmosphere of bickering and bad temper at Division. This was by no means unusual, but it was always to be regretted, was indeed the curse of the British Army; the fact that it was inevitable under the present system of promotion did not make it any the easier to bear. It was a thundering pity really, Dornoch thought, that Fort Gazai should have that plateau on its eastern flank; without it, in country that was mountainous everywhere else, Fettleworth could never have employed his confounded squares!

After the brief rest the column climbed to its weary legs again and moved on.

*   *   *

Makepeace was riding the limber of Number One gun of the leading battery; there was a new look in the old man's eye as he came slowly nearer the battle zone, a look of keen anticipation, and he seemed to cast off more and more of his frail weariness as he jogged along with Fettleworth's despised artillery. The guns were still being drawn along by elephants; in the case of the lighter mountain pieces the

297

guns had been dismantled and were being carried on the elephants' backs. In the main the gunners were riding on the limbers, or on the elephants, or on the bigger guns themselves. The bullocks plodded along behind, ready to take over the guns in action when required. The ground was treacherous and terrible, and Ogilvie felt that at any moment the guns must fall apart as they banged and rattled and twisted, rising and falling over hummocks and small boulders. Old Makepeace, he noticed, was having quite a job to hang on to the limber; but that old soldier didn't appear to mind his buffeting now that he was back with his beloved artillery. Ogilvie stumbled along beside him, but there was little conversation between them or between anyone else; they were too puffed. Now and again some of the guns had got stuck down on that difficult ground, wedged solid behind the rock, and not even the strength of the elephants could pull them clear without damage. It was a case of manpower when that happened, all hands to the task of freeing the wheels.

Their progress, Ogilvie thought, was damnably slow; they were climbing all the time through the narrow pass and the air was growing colder as they went. The men's faces had a pinched look as the wind off the distant snows funnelled through the pass—all except Sergeant Makepeace, who was staring ahead all the while with that rapt look in his red-rimmed eyes, pointing like a gun-dog towards the native hordes that waited at the end of the trail, the trail upon which, with an unerringly regained memory and sense of direction, he had himself put the batteries. Now that all they had to do was to go forward in a direct line for the firing position—and keep a close watch all along for any Pathans—Ogilvie was left with time, too much time, in which to think. Thought was inextricably mixed with worry now; he was only too well aware of what he had done and of the possible consequences. Each time he spoke to the Major, he suffered a sense of guilt about the ease of his deception. He had no doubts whatsoever in his mind that the guns would be of inestimable value to Fettleworth's column when it had fought through to Fort Gazai—indeed, he realized now that if any of the General's Staff Officers had known of the existence of this route of Makepeace's, they would almost certainly have advised Fettleworth to do precisely what was being done. But he knew the army structure, the rigidity of the chain of command, the retribution that attended inevitably upon insubordination. Success, of course, was a golden thing; but it was going to be most damnably hard to convince authority that he could have mistaken whatever order it was that Archdale had to convey, for an order to detach all artillery support along a route unknown, probably, to the whole of the British Army in India! That particular thought had not occurred to him before; and it was too late now.

In another kind of panic, Ogilvie thought of Major Tom Archdale. If Archdale had died back there along the main route, many considerations arose. He knew very well that Mary wouldn't mourn her husband in her heart. She would do the right thing, of course, would retire from the social scene and put on her widow's weeds of deepest black, would almost certainly go home to England. But not entirely certainly; Mary was an unconventional woman and though even she would observe the rigidity of a year's full mourning for a military husband who had died a soldier's death—if she didn't, she would naturally be ostracised by all military society both in India and at home— she might decide to remain out here until that year was up. James Ogilvie knew perfectly well that she was fond of him, and undoubtedly he was drawn to her in return. But if the question of marriage should ever crop up, he would face some very distracting decisions. The match would be highly unpopular to say the least.

Now, however, was not the time to worry about it; and all thought of social considerations died abruptly when a sudden shot rang out from a rifle ahead, echoing with shattering loudness off the surrounding hills. From the corner of his eye Ogilvie caught a movement, then saw a native fall from a peak clutching a long-barrelled rifle.

Ahead, Major Barrington, the artillery commander, lifted his hand and halted the batteries. Wheeling his horse, he rode down the line as the gunners stood by their small arms. Nothing more happened and after some five minutes the Major shrugged and turned his horse again. 'We never did expect to get through totally invisibly,' he said with a laugh, 'and we're lucky to have got that man before he got some of us. Good shooting. I shall bring this to the attention of Division. Get 'em on the move, please, Captain Soames.'

The batteries ground slowly on again. Ogilvie wondered if the dead native had managed to pass on the word of their advance. Surprise was fifty percent of success, and now, by Makepeace's estimate, they had only around ten more miles to go.

*   *   *

Fettleworth's column was now beginning its final leg, the ascent of the last high ridge of hills between its current position and its objective. They were now almost ten thousand feet above sea level, and the thinness of the air at such a height tired the weary bodies even more. Ahead, Lord Dornoch saw the winking heliograph from the signallers sent out with the advanced scouting party, which had reached the crest of the hills. The message told Division that the scouts were within sight of Fort Gazai. The column toiled on, sadly aware of that terrible nakedness without the guns. Reaching the summit, the 114th Highlanders' depleted ranks, in the van behind the Bengal Lancers, looked down on an awesome sight. Below them was the wide plateau; on its western flank lay Fort Gazai with the brooding mountains of the Hindu Kush behind, snow-capped, formidable, vast, seeming to reach up to grasp heaven by the hand. No wonder, Dornoch thought, that tremendous range had been named the Hindu Kush—the Hindu-breaker. This was the range that had been the physical barrier against the spread of Hinduism, the barrier that had kept the main impact of the religion to the east of the Indus River. On the dark tower of the fort itself the British flag fluttered still, and the men of the relieving force could make out the khaki tunics on the battlements, and the pipeclayed belts— the British sentries still keeping their perilous vigil. This was the time for cheering, perhaps, though the men in Fort Gazai could scarcely be expected to hear it. Wave upon wave of sound broke out, however, spontaneously, from the ranks as the regiments marched and rode downward to the plateau; all of a sudden, tiredness fell away like a discarded cloak. General Fettleworth rode pompously along the column, breaking into a gallop with his Staff

302

behind him as the track widened out at last. Reaching Lord Dornoch's side he said, 'There you are, Colonel. It's as I said. We shall soon see if they mean to attack or not!'

Below them, the natives' levies waited. Massed infantry, massed horsemen, ragged but ferocious men, Chitralis, stiffened by Afridis and other tribesmen from beyond the Khyber Pass. Firing broke out; they could see the puffs of smoke as rifles were discharged, but the range was as yet too great and no bullets reached the column. The firing was due merely to over-enthusiasm. As they watched a great standard was unfurled over a horseman, seated between two ranks of a mounted escort. Fettleworth's field-glasses went up. He said. 'That must be their leader, Shuja Khan.' He laid a hand on Dornoch's bridle. Emotionally he said, 'Colonel, you shall have the honour of playing us in. I have always admired the pipes,' he added, forgetting his opinion of the Scots as expressed earlier to his Chief of Staff, 'and they will stir the men's hearts. I shall leave the tune to your own choice.'

'The Queen's Own Royal Strathspeys, sir, *always* go into battle playing the one tune— "Cock o' the North".' Lord Dornoch turned in his saddle, looking hawk-like down the line. He sent a runner to Pipe-Major Ross. A few moments later there came the curious familiar sigh as wind was blown into the bagpipes and then the surge of warlike sound swept back over the Division toiling up the hillside as the pipes and drums of the 114th Highlanders beat into full voice to lead the infantry regiments and the squadrons of cavalry down onto Fort Gazai. Dornoch felt a lump rise in his throat; it was moments such as these that made the army so splendid a calling for a man; there was no thought now of bungling, or even of fear for the outcome of the engagement for which they were marching. They were as one now behind their General Officer Commanding. The pipes of Scotland were a promise, a guarantee of victory. Dornoch suddenly swept his helmet from his head and waved it in the air. 'Follow on, the 114th!' he called. 'Don't leave a man-jack of 'em alive!'

To go into battle like this, with the twentieth century clutching the nineteenth by the coat-tails, was in a sense absurd and outrageous; but by God, Dornoch thought exultantly, it was also thoroughly magnificent!

* * *

The Battery Sergeant-Major had gone on ahead of the guns with the scouts, and now he came running and sliding back along the pass to report to the Major. 'Gunfire ahead, sir,' he said breathlessly. 'Rifles, sir. Distant but unmistakable.'

Barrington nodded, and once again lifted his hand to halt the batteries. He rode down for a word with Makepeace. 'We're not far off now, Sergeant,' he said. 'I believe the Division is already in action. What's your estimate of the distance now?'

'If I remember rightly, sir, we should start to come down on the plateau after we round the bend ahead there.' The old man pointed along the pass with a shaking finger. 'It'll not be far.'

'Right,' Barrington said. He backed his horse, stood clear of the guns and called down the line to the gunners. 'You all know the drill, men. As soon as we clear the pass, the elephants are to be taken out of the traces and the bullocks yoked on. When that's done we close the plateau until we're within range—there won't be far to go, I gather—and then we wheel into line for action. I shall give the order to open, and after that you take your orders from your section commanders. That's all . . . except that I wish you all good luck and good shooting. Remember, the whole column will be depending upon you.'

He spurred his horse towards the head of the line of guns and beckoned to Ogilvie. 'I'd be glad if you'd keep close by me, Ogilvie,' he called. 'I may find a use for you suddenly, even if it's only to take over as a number in a gun's crew. Can you cope with that if necessary?'

'Yes, sir. I'd be delighted.' Makepeace had fired him with an enthusiasm for the batteries. He asked, 'What about Sergeant Makepeace?'

Barrington chuckled. 'Oh, he's in his

seventh heaven! I've promised to make use of him as a casualty replacement, and he can't wait to get his eye behind a gun-sight. It's a sad thing in a way, Ogilvie. You can see he's thinking of all he's lost to those devils—as well as of doing all he can for the people in the fort. It's going to be his last chance to even the account.'

A few moments later the batteries moved on again, closing the bend in the pass with men standing by to begin loosing the cumbersome, lumbering elephants.

*   *   *

The infantry wound down the hillside, making all speed possible for the plateau, under the eyes and rifles of the assembled native force that was still firing wildly in the air. Every man in the column was well enough aware of what the tension must be in Fort Gazai as its defenders watched so helplessly. Almost certainly by this time, the garrison would be too weakened, too depleted in number, to be able to mount any effective support. Indeed, as much was soon confirmed by heliograph from the fort itself; the besieged commander reported his numbers down to no more than seventy-eight fit men, while there was not enough ammunition left to provide more than five rounds per man. Nevertheless, the commander signalled that he would do all possible to assist if needed.

'Stout fellow,' Fettleworth said when this was reported to him. 'Signal that he's to remain inside the fort until we march through. I shall require no assistance.'

Brave words, and bravely uttered; but the enemy force was a very formidable one. The British column came down to the plateau and effectively under the fire from the Chitralis and Pathans. Orders were passed from the General that the infantry was to break off and start trenching five hundred yards to the left of the line of advance. The order was obeyed and the men got to work with gabions, pickaxes and *bildars*, implements largely in use in pre-Mutiny days, scraping and hacking at the hard ground and cursing frustratedly as they did so. The trenching operation did not in fact last long and for this there were three reasons, and good ones at that: firstly Fettleworth, in spite of the warning from Captain Hopkiss, had not chosen his ground well and, below a thin topsoil, much of that ground was solid rock and thus impervious to the antique entrenching tools, or any others; secondly the fire of the enemy was causing far too many casualties; and thirdly the Chitralis were making obvious preparations for a combined infantry and cavalry assault.

All this became quite clear to Major-General Fettleworth within half an hour and he at once negatived the trenching and

307

proceeded towards his panacea. Rubbing his hands briskly together and showing his teeth he said, 'We shall form square, gentlemen. Pass the orders immediately.'

*　　　*　　　*

The Royal Strathspeys were on the left of the line, forming up where the advance in column of route had taken them, when the Division turned to face the enemy's front. Over the squares when they had formed, the colours of the regiments floated. The enemy horsemen swept down on them like a never-ending tide, riding superbly, fighting bravely and with effect. Within minutes the Royal Strathspeys were under very bloody attack indeed; wave upon wave of yelling, screaming tribesmen rode down upon their square, where the horses were impaled on the bayonets of the kneeling Scots in the front rank, or cut up by the sustained rifle fire from the men standing shoulder to shoulder behind. As men in the front rank fell, others moved in to take their places; the steel line of the bayonets held against the charge, blood-soaked but steady. Behind the cavalry, the native infantry came on, running, yelling. So far as it went, the square formation worked. None of the regiments gave an inch, though the casualties were heavy. They much reduced the number of the enemy, but the initial preponderance of the native force gave the enemy the advantage still, and it was clear to Dornoch, and to the other colonels, that time would give them the victory as well if the present formation should be long maintained. Squares were still an effective method of defence; but scarcely of attack. Attack was not in their nature. And this operation was of necessity one of attack, thus the nature of the tactics and the objective were at variance basically. Dornoch groaned aloud as he saw his men fall around him; if only they had the guns with them . . . and if only Fettleworth would have used them if they had! There was little in the way of enemy artillery, so far as could be seen, and it appeared unlikely now that the Division's batteries had fallen into the hands of the native army, though God alone knew what *had* happened to them—and to Ogilvie . . .

At Division, the views of the Staff were showing a remarkable accord with those of Lord Dornoch. Fettleworth, though at last showing some signs of anxiety and an awareness that all was not so well as he had hoped, was parrying them. 'You've said all this before, Brigadier-General Forrestier,' he was saying stiffly, as he sat his horse some distance behind the squares of infantry. 'You know my answer—you all know my answer, gentlemen. I wish to wear out the enemy so that he is depleted by his useless efforts. *Then* I shall attack!'

'There is a distinct danger, sir, that it is *us* who will be worn out first.'

'Pish! I think, sir, you underestimate our men. To talk of defeat is not to win wars, Brigadier.'

'Neither, by God, sir, is this!'

'I beg your pardon?' Fettleworth bristled with anger, taking no notice of the shots that came in his direction. 'What was that?'

'I'm sorry, sir. I feel deeply about this action.' The Chief of Staff's voice rose high. 'I believe I can say I had a reputation once. You are destroying it.'

Fettleworth's face grew mottled and he blew out his moustache. Then he said, 'Dammit, man, you're nothing but a blasted hysterical prima donna,' and he turned his back ostentatiously. Still scarlet in the face he rode his horse a few paces to the front, where he reined the animal in and sat glaring through his field-glasses at the battle. Even to Fettleworth, it was in fact quite plain now that his tactics were not paying off, that the squares had lost not far short of a quarter of their strength dead and wounded.

Of course, it would never do.

Fettleworth gnawed angrily at his moustache, wondering how best he could back down. After some minutes he let out his breath in a hiss and, his face set firmly, rode back towards the Staff. 'Very well, gentlemen,' he said briskly. 'I have determined on a change of

310

tactics at this stage. Chief of Staff, the infantry will break square. They are to re-form in line to the rear behind the cavalry. The cavalry will re-deploy in readiness to charge, and the infantry will follow up behind the squadrons. See to that, if you please.'

'Very good, sir.' Forrestier passed the orders, catching as he did so the very sardonic eye of General Preston. It was obvious to both men that Fettleworth was sedulously taking his battle tactics from the native example. It might work out, and it might not, but in all conscience there was little else that could be done now. The slaughter on the plateau was tremendous, with the dead lying in heaps where the squares had been, as the infantry withdrew in obedience to the bugles from Division, the bugles whose strident calls echoed harshly off the surrounding mountain ranges. As the regiments moved back from their dead and wounded, Lord Dornoch found himself in the middle of running men, men bloody with bullet wounds and knife thrusts, men eager to get their revenge as speedily as possible. In double quick time, while the cavalry continued to harass the native flanks and then to prepare for the charge, the regiments re-formed into line and stood ready behind their officers, awaiting the word to advance. When the bugles sounded, they went forward as one, line upon line, with the cavalry now charging thunderously along the entire

311

front ahead of them while a band somewhere struck up 'Bonnie Dundee', time-honoured cavalry canter of the British Army—though they were scarcely moving at anything as genteel as a canter at that moment. The Guides and Lancers swept forward, their sabres gleaming until they met the tribesmen in head-on collision courses, after which those blades became stained red with heathen blood. They swept on and on until they had carved a path right through the enemy and had come up behind, and then they turned and charged again through the centre, cutting the force into sectors. The Chitralis and Pathans, however, with the standard of Shuja Khan in their middle, fought on regardless, using their still overwhelmingly superior numbers to good effect, meeting the British infantry in a clash of steel and rifle fire. They still had the day going very well in their favour; indeed they had an even greater preponderance of numbers now, thanks to the decimation of the squares earlier. It began to seem as though Fettleworth's change of mind had come too late. Dornoch's spirits were low when there was a diversion—very sudden, and totally unexpected. There was a bull-like bellow along the Scots line from the Regimental Sergeant-Major:

'The guns! God be praised, it's the guns!'

CHAPTER TWELVE

The batteries had made good time along the last leg of the pass and the moment the Major sighted the broad plateau ahead the elephants were taken from the traces and the bullocks, who were better able to withstand the noise and pandemonium of battle, were yoked on instead. Urged on by the sticks and cries of the native drivers, they trundled ahead in column until Barrington was satisfied with the range, and then, apparently unseen still in the confusion of the battle below, they wheeled into line, with the massed gun-barrels pointing towards the native levies. In the moment that they were observed from the Scots line, Barrington passed the order to open. The heavy batteries, together with the lighter mountain pieces, opened with sheerly devastating effect, dropping their shells into the massed tribesmen, cutting the yelling, screaming mob—as it quickly became—to ribbons with the lyddite, case and shrapnel, ploughing wide swathes through the mass. The gunners worked like fiends blackened by their own gunsmoke, working off the frustrations of the long march when they had been the despised cinderellas of Division. It was a sustained bombardment that went on and on— but the standard of Shuja Khan, Ogilvie saw, was still floating over the heads of his followers.

When the first shock had passed, Shuja Khan seemed to rally his men; his cavalry re-formed, and wheeled to charge the guns, and at the same time a barrage of rifle fire spattered the dust around the batteries. There were many casualties among the gunners; as a man close by him fell, Ogilvie ran to take his place, and saw that Sergeant Makepeace, his face alight with the battle lust, had already taken over as layer on Number Two gun of C Battery close by. As the native cavalry thundered up the slope towards them, Makepeace sent a shell straight into the squadron. The force seemed to disintegrate into smoke and flame and blood, and the debris of dead men and horses and only a handful of riders on the flanks were left to carry on the charge. They were met by revolver fire from the gunner officers, and from Ogilvie, and not one of them reached the batteries alive. As Ogilvie watched through a red, bloody mist he saw the enemy on the plateau break and run under the rain of shells and the swift following thrusts of the British cavalry squadrons. Then he saw, and saw with tremendous pride, through the smoke and the flame, the splendid, stirring sight of the Queen's Own Royal Strathspeys moving in for the kill in the van of the general infantry advance, charging behind their gleaming bayonets, led by Lord Dornoch with John Hay beside him, and the pipes wailing in triumph. Shells from the batteries were still dropping

314

into the native rear line, but, as the British force cut into them and the fighting became more confused, the artillery bombardment slackened. A yelling mob of retreating tribesmen came up the slope towards them, making for the escape route of the pass, and the hand-to-hand fighting started. Ogilvie saw Makepeace leave his gun and snatch up a rifle dropped by a native who had just been shot by a gunner subaltern; the old man, moving like a youngster now, drove the long, snaky bayonet home into a man's groin. Then Ogilvie was fighting his own way through, desperately, using his revolver, his broadsword, taking punishment from the fleeing Pathans and Chitralis without even being aware of it.

As the native remnants streamed past the guns and along the pass behind them, Ogilvie, feeling a sudden lurch in his heart, saw the rider detach from Fettleworth's Staff and come towards the batteries.

*   *   *

Fettleworth's face was a study; he was struggling with himself inwardly, and it showed. The enemy had broken, there was positively no doubt about that. Pursued by the British infantry and cavalry, they were making off in a most disorderly fashion for the hills, with Shuja Khan's standard—unfortunately—still in their centre. Fettleworth realized that

315

he had won a victory and a notable one; and soon now he would form up the Division to march in triumph into Fort Gazai. So far, so good—naturally! Honours, promotion, peerages even, loomed before him. There might be a bar to his D.S.O. But he was in a quandary—a dreadful quandary. The guns, appearing as if by magic from God alone knew where, had swung the whole action and just in time too—he could see that now, quite clearly, and he couldn't disguise it even from himself. He shrugged; one lived and learned. He had been wrong; but he was damned if he was going to admit it! He still felt a deep-seated mistrust of the gunners, who had stolen the glory from the cavalry, and more especially from the infantry.

And he had given no order to the guns.

He couldn't; he hadn't known where in Hades they were.

He would dearly like to know the sequence of events that had brought the guns into the battle! Somebody had blundered; but it would be most difficult to apportion blame for a blunder that had led to victory on this scale. Churlish, too. Even more important—unwise. It was a great victory . . . it was going to be a very long time before the hill tribes rose again to cock any snooks at British arms and impudently challenge the absolute supremacy of the British Raj. And who, other than himself, would be responsible for that?

316

Someone—someone as yet unknown.

General Fettleworth blew through his moustache and turned to the Chief of Staff, whose right sleeve was stiff and discoloured with drying blood. 'They did surprisingly well,' he said.

'Who in particular, sir?'

'The guns. Yes, I have to confess . . . the guns.'

'I fail to be surprised at that, sir. Except . . .'

'Yes, Forrestier?'

'Where the devil did they turn up from?'

'H'm. Forrestier . . . kindly send at once for the senior battery commander.'

* * *

'You and Makepeace had better come along to Division with me, Ogilvie,' Barrington said. 'You brought the orders and old Makepeace got us here. Credit where it's due!'

Ogilvie wiped blood from his face; there was a gash over his eye that was giving him trouble, and another in the calf of his left leg. He asked, 'What d'you think the General wants, sir?'

Barrington grinned, and clapped him on the shoulder. 'I dare say a word of congratulation's occurred to him,' he said. 'We don't seek honours, do we, but it's always nice to know one's appreciated . . . especially if you happen to be a poor wretched gunner under Bloody

317

Francis!'

Ogilvie made no response to that; the forthcoming interview, he felt, was going to be a damn sight worse than any battle.

* * *

'But what, exactly, did Major Archdale *say*, Mr. Ogilvie?'

Ogilvie's hands were shaking badly. He said, 'Sir, Major Archdale had been badly wounded. I ... found it hard to hear him, sir. I—I gathered you wished us to do what we did, sir—detach along the other track and reach the plateau independently. That was the message I passed to Major Barrington, sir.'

'Ha,' Fettleworth said. The young Scots officer had side-stepped the question and Fettleworth knew it, but didn't propose to press. Glancing sideways at his Chief of Staff, he met a very blank stare. Forrestier had known quite well what his order had actually been. This was a most difficult situation. Fettleworth felt suddenly angry, as though the whole thing was unfair; always, one had to compromise somewhere along the line to high places and it was obvious he would do well to make the best he could of this ... no doubt the orders had become misinterpreted somewhere, such often happened in the heat of battle and he would probably never get to the bottom of it anyway now Archdale—who could

318

conceivably have botched the message himself—was dead. Nor would anyone else, and he could very easily stifle any suggestions of an enquiry. Yes—far better, really, not to probe too deeply. He could deal with Forrestier later.

He turned to Barrington. 'You did well, Major. Very well. I shall see your gallant action does not go unremarked, you may be sure.'

'Thank you, sir.'

'And you, Mr. Ogilvie. Well done—well done, indeed. The orders were not precisely as I had given,' Fettleworth said, avoiding the eye of his Chief of Staff, 'but they were near enough—near enough! The intent, you understand, the gist. I am indebted to you for so bravely taking my orders on, Mr. Ogilvie. I shall mention this in my despatch to the Commander-in-Chief.'

Ogilvie gaped, recovered smartly, and said, 'Thank you, sir.'

'And you, Makepeace. The man who guided the guns through! You may be sure this will count in your favour. I congratulate you on your excellent memory—but am at a loss to understand how it was that you failed to report this alternative route to me when we spoke together earlier—hey?'

Makepeace, standing rigidly at attention with his tattered old blue jacket flapping around his scraggy body, said, 'Sir! I had not remembered at that time. It was only when I came upon the entry to the track again that I recollected a journey up this way, sir.'

'Yes, I see. Yes, it's understandable, of course. You're an old man, Sergeant—but a very gallant one as things have turned out.' Briefly, he smiled. 'Did you have a crack yourself at the damn heathen, Makepeace?'

'That I *did*, sir!' Makepeace answered with relish. 'I put some shells where they were not wasted, sir. It was grand to be working a British gun again, sir!'

'Yes, no doubt. Well done.' Fettleworth gave a stiff nod, a nod of dismissal to all three. 'That is all, gentlemen. Carry on, if you please.'

They saluted and turned away. Fettleworth caught Forrestier's sardonic eye. The Chief of Staff said, 'The orders you gave, sir, sounded to me very different from the effect given them.'

'Different, Brigadier?' Fettleworth smiled thinly. 'You're deaf, man, deaf as a post! As deaf as I may be ... when it comes to remembrance of certain damned impertinences earlier. D'you understand me?'

The Chief of Staff glared back at him and edged his horse closer. In a hissing whisper he said, 'By God, sir, this is no way to run an army!'

'There are many ways to run an army, Brigadier,' Fettleworth said smugly, 'as you will find out when you are called upon to command a Division of your own.' His smile after this became benign. 'You may well be so called in the fullness of time. You have been a great support to me, Brigadier—a great support. My despatches to Murree and Calcutta will reflect this, very possibly. Yes, I think we shall both do well to settle for a little deafness. And now, if you will be so kind as to pass the word, I wish the Division to be formed into column at once, and to do so smartly, for our entry to Fort Gazai.'

Fettleworth, the tiresome affair settled, rode his horse forward.

*   *   *

Rejoining his regiment as the column formed for the last march, with its wounded in the *doolies* or staggering along supported by the fit men, Ogilvie felt many eyes upon him; notably his Colonel, and Cousin Hector, and Captain Andrew Black, and Urquhart, the latter whispering to a couple of his brother subalterns. Urquhart, of course, knew what had happened; but Ogilvie felt he could be trusted to hold his tongue about that, even though the truth would undoubtedly be enough for its bearer to dine out on for the rest of his life. There was even a touch of envy, of jealousy in Alec Urquhart's eyes as he grinned across at Ogilvie, broke off his whispering, and made his way towards his half-company.

321

For Black, it was bitter as gall. There was a rather ironic constraint about the attitude of some of the subalterns, Ogilvie was to find later, as though they had guessed the truth and thought him abnormally lucky to have got away with such an enormous act of, in effect, disobedience of orders; but Black was showing no constraint as he rode his horse savagely up the regimental line, scowling and snapping. Ogilvie was clearly due for much acclamation from the men, who would see him as their very own salvation—it was in the nature of things that he, rather than the gunners themselves, should be the immediate hero of the 114th Highlanders; which was a lot for Captain Andrew Black to stomach. As spontaneous cheering broke out in the ranks, Black wheeled savagely to put a stop to it, his face working and a strange mad look in his dark eyes. Ogilvie watched the adjutant as the latter urged the battle-weary Scots into column of route; he had an idea Black was looking for someone in particular, and it was not hard to guess that the someone was Sergeant Makepeace. But Makepeace, miraculously unscathed in the action, was out of harm's way for the time being: he had pleaded with Ogilvie to allow him to march in with the guns, and Ogilvie, who knew that in basis the whole success of the artillery action was due to the old man, had at once agreed.

The entry to Fort Gazai was something

James Ogilvie was to remember for a long time. The original formation of the column had been preserved, and the pipes and drums led the Division across the drawbridge and into the fort, the wild Highland music beating and reverberating off the age-old walls. Their welcome was fantastic, tumultuous, the starved and depleted garrison rushing forward with their wild-eyed, shabby women and children to shake the men by the hand as they marched in. It was a time of great emotion and a time of pride in their race, a time to thrill to the hardihood and doggedness, the courage and sheer tenacity of ordinary British soldiers. It had been, if ever there was one, a private soldier's march and a private soldier's victory, and a high price had been paid in dead and wounded.

*　　*　　*

Later, when the regiments had been dismissed to quarters and the shadows of the night had fallen over the walls, Lord Dornoch sent for Ogilvie to join him on the battlements. Ogilvie found him standing motionless in the moonlight, looking out towards the darkness of the distant hills. The Colonel's right arm was in a sling and his head was bandaged, and there was something in his stance that spoke of a stiffness in the legs.

Ogilvie halted and saluted. 'You sent for me,

Colonel.'

'Yes, James. As you'll have seen, our accommodation is rather wretched. What I have to say, I can say better up here.' He paused, looking somewhat wistfully out towards the long route through from Peshawar. 'We've come a long way together,' he said abruptly. 'The regiment has been badly mauled. That's a great sorrow to me. But it would have been a great deal worse if ... if the guns had not gone into action when they did. You realize that, of course.'

Ogilvie waited; Dornoch went on, 'I'd like you to be honest with me. It will go no further, I promise you. I have formed a certain picture of what happened ... I think you understand me without my having to go into more detail?'

'Yes, Colonel.'

'Well? Is my picture the right one? You need only answer yes or no, James.'

'Then the answer's yes, Colonel.'

Dornoch nodded. 'Very well. I have only this to say. Victory is a most wonderful excuser of, among other things, a flagrant disregard of one's General's wishes. Defeat is not. Had things gone wrong today, somebody—let us not be too precise—*somebody* would have been cashiered.'

'Yes, Colonel.'

'I'm glad you understand me.' Their eyes met and held. Quietly Dornoch said, 'Damn well done, boy. Thank God you had the guts to do it—that's all! But from now on—I don't really need to tell you—keep your mouth tight shut. And make up your mind you'll have to take some long faces from your fellow subalterns when the truth gradually dawns, as I dare say it will within the regiment. A young officer who gets away with it is never precisely popular, James! Bear that in mind, and make allowances accordingly.' He paused, looking out once again across the wind-swept plateau where the fighting had taken place, and away to the hills. Then, with a change in his tone, he asked, 'Tell me, have you had time for a word with your cousin since you rejoined?'

'Very briefly, Colonel.'

'What did you think of him?'

Ogilvie hesitated, then smiled. 'I think his experiences have done him a lot of good, Colonel. The bounce has gone . . . so has some of the primness!'

Dornoch laughed. 'Yes, that's true. He's learned much about our way of life. He gave a good account of himself in action, too. I saw that he was armed, and sent back to the commissariat, and I'm told he was quite an asset to the defence of the supplies, or what was left of them.' He added, 'I believe we've all been changed in some degree by that march.'

*　　　*　　　*

At his headquarters in Murree three weeks

later Lieutenant-General Sir Iain Ogilvie pushed back his chair, got to his feet and walked across a deep carpet to the window. While the Staff Major who was currently waiting upon him stared at his broad, scarlet-clad back, Sir Iain stared out upon the dust and heat and sounds and smells of Murree. After a longish silence, he swung round and said, 'That curious old sergeant my son dug up—Makepeace. A very sad case, that. Dreadful. I only wish we could make some recompense.'

'I see no reason why we should not, sir. If the enquiry shows—'

'There'll be no enquiry. Too damn late—haven't you heard?'

'Heard what, sir?'

Sir Iain walked back to his desk and ruffled through some papers. Selecting one, he held it out. 'Despatch from Fort Gazai—came in this morning. Makepeace got hold of a gun, no one seems to know quite how yet, and shot himself. In a sense it's the best way out for him, I suppose. I gather he had no wish to live, once he'd had the satisfaction of working the guns again against the heathen devils. No family left—only wretched memories.' He drummed his fingers on the desk, looking abstractedly into space.

The Staff Major asked, 'What's the procedure now, sir?'

'The procedure?'

'Presumably there'll be an enquiry into the suicide and how he—'

'Oh—yes. Yes, certainly. I don't know about an *enquiry*. The 114th's Colonel has asked for a Court Martial. A Colour-Sergeant Barr, charged with negligence in allowing a prisoner in his care to get possession of a firearm. Don't like it—my old regiment, you know. But there it is.' He sighed. 'Dare say we'll have to strip Barr down to private.'

'And Sergeant Makepeace, sir?'

'Buried in Fort Gazai with full military honours. Gun carriage and a Captain's Escort. Pipes and drums of the 114th. And God rest his soul! I'm delighted Dornoch did it that way.'

That same evening Sir Iain took a stroll in his garden with his wife, who had joined him from Simla a few days after the first news had come in of the relief of Fort Gazai. He took her arm as they walked in the brief Indian twilight beneath the tall deodars, and as he did so he felt a tremor run through her body. He said abruptly, for he knew the reason for that tremor only too well, 'My dear, do stop thinking about it.'

'I can't, Iain,' she said. 'That woman ... it was so obvious she didn't care twopence about the news. So long as she remains in India, she's a threat.' Another shiver ran through her. 'Can't you have her sent home?'

'I've told you ... I don't know that my

327

powers extend to widows, my dear. It's her choice. She's a free woman, after all.'

'Don't say it like that.'

'I'm sorry.' Awkwardly, the General patted his wife's arm. They stopped, listening to the distant bugles sounding Sunset; in the fading light the British flags were being lowered on another day, one more day in the long life of the Raj. Last Post, which over the agonizing years of Empire had sounded over so many graves, cut poignantly through the Indian evening. Sir Iain's heart swelled with emotion beneath the starched shirt-front of his mess uniform, lifting the closely-hanging miniature medals and decorations against the blue and scarlet cloth. He spoke again, quietly, kindly. 'Listen to me, Fiona my dearest. We know that young Shuja Khan escaped into the hills . . . we can take it he'll have made his way back with plenty of his followers through the passes into Afghanistan and his father's stronghold. Now, there's a father who'll be glad to reflect that he who fought and ran away . . . my dear, the Frontier will probably *never* be finally settled, there will always be wars, and quite possibly that march from Peshawar will need to be repeated before very long. What I'm trying to say is this—we're lucky in that the boy's come through this time. We may not always be so lucky. Let us count our blessings while we can, my dear—and not dwell too much on other things. It's not as bad as all that, you know.'

This time, he pressed her arm hard. 'This sort of thing doesn't come very easily to me. I'm no hand at speechmaking. But try to—to let your mind be at peace.'

'Peace?' She gave a quiet humourless laugh and when he looked into her face he saw that her eyes were shining through tears. 'Iain, there's no peace, ever, for a soldier of the Queen—or for his mother. Or his wife,' she added, putting her hand gently on her husband's.

We hope you have enjoyed this Large Print book. Other Chivers Press or Thorndike Press Large Print books are available at your library or directly from the publishers.

For more information about current and forthcoming titles, please call or write, without obligation, to:

Chivers Press Limited
Windsor Bridge Road
Bath BA2 3AX
England
Tel. (01225) 335336

OR

Thorndike Press
P.O. Box 159
Thorndike, Maine 04986
USA
Tel. (800) 223-2336

All our Large Print titles are designed for easy reading, and all our books are made to last.